An
Kalash

Divya Narain Upadhyaya is a medical doctor and a professor of plastic surgery at King George's Medical University, Lucknow, India. His fields of interest in clinical medicine are cleft and craniofacial surgery and treating brachial plexus injuries. He is a fellow of the American College of Surgeons and has trained extensively in cranio-maxillofacial and paediatric plastic surgery from the United States and Switzerland. He is an international fellow of the American Society of Maxillofacial Surgeons and an AO-CMF Fellow.

His primary literary interests lie in Indian scriptures, Indic religions and Indian history. He writes about a variety of topics. He has previously authored three books, *The Battle of Panchavati and Other Short Stories from Indian Scriptures* (2019), *Daffodils: A Bouquet of Short Stories* (2020) and *Finding Shankara: A Dramatized Biography of Adi Shankaracharya* (2025).

शान्ताकारं भुजगशयनं पद्मनाभं सुरेशं
विश्वाधारं गगनसदृशं मेघवर्णं शुभाङ्गम् ।
लक्ष्मीकान्तं कमलनयनं योगिभिर्ध्यानगम्यं
वन्दे विष्णुं भवभयहरं सर्वलोकैकनाथम् ।।

He, who is the foundation of the whole universe, who is infinite like the sky, whose colour is dark like the clouds, and whose limbs radiate auspiciousness.

He who is the beloved of Sri (Goddess Lakshmi), whose eyes are beautiful like lotus petals, who is attainable by the Yogis only through deep meditation.

I worship Vishnu, who rids us of the fears of this mortal world, and who is the One Lord of all the Worlds.

***Vishnu Dhyanam*—Prayer to Lord Vishnu, authored by Maharishi Ved Vyas.**

(Appears before the 'Vishnu Sahasranamam' in the 'Anushasanika Parva' of the Mahabharata, the great Indian epic)

Amrit Kalash

Greatest Tales from Indian Mythology

Divya Narain Upadhyaya

RUPA

Published by
Rupa Publications India Pvt. Ltd 2025
161-B/4, Gulmohar House,
Yusuf Sarai Community Centre,
New Delhi 110049

Sales centres:
Bengaluru Chennai
Hyderabad Kolkata Mumbai

P-ISBN: 978-93-7003-381-8
E-ISBN: 978-93-7003-922-3

First impression 2025

10 9 8 7 6 5 4 3 2 1

Printed in India

Dedicated to my mother, for making me sit in her lap and telling me all the stories she did. It is your spirit, Mother, that shines through me, and will continue to shine through my children and their children. God willing!

Contents

Introduction

As I sit down to write the introduction to this book, I am reminded of an amusing incident. On 2 February 1835, Thomas Babington Macaulay, while making a case for European learning and the English language as a medium of education in colonial India, famously remarked in his 'Minute on Education', 'A single shelf of a good European library is worth the whole of native literature of India and Arabia.'

I will not be presumptuous enough to even begin to assess the erudition or the veracity of Macaulay's statement, or even its repercussions on India and her education system, since that is not my field of knowledge or my area of expertise. I am, after all, a storyteller. But this book is my effort to fill that 'single shelf of a good European library' Macaulay alluded to.

Ancient Indian literature is a vast and unfathomable ocean which can broadly be classified into *shrutis* and *smritis*. The shrutis are 'revealed knowledge', heard by the sages when the world was still young, and when the gods still talked to men. The smritis, on the other hand, are texts created by men that were passed down the generations by memorization and oral transmission.

The shrutis consist of the Vedas, the Upavedas, the Vedangas, the Samhitas, the Brahmanas, the Aranyakas and the Upanishads. The core text of the shrutis are the

Vedas; the other texts revolve around them.

The smritis consist of the more famous Itihasas, the Puranas, the Nibandhs and the Vedantas or the six philosophical schools of ancient Hindu thought. Of these, most of the stories, legends if you will, that we have heard or read, come from either the Itihasas, which are the epics, or the Puranas, which deal with the creation of the universe and have accounts of the lifespans of gods as well as their incarnations. This book, like most other story books, derives its stories from the Itihasas and the Puranas.

The stories, whether taken from the Itihasas or the Puranas, have been dramatized to make them more interesting for the modern reader without taking away their originality and 'true essence'. Ignoring the spirit of these stories would be a great disservice to the readers of Indian mythology. Additionally, several footnotes have been added throughout the text of the stories to explain Sanskrit terms or concepts which the reader may not be familiar with. Another purpose of the footnotes is to supply the reader with tidbits of interesting information or the author's opinion. They have been left unreferenced deliberately so that the readers may be inspired to do some further reading of their own.

The purpose of repackaging these immortal stories from our epics is to give the readers a snapshot into the rich world of ancient Indian literature and push them to dive into this unfathomable waters—to churn the ocean, so to speak.

The book is divided into three sections: *Prathamah* (First), *Dwitiyah* (Second) and *Tritiyah* (Third).

The first section has two stories sourced from the

Mahabharata, one of the great Indian epics, or Itihasa. *Prathamah*'s stories are about two great characters who appear in this epic: Gangaputra Bhisma, the Kuru patriarch and Brihannala, the eunuch who is Arjun during the period of his incognito existence while in exile.

The second section is sourced from the Shiva Purana and describes the two different types of dances of Shiva—the Rudra Tandava and the Ananda Tandava. One of the stories in *Dwitiyah*, 'The Cosmic Dance: *Rudra*', also appears in my previous book *The Battle of Panchavati and Other Stories from Indian Scriptures*'. The original story has been edited, extended and added here to complete its context and provide a better perspective when describing the different dances of Shiva.

The third section is based mainly, but not exclusively, on the Bhagwat Purana and has stories about the different incarnations of Vishnu—from Varaha, the boar to Vamana, the midget. Along with the incarnations of Vishnu, *Tritiyah* also describes the rise and fall of the great *daitya* leaders, from Hiranyakashyap to Mahabali.

However, the titular story of the book, also its longest, is one of the most enduring images of Indian mythology—the Saagara Manthan, or the churning of the ocean. The story, '*Amrit Kalash*: The Pot of Nectar', describes this event in detail and forms the second of the three mega-stories in the third section.

I sincerely hope, and pray to the Almighty, that the book is successful in its attempt to entice readers toward the lodestone of ancient Indian literature.

'*Namah Shivaay*'

PART ONE

PRATHAMAH: MAHABHARATA

Bhishma

1

Rishi Vashishtha was angry! His cow Nandini was missing from his hermitage. No ordinary cow, Nandini was a Kamadhenu, a wish-fulfilling cow, and she had always roamed free in the grasslands surrounding his ashrama. So far, no one had ever troubled her. Everyone knew about the great sage and his love for his cow. Hence no one had dared to come anywhere near her, which is why her disappearance was so strange. Who could be foolish enough to steal her?

The hermit resolved to find out who had committed this felony and to punish them suitably. So, he sat down in meditation and looked deep within. As he descended deeper and deeper into his *dhyanam,*[1] the layers of *maya*[2] fell away, and time and space ceased to exist. He looked into the past, present and future.

He saw the eight Vasus[3] roaming the verdant fields near his hermitage. The element gods had descended to

[1]Meditation

[2]The illusion that surrounds the mortals and keeps deviating them from the true path of finding the Brahman, or the supreme consciousness.

[3]The element gods in ancient Vedic literature. They, along with the twelve Adityas, eleven Rudras and the two Ashvins, make up the thirty-three gods of the Vedic pantheon.

the earth along with their wives to frolic in its beautiful orchards and gardens, enjoy the heavenly mountain air, and bathe in the clear water of the mountain streams. While they bathed, played and enjoyed themselves, one of the women noticed a beautiful cow grazing by the riverside, bearing all the auspicious marks, her horns embellished with gold. The gods immediately knew that this was no ordinary creature, but a wish-fulfilling cow.[4] The woman who had noticed it first went to her husband Prabhas,[5] the leader of the Vasus, and requested him to take the cow with them to the heavens so that she could fulfil their wishes. Prabhas, however, was reluctant since he knew that the cow belonged to the great sage Vashishtha. He tried to convince the women, but they would have none of it. In the end the Vasus relented, and led by Prabhas, they stole the hermit's cow.

Vashishtha was angry. He now knew who had done the deed, and how they were to be punished. It was what

---

[4]The cow occupies an important place in Vedic lore, being the centre of the household, as well as a measure of the prosperity of any kingdom. This fixation with the cow continues in the Indian ethos and the animal still occupies a central place in the rural Indian household. She helps with agriculture; the milk she gives provides nourishment for the whole family; cow-dung is used as manure as well as a source of fuel to cook. The rural household economy, thus, revolves around the cow.

[5]The sky god in Vedic literature. He is also known as Dyaus or Dyaus Pitr; *pitr* meaning 'ancestor'. In the Indo-Iranian or Indo-European family of languages and in cultures which have parallels to Vedic culture, like Greek culture, he is also known as Zeus Pater, the patron deity of the Greek pantheon of Gods. Zeus is also a sky god and wields the lightning bolt as his weapon. 'Pitr' or 'pater' is the root of words like 'father' in English, and *pita* in Hindi.

Hari[6] had intended for the world, it was His wish, and it must be done! He cursed the Vasus to be born as men in the realm of the mortals, since, by stealing his cow out of greed, they had behaved like mortals. The Vasus learnt of the curse and went to the hermit in supplication, repentant. The *rishi*, the epitome of kindness and forgiveness, took pity on them and mitigated the curse.

'The curse cannot be nullified,' he said. 'However, since you have repented, it will be such that the seven of you who helped Prabhas steal the cow will be freed from the curse soon after being born in the mortal realm. Prabhas's sin, however, is greater as he instigated others to commit this crime. He will have to live his full life on earth but he shall be illustrious upright, and a great warrior.'

Thus, the sage bade them to go to Mother Ganga, the divine river which flows in the three realms,[7] and request her to be their mother on earth to deliver them from their curse once they were born.

Shantanu was the king of Hastinapur, the capital of the Kuru Empire. He was Yayati[8] and Puru's descendant. Once, while he was camping by the side of the Ganga

[6]The dark-skinned god who lies on the infinite serpent. He is also called Vishnu or Padmanabha.

[7]Heaven, earth and the nether regions

[8]Yayati, through his wives Devyani and Sharmishtha, had five sons—Anu, Puru, Druhyu, Yadu and Turvasu. Sons of Yadu came to be known as the Yadavas, and those of Puru were known as Pauravas or Purus, and later as Kurus, the royal line to which both the Kauravas and Pandavas belonged. King Porus, who faced Alexander the Great when he tried to enter India, was probably a descendant of this line; hence the name Porus.

River, he saw a divine beauty dressed in white who lit up everything around her with her radiance. She had arched eyebrows, dainty limbs, a supple waist and white, pearl-like teeth which sparkled when she smiled. Her long, curly hair was strung with jasmine flowers which could be smelled from a *yojana*[9] away. She was roaming leisurely by the side of the river and seemed to attract even the animals, birds and beasts of prey, who wandered lovingly around her as if she was one of them. Shantanu fell madly in love with this heavenly beauty and approached her.

'O divine lady, who are you? Where do you come from? Which *kula*[10] do you belong to? Are you an *apsara,*[11] or are you an embodiment of Sri, the goddess of prosperity and wealth? I have never seen anyone as beautiful as you,' he asked her in wonder. 'I am Shantanu, the king of Hastinapur. I am a descendant of the illustrious Yayati and Puru, and desire a suitable match for myself. A beauty such as yourself should be the queen of Hastinapur. I beg for your hand in marriage. Will you please be my queen?'

The woman laughed gently upon hearing Shantanu's propoal. It sounded like the tinkling of bells, like the soft opening of rose buds, titillating Shantanu with its happy sound. Her eyes shone like emeralds, their blue-green colour deep like the ocean, the lord of all the rivers.

'I know who you are, Shantanu,' she said in a melodious voice.

'My name is Ganga. I come from the Himalayas, the

---

[9]Approximately 13 km in the modern metric system
[10]Family
[11]Celestial dancer

abode of the gods. I'm happy to be your queen, on the condition that no one, including yourself, shall ever question anything I do or say. No one is to stop me from going anywhere or doing anything that I want to. If you take a vow to honour this pledge, I shall marry you happily. If you ever break your vow after marriage, I shall leave you immediately.'

Shantanu was in love and was more than happy to accede to her wishes, however inscrutable and bizarre they sounded.

'I am happy to accept your conditions, Ganga. No one shall ever question your actions or your decisions. You will have full freedom to come and go as you please, and to do whatever you want,' Shantanu promised.

Shantanu and Ganga were soon married and they started to live happily, immersed in each other's love. Ganga was the embodiment of love and kindness, and she soon won the admiration of everyone in the palace as well as the kingdom. The courtiers, the ushers, the maids and the members of the royal family were all happy at Shantanu's choice of queen and remarked how the two looked like they were made for each other.

In due course of time, Ganga delivered a healthy baby boy, radiant as an angel descended from the heavens. Shantanu was overjoyed. He distributed alms all over the kingdom and propitiated the gods by performing various ceremonies in the temples across Hastinapur.

The morning after the child's delivery, when Shantanu rose from his sleep, he saw Ganga silently pick up the infant and secretly head out of the palace. It was still very dark outside and the palace was not stirring yet. A few birds chirped merrily, indicating the imminent arrival of dawn, but the city was still asleep, tired after a day of festivities.

'Where is she going with the baby when she should be resting?' Shantanu thought, and resolved to follow her quietly.

Ganga left the palace, hidden from the public eye and quickly made her way out of the city. Shantanu followed her silently, his heart beating with anxiety, his mind reeling with questions. Shortly, Ganga reached the banks of the river which bore her name, with Shantanu following close behind. As he watched in horror, Ganga held the child over her head, looked at the sky as if offering him to the gods, murmured a few words of invocation and threw him into the water. The river rose like a receptacle, as if to receive the newborn with her watery hands, and then with a great rumbling sound, the river accepted the offering. The child was gone!

Shantanu went white with shock and ran like a mad man towards Ganga to try and save the boy, but it was too late. The waters swallowed his child without a trace and the river flowed smoothly, without a ripple, as if nothing had happened. Everything was quiet again in an instant. As Ganga turned after performing the unimaginably heinous act, unconsciously smiling, she saw the anger, accusation and query in Shantanu's eyes.

'O Great King,' she said gently, unperturbed by Shantanu's agitation, 'remember that I will do certain things that you may not be able to understand. But if you interfere or stop me from doing them, I will leave Hastinapur immediately, as I have promised to do. If you want me to stay with you, please do not question me. Trust me when I say that whatever I do is for everyone's good. Come, let us go back to the palace; it is almost dawn now and people will soon start to miss us.'

Shantanu could not believe his ears. How could a woman so beautiful, kind and sweet be so unimaginably cruel? He wanted to say so many things, ask so many questions, to reprimand her, but he kept his peace and accepted her inexplicable act of cruelty. His love for Ganga and his faith in her innate goodness fanned a flicker of hope in his heart that things would fall into place with time. For now, however, he would swallow his anger and pride and hope for the best. With a heavy heart he returned to the palace, following Ganga meekly like a lamb; depressed, crestfallen.

As news of the untimely and mysterious loss of the newborn prince spread throughout the city, the festivities died down, and Hastinapur was engulfed in a pall of gloom. Shantanu tried his best to hide Ganga's role in this tragedy, and thus several stories were circulated among the courtiers and the palace staff about how and why the child had died as well as where he had been hurriedly cremated. The king, though trying to limit the damage to the reputation of his queen and royal household, was himself sad beyond measure; but Ganga stayed her cheerful self and tried to cheer Shantanu up too. He could not understand this cold-hearted attitude of a lady who was otherwise the embodiment of kindness and love. The palace staff and other family members thought Ganga was being an ideal wife, trying to help her husband recover from this tragic loss.

As the years went by, Ganga conceived and delivered six more children, all baby boys, all of them meeting the same fate. The people inside the palace were shocked beyond belief at the frequency of this mysterious loss of royal babies. They stopped believing in the stories which were deliberately circulated in the palace. Tongues wagged and secrets were whispered; the truth could not be hidden any longer.

The king himself was almost insane with grief when she did this to their seventh son, and he resolved that despite the risk of losing Ganga, or creating a public ruckus in his palace, he had to know the truth behind her actions, and he had to stop her. Thus, when Ganga delivered their eighth son, Shantanu went to her chamber to talk with her.

'Why are you doing this to me, Ganga? Have I done anything wrong that you are punishing me thus? I will not let you kill any more babies even if you decide to leave me for this. You must answer for your actions,' the king said.

Ganga smiled and said, 'It is not your fault, Shantanu, you have not done anything wrong. On the contrary, it is your good fortune that you have had me as your wife and the Vasus as your children.' She then went on to explain further as Shantanu listened, open-mouthed with wonder.

'The eight Vasus were cursed by Sage Vashishtha to be born as mortals. Later, he mitigated the curses of seven of them so that they could return to the heavens as soon as they were born. But the eighth one, Dyaus, the sky god, had a greater proportion of sin and was thus cursed to live his full life as a mortal. Thus, he will live on this earth as your son and suffer all the ills that mortals are subject to. However, he shall be very illustrious. He shall be learned and become a great warrior. He shall spread the fame of the Kuru Empire all over the world before he chooses to return to the heavens,' Ganga revealed.

'I am no ordinary woman, O King, but the human personification of the heavenly Ganga—the river with the three sacred flows. I chose to be your wife so that I could give birth to the Vasus in this mortal realm and return them to where they belong by immersing them in my waters. I am only a medium, O King, carrying out the orders of the gods. I must now return to the realm of the gods as my work here is done. I will take your eighth son with me to the kingdom of the *devas* so that he can learn the arts of politics, state craft, diplomacy, warfare and philosophy from the best teachers in this world. He shall live with the gods and shall receive the best possible education from the likes of Brihaspati,[12] Shukracharya,[13] Parashuram[14] and Indra.[15] Once his education is completed, I shall come back to the earth, and reunite him with you so that he can take his rightful place in the Kuru Empire.'

Saying this, Ganga bid farewell to a surprised and teary-eyed Shantanu, leaving for the heavens along with her son Devavrata.

Several years later, Shantanu was strolling by the banks of the Ganga River, when he noticed that the water level was unusually low. On walking further upriver to investigate the cause of this weakening of her flow, he came upon a place where the mighty river had been

[12]The preceptor of the devas

[13]The preceptor of the *asuras*

[14]The warrior sage, also regarded as an incarnation of Vishnu

[15]The king of the devas

dammed by a barrage of arrows. Shantanu was surprised beyond words. He did not know of any archer in the whole of Bharatavarsha[16] who could accomplish such a feat.

'How is it possible to dam a river and stop her flow merely by knitting arrows together? This must be the work of gods, for no mortal can achieve such a feat!' Shantanu wondered.

In his curiosity, he looked around for the person, mortal or divine, responsible for this impossible feat. He did not have to go far. Soon enough, he came upon a handsome young man, tall and well-built like a warrior, who was dressed in white and carried divine weapons. His eyes shone brightly from beneath arched eyebrows, and he illuminated every direction with his radiance as he roamed the banks of the Ganga. His stride was long, his gait confident, and his shoulders broad and strong like those of a bull. He held his weapons with ease, as if he had been born with them. He carried a bow in his left hand and a quiver full of arrows was strapped to his back. To his waist was strapped a scabbard carrying a sword with a silver hilt, studded with several precious gems.

'Is he a deva or a demigod?' Shantanu wondered. 'I have never seen him before in my kingdom. He must be an outsider. Is he an invader? Or a celestial visitor?'

Thinking thus, Shantanu was about to confront the young man when suddenly Ganga appeared before him, smiling radiantly, youthful as ever. Looking at her, Shantanu forgot everything about the young man, forgot

---

[16]Ancient name of India, derived from the name of King Bharata of the Lunar line of kings, the son of Dushyant and Shakuntala

about all the time that had elapsed since she had left him, forgot all his heartache and loneliness, and stood looking at her with love and longing in his eyes.

'Ganga,' Shantanu exclaimed, and then could say no more, overcome with emotion.

'O Great King,' Ganga said, her divine beauty unchanged. 'I have come back as I had promised, and I have brought you a gift from the gods.'

Ganga then presented the young man to Shantanu and said, 'This is your son, Devavrata. His education is now complete; therefore I am leaving him under your care so that he may fulfil his earthly responsibilities. Being the son of a goddess, he shall always be abler than the mortals and shall extend the fame of the Kurus all over the world. Take him with you, for he is your flesh and blood, and make him your prince.'

Thus, Ganga handed over her son to Shantanu and then blessed Devavrata.

'Son,' she said, 'go with your father and serve him well. Obey his wishes as you have obeyed mine. Always look after his interests and the interests of the Kuru Empire. From now on, Hastinapur is your home and King Shantanu your father as well as your king. I must go back to the heavens now but I shall always look over you, for you are my child. Whenever you feel lonely or need my company, come to the banks of this river that bears my name. You shall always find me here in spirit, and these waters will give you solace and inspiration. May the gods always bless you, my son!'

Saying so, the divine Ganga kissed Devavrata's forehead and bid goodbye to Shantanu, before disappearing into the waters of the river like the morning fog melts into air after sunrise. Shantanu was left standing with Devavrata.

Later, father and son returned to Hastinapur, and Shantanu happily crowned Devavrata prince, declaring him the heir apparent. He was happy that the future of the empire was in Devavrata's capable hands. But alas, destiny had other plans for the Gangaputra.[17]

2

Shantanu did not remarry after Ganga left him. Her memory was enough for him. Moreover, no woman could fill the void that Ganga had left in his heart. Over time, however, he grew increasingly lonely and missed the simple pleasures of companionship. His loneliness did not last long, for destiny, as always, intervened to change the course of history.

Several years after he had ordained Devavrata as the crown prince of Hastinapur, another woman won his heart. He had been riding his horse near the banks of the Yamuna River one evening when he saw a dark, earthy beauty, the daughter of a fisherman, who smelled like a musk deer. She stirred long-forgotten feelings in his heart and he immediately fell in love. He started to visit her secretly in plain clothes without letting her know who he was. He would sit by the bank of the river in the evenings, watching her and talking to her. He enjoyed her fragrance as she ferried him across the river in her boat. Later, as is proper, he introduced himself to the young girl and her father and asked for her hand in marriage. However, her father, the old fisherman, imposed an impossible condition on their union, which

---

[17]Son of Ganga

Shantanu could not fulfil. Thus, he stopped seeing to see her from that day onwards, for what was the use of meeting her if he could not marry her?

But not seeing her, not talking to her, was killing him inside. He wasted away, yearning for that young fisherwoman, the fire of desire scorching his heart, eating him away. His life force seemed to ebb; he lost interest in everything around him and confined himself to his chambers, pining away for Kasturigandhi,[18] for that was her name, and not being able to have her as his wife was upsetting him beyond measure.

Dasaraj was the leader of the fishermen, a minor king of sorts. His people had manned the boats across the Yamuna River, and caught and sold fish for generations. They were a semi-autonomous *jana*[19] spread across the length and breadth of the Yamuna and had alliances with several kingdoms. These kingdoms ranged from the Kuru and the Panchala in the north to the Vatsa and the Chedi in the south. These people kept moving along the river and were not permanent residents of any one region.

Once, while living near the Chedi Empire, their people found a huge fish which they brought to Dasaraj as a gift. When the belly of the fish was cut open, Dasaraj

[18]Literally, 'one who smells like musk'

[19]*Jana* simply means 'people', and can be understood as a 'community' of people. This community can be organized as either a village or a town or a city. The term jana carries no racial or religious connotations; it simply refers to a group of people living together as a cohesive cultural or familial unit. Jana is also the source word for *janapada*, more easily understood as 'republic'.

was surprised to find a boy and a girl inside. They were both alive and well. As per the prevailing customs, Dasaraj went to the Chedi king to report this mysterious event and presented him with the magical babies found inside the fish's belly. Being childless at the time, the Chedi king adopted the boy and named him Matsya,[20] and gave the girl away to Dasaraj, to be brought up as his daughter.

Dasaraj and his people later moved further north and settled near the Kuru Empire. He named the girl Kali as she was dark-complexioned, and raised her with affection as she was his only child. She was also known among the fishermen as Matsyagandhi[21] or Yojanagandhi.[22] Even though she smelled like fish, Kali grew up to be a very beautiful woman, with dark eyes and long eyelashes. She was very attractive and her mannerisms enamoured her to many prospective suitors. However, her father was very protective of her and would not let any fishermen woo her. He would accept only the very best for his Matsyagandhi!

When she grew up, Kali started ferrying people across the Yamuna in her boat to help her father. One person who availed her ferry service frequently was Parashar Muni.[23] He was a learned rishi and could tap into the universal consciousness to look beyond the present.

---

[20]*Matsya* means 'fish'. This child, Matsya, later established the Matsya kingdom, about which we hear in the Mahabharata, especially in the 'Virat Parva', when the Pandavas live incognito in the court of the Matsya king, Virat.

[21]Literally, 'one who smells like fish'

[22]One who can be smelled from one yojana away, a yojana being approximately 13 km in the metric system.

[23]Hermit or renunciant

Over the years, he had grown fond of Matsyagandhi, and thus, when he wanted a son to whom he could pass on his heritage and an important responsibility, he chose Matsyagandhi to be his consort.

'As soon as my son is born to you, Matsyagandhi, you will become a virgin again and your body odour will change to musk which will spread across one yojana. My illustrious son will become a grown man as soon as he is born and shall then leave this place to pursue his penance and his austerities.'

The sage blessed Kali when she agreed to bear him a son.

Parashara and Matsyagandhi's son was born on an island in the middle of the dark waters of the Yamuna, and he instantly grew up to be an adult right after his birth. Bowing his head in front of his mother, he put his palms together and said, 'Permit me Mother, for I must go to perform my austerities. The Universal Father has entrusted me with very important tasks. But I shall come whenever you need me. You only have to call my name and I shall be there.' Saying this, Matsyagandhi's son left to perform his penance.

Mastyagandhi named her son Krishna since he was dark-complexioned. He was also known as Dwaipayan, for he was born on a *dwipa* or island. He would later become one of the most illustrious poet-saints India has ever known and would be honoured with the title of Ved Vyas.[24]

---

[24]Ved Vyas is probably a generic title, rather than the name of a single person. The title of Ved Vyas was conferred upon Krishna Dwaipayan since he was the one to organize the Vedas into four parts. He also composed the Mahabharata and organized the Puranas.

As per Rishi Parashar's blessing, Matsyagandhi regained her virginal form after her son was born and her body, which smelled of fish, started smelling of *kasturi* or musk. Due to this, she came to be known as Kasturigandhi in time.

When her father asked her the cause of this curious change in her body odour, she truthfully shared her secret with her father and told him of the son she had produced through Parashar Muni. Her father was happy with her truthfulness and named her Satyawati, a name which stuck among the others. He only had one worry—who would marry his daughter after knowing that she had already borne a son to Parashar Muni?

It was this Kasturigandhi whose sight and smell had driven King Shantanu crazy, and he had approached her father for her hand. The two men had talked in Dasaraj's humble dwelling as Satyawati watched from behind a wooden partition.

'It is my fortune, O Great King,' Dasaraj said, his body enfeebled with age but his mind as sharp as ever, 'that you seek the hand of my daughter in marriage. Though she is not my real daughter but that of the king of Chedi, I have brought her up as my own. Her brother Matsya is the prince of Chedi. But it is her misfortune that she, a princess, has been brought up as the daughter of a fisherman. I had always hoped that she would get married in a royal household so that she could have what is rightfully hers, a royal lifestyle. I am thankful to the gods that I have been able to see this day with my eyes before I die.'

'But I have only one concern,' he continued.

'Please ask me for anything you want, Dasaraj. I will grant you any wish to marry Satyawati,' Shantanu said, eager to please the father of his prospective bride.

'What I ask for is not difficult for you to give, O King. Please promise me that the sons you beget through my daughter Satyawati shall be the ones to sit on the throne of Hastinapur. If you can promise me this, O King, I shall be happy to give her hand in marriage to you,' Dasaraj said.

Shantanu was shocked. He had not expected such an impossible demand from the girl's father, considering he was a lowly fisherman. No matter how much he loved Satyawati, he could not take away from Devavrata what was rightfully his and promise it to her unborn son. He tried to reason with Dasaraj and then pleaded with him to no avail. He would not budge. And so, the king came back empty-handed and spent his days pining away for his love. He could not eat properly, nor could he sleep well. He lay face down on his bed all day and sighed like forlorn lovers do.

When Devavrata did not see his father for a long time, he enquired if King Shantanu was unwell. What he came to know—his father's attendants informing him in hushed whispers—surprised him. He was immediately guilt-ridden and full of love for his father. How could he, Devavrata, enjoy life and the power of the Kuru throne while his father pined away for his beloved? Why had his father not shared this anguish with him? Then he learnt of the reason—the Kuru throne stood in the way.

Devavrata was the son of a goddess; his heart was full of noble emotions. He felt bad that his father, whom he revered as a god on earth, was unhappy. It was due to him that his father was unable to promise the kingdom to his beloved. Devavrata's heart swelled with love and pride for Shantanu. To see him enthroned, his father had denied himself a simple and basic human emotion—the feeling of being loved, the pleasure of companionship. He had performed his duty towards his son, but had his son performed his duty towards his father? This thought assailed Gangaputra's noble heart.

'Get me my chariot,' Devavrata instructed his servants. 'I shall go and see if things can be helped by my intervention.'

His silver-coloured chariot was prepared with four white horses yoked to it. Off he went, riding as quickly as the horses would take him. Dressed in white with his forehead marked by a tilak, Devavrata looked very much like the demigod he was. His sword strapped to his waist, his bow and arrow stashed in the chariot, and his royal insignia fluttering atop the canopy, Devavrata hurried towards the banks of the great Yamuna where the fishermen dwelt.

Devavrata's reputation as a valiant warrior preceded him, and it sent a wave of terror through the small village of fishermen when he arrived in full regalia. People thought he had come to avenge his father's dishonour at the hands of Dasaraj, and they panicked, fearing an attack. A deathly silence greeted him when he entered the small, deserted village of the fishermen. Unaware of this terror, Devavrata proceeded to find Dasaraj's humble dwelling. He called for the leader of the fishermen.

'Dasaraj, I bring you greetings from the Kuru king Shantanu. I am his son, Gangaputra Devavrata, and I request you to please grant me an audience.'

The king of the fishermen came out of his house, his hands folded, his head bowed.

'May the almighty bless the great Kuru warrior Devavrata. This humble dwelling has been honoured by your presence, O Prince. Please do come in and sit down,' Dasaraj led the prince inside his humble dwelling.

When they were finally seated and Devavrata had been suitably honoured, the two men began talking.

'You do know why I am here, don't you, Dasaraj?' Devavrata quizzed the fisherman, looking him squarely in the eye.

'I am not sure, sir, and I will not be so bold as to presume the purpose of your visit,' Satyawati's father replied slyly, not revealing his cards.

'The man is shrewd and fearless,' Devavrata thought, looking at the frail frame of the old fisherman. 'No wonder he drove such a hard bargain with my father.'

'My father seeks the hand of your daughter Satyawati in marriage, Dasaraj. I have come to convince you to agree to his proposal,' Devavrata said, his voice full of authority.

'If the prince will spare my life, may I speak freely?' the old man asked, looking sideways at the prince, acutely aware that if things went go, he would lose much more than his daughter. Devavrata's anger was legendary, as were his skills with his weapons. Dasaraj was treading a very thin line here; he had to play this well.

'I grant you *abhaya*,[25] Dasaraj. Please speak freely,' Devavrata said, his right hand raised, palm facing the elderly fisherman in a gesture of forgiveness and peace.

Dasaraj hesitated, wisely choosing his words.

'Prince Devavrata,' the old man said, his grey eyebrows knotted in the centre of his creased forehead and his bald head beaded with perspiration, 'I would not have hesitated even once had it been you who had come asking for my daughter's hand in marriage. But with your father, it is a different matter altogether.'

'And why is that, please do tell me,' Devavrata said, irritated at the old man's insinuation that Shantanu was an unsuitable match for his daughter.

'You will agree, my prince, that every father wishes the best for his child?'

Devavrata nodded.

'You will also agree that I am doing nothing wrong if I am looking out for the interests of my daughter? This is sanctioned by dharma, isn't it, my prince?'

'Yes. Looking after the interests of the child is sanctioned by dharma, Dasaraj,' Devavrata said, not sure where the conversation was leading.

'My only wish is that my daughter should live prosperously and that her progeny should also live happily and free from fear. In royal households, you will know, only those in power are happy and secure. Therefore, if you would have asked for her hand in marriage, I would have been happy to say yes, knowing you are the heir apparent to the throne, and my daughter would become the queen, with her children

[25]Freedom from fear

being princes and princesses. But if she gets married to your father Shantanu, this future is not assured, and she will always be a secondary wife to the king, her children never wielding power. They will always be vassals of your children and will always remain at their mercy. Hence, my dharma dictates that in the interest of my daughter's future, I should refuse the king's offer unless he can assure me that Satyawati's children will inherit the throne,' the old man explained.

He paused and looked at Devavrata worriedly, trying to gauge what his reaction might be. If Devavrata was worried or confused, he did not show it. His face shone with clarity of thought and the radiance of firm resolve.

'This problem is easily solved, dear Dasaraj. My father may have hesitated in promising this to you, which is understandable considering his love for his son, but I can easily promise this to you. I vow to you on the souls of my ancestors that I shall renounce my claim to the Kuru throne in favour of the sons of Satyawati,' Devavrata said, his face shining, his voice thundering and booming like the clouds which had gathered outside.

But his test was not over yet. The gods had planned an even more elaborate ordeal for him. They gathered in the heavens with Devavrata's mother Ganga in attendance to see how things would turn out, and how Gangaputra would respond to the dilemma about to be presented to him. Would he give in to temptation, a human trait? Or would he take the path of renunciation and show his true character as a god? The clouds rumbled outside and the holy river Yamuna's waves crashed at her shores, impatient, as Devavrata waited for Dasaraj to respond to his promise. Would he now consent to let his daughter marry Shantanu?

After a pause, Dasaraj spoke again.

'I am happy to hear that you are ready to renounce your claim to the throne in favour of the sons of Satyawati, O Prince. It is a great sacrifice and a noble gesture, but your renunciation will not solve my problem. Even though you refuse to accept the throne voluntarily, what is to stop King Shantanu from bequeathing it to you or convincing you to share it with Satyawati's sons? That will defeat my purpose, my Prince.'

Devavrata smiled. The old man was very persistent, but he could not be blamed for thinking about the welfare of his only child.

'Not only do I renounce the throne, Dasaraj, but I also promise to convince my father to hand over the kingdom to Satyawati's sons. I give you my word that I will see to it that they sit on the throne of Hastinapur. Are you happy now, Dasaraj?' Devavrata assured him.

Dasaraj felt a surge of happiness and he could hear his daughter chuckle from behind the wooden screen. He had done well, and his daughter would become the queen of Hastinapur after all. However, he was a man of the world; he knew better than to celebrate prematurely. Something more needed to be done before he could breathe a sigh of relief.

Meanwhile, a storm had begun outside. The angry rumble of thunder and the sounds of the Yamuna crashing against her banks were making conversation difficult. The tempest outside prophesied the tempestuous times that were in store for the kingdom of the Kurus.

Dasaraj spoke again, 'My dear Prince, I have just

one doubt left. If you can address this doubt, I shall be happy to hand over my daughter to you to take her to Hastinapur to be wedded to the King.'

'Speak up Dasaraj, you need not fear,' Devavrata said.

'You may renounce the throne, Prince, and you may convince your father to hand over the empire to the sons of Satyawati, but what will happen when you have sons of your own? You are a valiant hero, O Prince, the son of a goddess. I do not doubt that your sons will be valiant too. Will they not, after you are gone, fight with Satyawati's sons for the throne, which should rightfully have been theirs? I am sure, being your sons, they will easily be able to defeat them and claim the throne. Your promise will then be falsified, O Prince,' the old man paused, out of breath, waiting to see what Devavrata would say.

A cloud of doubt hovered over his mind; maybe he had gone too far this time. Maybe Devavrata would lose his temper, behead him and carry away his daughter. But a voice inside him, an uncanny sense of diplomacy developed over the years, told him to hold on just a little more. It told him that he would win the bargain, that the deal with Devavrata would be sweet beyond imagination if he takes this final bait.

Devavrata thought for a moment and the clouds outside also paused. The Yamuna was also quiet, listening to what Gangaputra would say. But Devavrata had made up his mind. He smiled and stood up, looking directly at Dasaraj, who stared meekly, as if afraid that he might be killed any time. Devavrata drew himself to his full height. With one hand he touched his holy thread[26] while the other he raised to the sky. Looking towards the heavens, he said in a voice that sounded like the clouds growling outside, 'Dasaraj, may the *panchabhoot*,[27] and all the gods in the heavens be my witnesses. May my mother, the holy Ganga, who washes the sins of even the celestials, be my witness. May the holy fire, which creates and nourishes and destroys this world, be my witness. I swear in the name of all my ancestors that I shall never marry, and I shall never have children who can compete for the throne of Hastinapur. I renounce the throne for all posterity and I shall forever serve it as a faithful servant, looking after its interests and of those who sit on it till my breath leaves this body.'

All hell broke loose. Thunder crashed and a bolt of lightning seared the sky as if Indra himself were attesting to Devavrata's Bhishma[28] oath. The Yamuna broke her banks and washed the feet of this demigod who had done what no mortal could do, who had taken the Bhishma vow. Dasaraj put his head on Devavrata's feet and wept tears of joy.

Devavrata's Bhishma vow earned his father a bride and the name of Bhishma for himself; a name he would carry till his end on a bed of arrows on the battlefield of Kurukshetra. Bhishma's vow also served to change the course of Kuru history and finally led to the great fratricidal war of the Mahabharata on the plains of Kurukshetra. His vow, given in good faith, became the

---

[26]The scared thread was worn by many Hindus after the *upanayana sanskara*, also popularly known as the *janeu*.

[27]The five elements that make up the human body

[28]*Bhishma* means terrible

'original sin' which started the cascade of events leading up to the great war!

Author's Note

Bhishma, or Bhishma Pitamah, as he was lovingly called by both the Kauravas and the Pandavas, remains a central figure of the Mahabharata. He led the Kaurava forces as their commander-in-chief in the great war for ten of the eighteen days it lasted. He was shot down by Arjun, his favourite grandchild and disciple, but remained alive on the *shar shaiyya*, or the bed of arrows, for fifty-eight more days. He chose to leave this world on the day of the winter solstice when the sun starts its northward migration, an auspicious day in the Hindu calendar. While on the shar shaiyya, he instructed Yudhishthira in the tenets of administration and royal duty, and revealed to him the Vishnu Sahasranamam the thousand names of Vishnu. Hindus all over India still observe this day as a day of fasting and penance on Magha Shukla Ashtami, the eighth day of the dark fortnight in the month of Magha, which falls approximately during January–February according to the Gregorian calendar. This apparent discrepancy between the current winter solstice and the month of Magha is due to the migration of the calendar, which occurs over thousands of years. Scholars can use this 'migration' of the dates mentioned in the great epic to pinpoint the year when the great war of Mahabharata was fought.

Brihannala

1

The grapevine was abuzz in Matsyadesh, as well as in the other parts of Bharatavarsha, the land of the Aryas.[29]

Ever since the mysterious death of Keechak, the powerful Matsya commander and the queen's brother, people kept relentlessly talking about Sairandhri and her *gandharva* husband who had killed Keechak so mercilessly. Sairandhri herself had happily encouraged these rumours and even helped spread them with the help of Kanka, Ballabh, Brihannala, Granthika and Tantipala,[30] so that the suspicion for Keechak's killing was deflected from herself and the Pandavas, who were hiding in King Virat's court for almost a year now.

Following a gambling match, which Yudhishthira had lost, the Pandavas and Draupadi were forced to spend twelve years in *vanvaas*[31] and one year in *agyaatvaas.*[32]

---

[29]Despite the common misconception of the meaning of the word *arya* as a 'race' of people who came to India in the second millennium BCE, in common parlance as well as in the Sanskrit language, arya has most often meant 'civilized people' who uphold the cosmic balance, also known as *ritam.*

[30]The pseudonyms of the Pandavas in exile

[31] *Van* means 'forest'; *vaas* can mean both 'house' or 'abode' and 'to live'. It is thus both a noun as well as a verb. *Vanvaas* thus means 'to live in the forests either as a form of penance or in exile'.

[32]*Agyaat* means 'unknown'. *Agyaatvaas* thus means 'to live incognito'.

The terms of the gambling match dictated that if they were caught during the period of their incognito existence, the whole cycle of thirteen years would have to be repeated once again. Hence, when their agyaatvaas began, Duryodhana, the eldest of the Kauravas, and his uncle Shakuni let loose their best spies throughout the Jambudwipa[33] to look for the Pandavas and Draupadi.

The Pandavas and Draupadi had disguised themselves as courtiers and servants in the court of King Virat of Matsyadesh.[34] Yudhishthira had become Kanka, the courtier, Bheem had become Ballabh, the cook, Arjun had become Brihannala, the eunuch and dance master to Uttara, the princess, and Nakul and Sahadev had become Granthika and Tantipala, looking after the horses and the cows owned by the royal family. Draupadi had disguised herself as Sairandhri, the queen's handmaiden. They thought they would be able to spend their days quietly this way, but this was not meant to be. Keechak had noticed Sairandhri and tried to molest her. When things worsened to the point where they could no longer be ignored, the Pandavas and Draupadi decided to kill Keechak in a way that would be least likely to draw attention to them. Thus, Sairandhri had lured Keechak to her bedroom late one night, and there Ballabh had pulverized the life out of him.

---

[33]*Dwipa* refers to a land surrounded by sea, while *jambu* refers to jamun, a berry found exclusively in the Indian subcontinent, also known as Indian blackberry or java plum. *Jambudwipa,* hence, is an old Sanskrit name for the Indian Subcontinent.

[34]Located somewhere in present-day Rajasthan. The subjects of Matsyadesh were called the Matsya people and are probably known as Meena today. *Meena* in Sanskrit means 'fish', as does *matsya.*

The next day Sairandhri and the Pandavas spread the rumour about Sairandhri's gandharva husband killing Keechak, to deflect any suspicion from her and the Pandavas.

Their planted story had been successful to a limited degree. Though no one troubled them anymore in King Virat's court and the king seemed satisfied with their explanation, the news of Keechak's mysterious death had spread from Matsyadesh and reached Hastinapur, the capital of the Kuru kingdom, finding the ears of Duryodhana and Shakuni.

Shakuni was not as gullible as King Virat and immediately smelled a rat.

'There has to be something more to this whole episode than what meets the eye,' he had confided to Duryodhana.

'Keechak was strong as a bull and an expert at both *mallayuddha*[35] and *gadayuddha.*[36] It is not easy to kill someone as powerful as him. In my reckoning, there are only two people in this world who are powerful enough to do something like this—Bheem and Balrama.[37] Don't mind, Duryodhana, but even you would have had a tough time fighting Keechak. Balrama, I know, is living in Dwarka[38] presently,' Shakuni said. 'So I

---

[35]The art of close combat or wrestling

[36]The art of fighting with the mace

[37]Balrama was the elder brother of Krishna, and the son of Nanda and Rohini.

[38]Dwarka, sometimes also referred to as Dwarawati, was the capital of the Yadus, the royal family to which Krishna belonged, and was situated on an island in the western ocean to protect it from frequent attacks by Jarasandha, the king of Magadha.

strongly suspect the Pandavas are hiding somewhere in Matsyadesh. I think Bheem killed Keechak. But, so far, our spies have had no success in finding out where they are, or their new identities. We need to do something to flush the Pandavas out of their hiding place before their period of incognito living is over so that we can send them to exile again for thirteen years,' he told Duryodhana, his evil mind already formulating a solution to this problem.

To discuss this matter, an urgent assembly of the royal court was summoned, with all the Kauravas and the elders of the royal family in conference, with Dhritrashtra—the blind king—presiding.

The Kuru royal court was a huge, pillared hall, rectangular in shape and lined by small couches along its sides for visitors or courtiers to sit on. At the far end of the hall were cushioned seats arranged in a semicircle on a raised platform, with the royal throne placed in the centre and smaller seats for the Kuru elders flanking it. In front of the throne was a small vacant area, an atrium, where suitors or visitors could stand and address the throne. This was the area where the infamous gambling match had been played. Beyond the atrium was another semicircular area, dotted with lavish seats facing the assembly and the seats of the Kuru elders, which were usually occupied by the princes or the members of the royal family. Beyond this was the U-shaped main hall, lined by ornate pillars, which was used by the courtiers, invitees, guests, ambassadors, or public called into the assembly or summoned to the royal court for some reason.

Behind the pillars of the general assembly, the hall

had a recessed area which ran throughout its length and which was used by servants to move up and down. The recessed corridor had a few hidden doors which could be used to climb up to the balcony above to observe the proceedings of the royal court, or to exit the premises without being observed. In front of the pillars neatly arranged were several couches set into exquisitely carved wooden frames, arranged neatly in rows where guests and other visitors to the court could sit or recline while the assembly was in session.

It was in this court that the Kuru royal family had assembled to discuss the issue of Keechak's murder. Dhritrashtra sat on the royal throne in the middle of the arc at the end of the hall, flanked by Bhishma, Drona, Kripacharya, Vidura and Karna.

Karna, a late addition to Duryodhana's circle of friends, had become a permanent fixture at the Kuru royal court, much to the distaste of Bhishma, who considered Karna to be nothing but an upstart; an arrogant, immoral and boorish person. It was Karna's constant encouragement and instigation of Duryodhana that continuously scuttled any chances of compromise between the Kauravas and the Pandavas. Karna, Bhishma felt, was trying to score his own points over the Pandavas through Duryodhana, who was foolish enough not to realize that he was being used. Bhishma also blamed Karna for his active encouragement of Duryodhana and Dushasana in disrobing Draupadi. Thus, Bhishma could never bring himself to like or even tolerate him. Karna also did not care much for the Kuru patriarch and thought that the old man was pretty much overrated and biased towards the Pandavas.

'The Pandavas are in hiding in the kingdom of Matsyadesh. This is apparent by the suspicious circumstances under which Keechak, the powerful commander of their forces, has died. I believe it is Bheem who has killed him. If my suspicion is true, King Virat, despite being our ally, has been helping the Pandavas behind our backs, and thus has effectively declared his sympathies for the opposite camp. We will need to attack his kingdom and punish him for this transgression. This attack will also flush out the Pandavas from hiding, as they will want to come to the rescue of King Virat when we attack. Thus their vow of incognito existence will be broken and we can send them back to exile again,' Shakuni said, looking at the Kuru elders seated in the court.

Dhritrashtra had always sided with Duryodhana. However, as the king, he could not openly side with something that was blatantly unjust and openly hostile to the Pandavas, who were after all the children of his brother Pandu and had been in his care after their father's untimely demise. Thus, he always sought the approval of the other Kuru elders in the court, like Bhishma, Drona, Kripacharya and Vidura, the last of whom was his political advisor as well as half-brother. Their approval bestowed sanctity on whatever decision the king took and also served to spread the blame if things didn't turn out as expected.

The elders of the court had always tried to placate both the Kauravas and the Pandavas, and talk sense into both Duryodhana and Shakuni whenever the duo came up with an evil plan. However, they had not been successful so far and the enmity between the two sides had only grown despite their efforts.

Things had come to a head when, after losing the gambling match, Duryodhana tried to have Draupadi disrobed in public in the Kaurava court; only a miracle had saved her honour. Later, the Pandavas were exiled for thirteen years and their kingdom was usurped by Duryodhana with Shakuni's help. Everyone knew that Duryodhana and Shakuni disliked the Pandavas and had always wanted to expel them from the Kuru Empire, taking it all for themselves.

However, now that the Pandavas had duly completed their exile, the Kauravas were again scheming to catch them during the period of their incognito existence and send them to exile again. This seemed unfair to most of the elders of the Kuru clan, and they advised Dhritrashtra to be fair and just. They urged him not to let Duryodhana and Shakuni's hatred start a war between brothers. But all their advice had fallen on deaf ears, since Dhritrashtra was too biased in favour of his son and too weak to resist the duo's pressures.

Bhishma and the other elders again tried to reason with Dhritrashtra and Duryodhana.

'King Virat has always been our ally, Maharaj. His family has also been related to ours for generations,' Bhishma said.

'It is not wise to attack a friendly kingdom without finding out the merits of the case. Even if the Pandavas are hiding in his kingdom, I doubt if King Virat has any knowledge of this, since they would be incognito as per the terms of their exile. Attacking him for a folly which he has not committed and has no knowledge of will not only be a political blunder, but it will also turn a friend into a foe. Moreover, it cannot be the stated policy of the Kuru Empire that our friends cannot help the Pandavas in their exile. We must remember that our friends are their friends too, since we are, after all, the same family. Therefore, punishing him for helping the Pandavas, which I believe is not a crime any way one looks at it, will not be politically wise and will not benefit the empire in the long run,' Bhishma continued.

'Besides, the Pandavas have, as per the rules of the gambling match, duly completed their thirteen years in exile. We should, in fact, welcome them back with open arms and give half of the kingdom back to them, instead of conspiring to send them back into exile. They have suffered enough and we should not prolong their agony. They are, after all, our own family and the children of your brother Pandu. Prolonging this enmity any further will not be beneficial to the Kuru Empire. The Pandavas are not only exemplary warriors but are also just and pious people who have not intentionally harmed anyone till date. Even the citizens of the Kuru Empire love them. It will, therefore, be unwise for the royal family to continue antagonizing them and risking a possible fratricidal war with them.'

'I agree with Bhishma Pitamah,' said Dronacharya, the warrior sage. 'He always has the best interests of the family at heart and has the greatest experience amongst all of us in matters of politics, diplomacy and statecraft. It will not be in the interests of the kingdom to ignore his advice.'

Dhritrashtra turned from Bhishma to Drona and then towards the other elders seated in the assembly, staring with blind eyes, knowing where they sat only because he recognized their voices. Kripacharya and Vidura also nodded their heads in agreement and made agreeable noises, supporting the statements of the other two elders.

'This is the sanest advice anyone could give. This is the only way to ensure lasting peace in the empire and the continuity of the royal line on both sides of the family. The impending war will destroy several kingdoms, interrupt the propagation of their lines, and scorch the earth like a plague,' Vidura warned.

Predictably, this advice did not go down well with Duryodhana.

'Pitamah,' he growled. 'With due respect, I think you and the other elders of this family who serve the throne are unfavourably biased against me. There is no other reason why all of you would give such foolish advice to us. However, Shakuni Mama[39] is not asking for your advice. He is simply informing the court of what we have decided to do. Please do remember your pledge to always serve the throne and help us carry out what we want to do. Consider this plan as *rajagya*[40] and comply accordingly!'

Listening to the arrogant brat, Bhishma's eyes blazed for a *nimesha*,[41] his sword arm twitching to give the impudent prince a befitting response, but then he controlled himself and gave in to his better judgement. Of late, Bhishma had had to exercise more and more

---

[39]Maternal uncle

[40]Royal command or proclamation

[41]In the ancient Indian or Vedic method of measurement of time, a *nimesha* is the time required to bat an eyelid, or eight-fifteenths of a second in the metric system.

restraint with the type of company that had gathered around the royal throne of the Kuru Empire. He rued the day when he had vowed to serve the throne to ensure the marriage of his father Shantanu to the fisherman's daughter Satyawati. It was his and his father's bad decisions which had now come to haunt the Kuru kingdom.

Taking a deep breath, he tried again, addressing the king directly while ignoring Duryodhana's haughtiness and thick-headedness. From the corner of his eye, he could see Karna giggling with Duryodhana, making fun of Bhishma's helplessness.

'Maharaj,' Bhishma repeated, 'this will not end well. You are wiser and a more seasoned administrator than Duryodhana and should try to stop him from the course that he has set himself on, with more than a little help from Shakuni.' Disgust and disdain, particularly towards Shakuni, were apparent in his tone and words.

Shakuni had come with his sister Gandhari from Gandhar[42] when she was married to Dhritrashtra and had stayed back in Hastinapur ever since, always creating trouble. The gambling match that had led to Draupadi's attempted disrobing and the exile of the Pandavas was Shakuni's idea. Bhishma had never forgiven him for it. But Bhishma's hands were tied, and there was not much he could do unless King Dhritrashtra agreed to it.

Dhritrashtra did not reply and only wrung his hands in apparent helplessness. This was a favourite ploy of

---

[42]What would eventually be recognized as North-West Frontier Province (present-day Khyber Pakhtunkhwa of Pakistan) and northeastern Afghanistan

his to deflect any responsibility from himself; to show himself as a helpless puppet, a blind monarch prisoner to the whims and fancies of his son, whereas the truth was something else. Dhritrashtra knew the difference between right and wrong; he also knew that what Bhishma was saying was right, but he wanted to indulge his son and have his desires for the kingdom fulfilled vicariously. Dhritrashtra had always resented that he wasn't given the reins of the kingdom because he was born blind. The desire to rule the Kuru Empire had slept coiled within his heart ever since, and in Duryodhana's brashness and Shakuni's evil plots, he saw the fulfilment of his heart's deep desire.

While Bhishma and the other elders kept pleading for sanity, Dhritrashtra sat deaf and mute to voices of reason. In the end, it was decided that Kuru forces would attack Matsya to punish the errant king. What they needed now was a strategy!

'King Virat is not a puppet, Duryodhana, and will give a good fight to our forces. Even though he is enfeebled due to the loss of his commander Keechak, defeating him will not be easy.' This was Susharma, the king of the Trigarta kingdom.[43]

'Let me lead my forces against King Virat from the north. I will attack his kingdom and draw the army and the king away from the city. While Virat is away fighting my forces in the field, the Kuru forces can attack Matsya from the east. This will force the Pandavas to come to

---

[43]Tentatively located in the present-day Indian states of north Punjab and Himachal Pradesh, roughly close to the city of Jalandhar, with its capital at Kangara

Virat's rescue,' Susharma suggested.

'Wonderful!' Duryodhana exclaimed, overjoyed. 'You are a genius, my dear friend Susharma. What do you say, Shakuni Mama?'

'I think this should work,' Shakuni said pensively.

'While Susharma draws out Virat's forces to the north, we will attack the kingdom from the east and herd away all their cattle.'[44]

'Even if the Pandavas do not come to Virat's rescue, which I think they will, we will still have taught him a lesson. On the other hand, if the Pandavas do come out of hiding to help Virat, they will be spotted and, according to the terms predecided, they will have to return to exile. Either way, we have nothing to lose,' Karna said, finally happy that he would be able to face Arjun in battle and prove his superiority, which he had been itching to do for a long time. Karna needed to prove his prowess with the bow and the arrow as well as his loyalty towards Duryodhana, who had lifted him out of abject poverty by bestowing upon him the title of King of Angadesh.[45] This was the reason Karna had always been unusually aggressive whenever anything related to the Pandavas was discussed in front of Duryodhana.

Bhishma, however, did not approve of Karna's unnecessarily belligerent attitude and sounded a word of caution again.

---

[44]Traditionally the wealth and prosperity of a kingdom was measured by the head of cattle the kingdom possessed, since the state's economy revolved around cattle. All through the epics and the legends of ancient India we repeatedly find this special emphasis on livestock, especially cows.

[45]Anga was an old kingdom to the east of the Kuru Empire, corresponding roughly to present-day Bihar.

'Be careful, Karna. The men who go looking for trouble usually find it. I know you are itching for a duel with Arjun, but you must remember that this Arjun is not the same one who sat hanging his head in shame when the gambling match was going on. This Arjun is one who has earned several divine weapons from various gods, the fire of revenge burning within his heart. It is my advice to you, son, as an elder of this royal house, that you should not think of picking a fight with Arjun, or you may have a surprise in store for you.'

Bhishma's well-meaning advice was not received well by the group that surrounded Duryodhana. Suddenly, pandemonium broke out, with allegations and counter-allegations flying from everywhere. Duryodhana, Karna and Shakuni accused Bhishma of being biased towards the Pandavas, especially Arjun, and raised doubts over his motives. Vidura and Kripacharya tried to pacify the trio while Bhishma and Drona looked on in consternation, embarrassed at the behaviour of their descendants. When things seemed back in control, Bhishma spoke again, addressing the throne, unwilling to speak to the ill-mannered and uncouth rabble of people like Shakuni and Karna.

'Maharaj, it is unfair to doubt my intentions. Everyone knows that I have taken a vow to always serve the Hastinapur throne, and I will never break my vow as long as I breathe. Thus, the fears of the prince and his friends are unfounded. What I say, what I advise them, is only due to my concern for their and the kingdom's well-being. If it comes to war with the Pandavas, you do know, Maharaj, that I will always fight on the side of the throne,' Bhishma thundered in a voice which made even the scheming Shakuni shudder and thank his stars that Bhishma was on their side.

'It is resolved then,' Dhritrashtra spoke, finding his voice after a long time. 'Shakuni, Karna and Duryodhana will exercise more restraint and discipline when addressing Pitamah, taking his advice in the proper spirit. We know that Pitamah is the pillar, the foundation upon which this empire stands today. It is foolish to doubt his intentions. On the other hand, Pitamah, we need to be more careful when dealing with Duryodhana and his friends. They are all hot-blooded and often do or say things they do not actually mean. It is also decided that we will attack Matsyadesh and try to flush out the Pandavas. If the Pandavas are discovered, they will have to go back to exile; if they remain incognito, we shall welcome them back to Hastinapur and give them their half of the empire. We are not doing this out of enmity, but the terms of the match dictate that we do everything in our power to try to discover them in exile. It is the duty of Kshatriyas to adhere to their dharma without fear or bias, and we are merely following our duty. Susharma will attack Matsya from the north and draw out Virat, following which the Kuru forces, under the leadership of Bhishma Pitamah, Dronacharya, Kripacharya, Karna, Shakuni and Duryodhana, will attack from the east. Does everyone agree?'

Everyone nodded their assent.

'We have only two weeks left till the completion of the agyaatvaas,' Susharma said. 'I will quickly assemble my forces and attack in ten days. I will send a messenger to Duryodhana to tell him when it is opportune for him to attack.'

'May the gods be with you, Susharma, my friend,' Duryodhana said, bidding farewell to the Trigarta king, who left promptly to prepare his forces.

'We have to be ready to leave for Matsyadesh within ten days, Pitamah,' Duryodhana said, addressing Bhishma.

'Don't worry, Duryodhana. It will be done,' Bhishma said as he walked out of the royal assembly, after bowing before the throne.

Meanwhile, in Matsyadesh, King Virat and the Pandavas had no inkling of the trial they were going to face soon.

2

King Virat, the ruler of Matsyadesh, was married to Queen Sudeshana and was the father of two children—a son named Uttar Kumar and a daughter named Uttara. The king himself, though valiant and cognizant of his duties to his subjects, was fond of gambling and thus used to spend a considerable amount of his time enjoying the company of gamblers, jesters, musicians and dancers. When Keechak, Virat's commander and Queen Sudeshana's brother, was alive, he had taken advantage of this habit to surreptitiously take charge of the affairs of the kingdom, thus becoming the de facto king, while Virat indulged himself.

However, after Keechak's death there had been a void, and Kanka (Yudhishthira) had tried to tend to the duties of the king in place of him. This had given Kanka a fair idea of the situation in Matsya. He had religiously looked after the welfare of the kingdom and the royal family, collecting taxes, watching over the treasury, keeping the armed forces in a state of readiness and interacting with the spies to help the kingdom get news of its friends and foes. It was through this network of spies that Kanka had learnt of the impending attack by the Kuru forces.

However, the Matsya spies were not as skilful as the Kuru spies and could not inform him of the attack plan in detail. Kanka, therefore, had no idea of the two-pronged attack that Duryodhana had planned for Matsya. However, since he knew that the attack was coming, Kanka had kept the forces ready. He had also informed Ballabh, Granthika and Tantipala about the same. After several secret parleys, it was decided that these four men would go with the royal army to help with their defence whenever the attack came, and that Sairandhri and Brihannala would stay behind.

All this while, the king spent his days in indulgence while Kanka prepared the army.

The king's son, Uttar Kumar, was a fine gentleman but was not cut out to be a warrior. Unfortunately, he was blissfully unaware of this and considered himself a warrior par excellence. The king and the other courtiers also indulged him, never having the heart to tell him that he was living in a fool's paradise.

Uttar Kumar's sister, Uttara, was a beautiful girl and a skilled dancer. Her knowledge of music, dance, court courtesy and knowledge of statecraft had grown by leaps and bounds ever since Brihannala had become her coach and mentor. She would chat with Brihannala about a variety of topics, ranging from art forms to warfare to qualities of kings and queens to fantastic stories about the Pandavas. Brihannala seemed to know a lot about the Pandavas and when Uttara quizzed her, she would say that she had worked in the court of the Pandavas for several years before they lost the gambling match and were sent into exile.

'After the Pandavas left Indraprastha, the city lost its lustre and became just a relic of its glorious past. The Kuru rulers treated the city in a stepmotherly fashion since it belonged to the Pandavas. Soon many noble families and merchants had left Indraprastha, and the city was consumed once more by the forest of Khandava.[46] I also left soon after the Pandavas were exiled,' Brihannala told Uttara.

Slowly, Uttara grew quite close to Brihannala and sought and respected her advice on many matters, either personal or those of the state. Brihannala also told Uttara how Kanka had held an important place in the court of the Pandavas and that they never ignored his sage advice. This valuable piece of information was, of course, duly conveyed to the king, and he always kept this in mind whenever Kanka gave him unsolicited advice or aired an opinion that the king and his courtiers didn't immediately understand.

Slowly, the king came to trust Kanka because he soon found out that whatever Kanka advised ultimately benefitted the kingdom. Under his expert guidance, Matsyadesh had prospered and the royal treasury had increased manifold.

It was also through Brihannala that Uttara, and in

[46]The Kuru Empire was initially equally divided between the Kauravas and the Pandavas to put an end to the enmity between the two sides. Dhritrashtra gave the Pandavas the area of the forest of Khandavaprastha. The forest was burnt down to make way for the new city of Indraprastha—modern-day Delhi—which became the capital of the part of the empire ruled by the Pandavas.

due course Virat, came to know that Ballabh, Granthika and Tantipala were also trained soldiers, having served in the army of the Pandavas. Brihannala had also told Uttara that these men could be trusted in times of need, when no help from any other quarter may seem forthcoming.

One day, when the court was in assembly and King Virat was sitting on the throne, the leader of the royal spies walked in. He bowed low to the king and pronounced the usual benediction.

'Raja Virat *ki jai ho* (Victory to King Virat). The forces of Trigarta threaten us, Maharaj. King Susharma has camped with his army of one *akshauhini*[47] two days' ride away from here. Their intentions are not noble as they ride with full battle gear, in formation, with their standards raised high and their conches blowing warning blasts.'

King Virat was rendered speechless for a moment. Kanka and his friends looked at the king with interest and a little amusement. Kanka had anticipated this and had made sure that Ballabh, Granthika and Tantipala were present in the royal court when this news was broken to the king. He looked around at the others now and saw a little smile playing on Ballabh's lips. He was probably amused at the prospect of finally seeing some action.

[47]A battle formation consisting of elephants, chariots, cavalry and infantry in the ratio of 1:1:3:5. Typically, an akshauhini will have 21,870 elephants, 21,870 chariots, 65,610 cavalry and 109,350 infantry. This would be a total of 218,700 warriors excluding the chariot and elephant drivers, who do not fight. This number, even by today's standards, is staggering.

After a moment's pause, the king broke his silence.

'It is strange that Susharma would want to attack us. We are not his enemies and have never done anything to offend him or harm the interests of his kingdom, yet he attacks us,' the king said, pausing for a moment. Looking at Kanka, he continued, 'What do you think we should do, Kanka? Should we send emissaries and press for parley or prepare for war?'

The king trusted Kanka completely and hence, in this time of need, he had turned to him for advice. Kanka stood in front of the royal throne, his hands folded, flanked by the other three—Ballabh, Granthika and Tantipala.

'Maharaj,' he said. 'King Susharma has attacked us without provocation, and he comes in battle formation. It is my opinion that people who attack without reason will not listen to reason, hence we need to be prepared for war. In fact, I would suggest that we do not wait for him to come to us, but we should go out and meet him on his way.'

'But his army is too big—we cannot fight it,' the king complained.

'Let me assure you, Maharaj, that with Ballabh, Granthika and Tantipala on our side, we need not be afraid, and even an army of one akshauhini can be routed easily. These are exemplary warriors who used to serve in the army of the legendary Pandavas and have never seen defeat in their lifetimes. Please put on your battle gear and let us head out to teach this errant king a lesson,' Kanka replied, brimming with confidence.

Kanka's confidence was infectious, and he, with Ballabh, Granthika and Tantipala standing behind him, looked so majestic that the whole court roared in approval, their confidence soaring. The morale of the royal family, courtiers and the armed forces was boosted and they mentally girded themselves for war.

'So be it,' Virat said, 'Let Susharma have a taste of his own medicine. We will ride out to meet him at one day's distance from here.'

With this Virat unsheathed his sword, raised it high in the air and bellowed, 'Har Har Mahadev.'

The court responded with war-like fervour, 'Har Har Mahadev.'

Orders were given and the forces were instructed to get ready and assemble outside the city walls, ready to march. Kanka had already kept the *chaturanga*[48] army ready, and it did not take much time to mobilize them. The king, meanwhile, went to his chambers to apprise his family of the developments. It was decided that Prince Uttar Kumar would stay back with a small contingent of soldiers to guard the gates of the walled city and the other men would leave with the army, with the king leading the charge.

Prince Uttar Kumar initially protested, but later relented as he thought that he was being assigned the

---

[48] *Chaturanga* means 'four–limbed' or 'comprising of four parts'. Thus, an army was called chaturanga if it had elephants (*gaja*), chariots (*ratha*), cavalry (*turanga*) and infantry (*pada sainik*). Chaturanga, incidentally, is the root for the modern Hindi/Urdu/Hindustani word *shatranja* or chess, which also has four types of board pieces besides the king and the queen—the rook, the bishop, the knight and the pawn. The composition of the board game thus reflects the composition of the army mentioned in the ancient Indian scriptures. It is a known fact today that chess originated in ancient India. In fact, chess pieces have been found during excavations of pre-historic sites in the Indus-Saraswati basin, also known as the Indus Valley Civilization.

important role of guarding the women of the royal household. His ego satisfied, he agreed to shoulder the responsibility with a great show of sacrifice. The queen and Princess Uttara were worried about the safety of the king, but Brihannala assured them that with Kanka, Ballabh, Granthika and Tantipala by his side, not even the devas would be able to harm Virat.

Brihannala's words infused some confidence among the ladies of the royal household and the queen started her preparations to see the king off.

Presently, King Virat stood in front of the queen, dressed in full body armour and chainmail, with his royal sword strapped to his side. The queen held a golden tray with lamps in her hands for the *niranjana*[49] and prayed for the success of the armies of Matsya. She marked his forehead with vermilion and, after doing a *pradakshina*,[50] showered him with rice grains and flower petals.

The king's procession exited from the palace, winding through the city's lanes, joining the army waiting for him outside the gates. He was happy to see Kanka, Ballabh, Granthika and Tantipala, similarly attired, their foreheads marked with vermilion, looking resplendent in their battle gear.

The king smiled at Kanka and assumed his place at the head of the army. The *purohit* (priest) accompanying the army blew his conch shell to indicate that the moment of departure had arrived, and the army moved forward, marching towards the place where Susharma's army had camped. From the walled city, the queen, the

---

[49]An auspicious ceremony to wish for good luck

[50]Clockwise perambulation around someone

princess Uttara and the eunuch Brihannala continued to look at the standards of the army till they faded away from view.

Before his army had pitched its camp in a field two days' ride away from Virat's palace, Susharma had dispatched a rider on a swift horse, carrying a message to Duryodhana.

The Kurus, meanwhile, had kept their forces in a state of readiness and were waiting for word from Susharma so that they could march towards Matsya. The army contingent had been kept small so that it could move swiftly and raid the outlying portions of Matsya, thus forcing whoever was inside the fort to come out and face them. Besides, the number of soldiers did not matter when the Kuru warriors accompanying them included names like Bhishma, Drona, Kripa, Karna, Duryodhana, Ashwatthama[51] and Shakuni. Each of these warriors was enough to hold off an army on his own, hence Duryodhana was not worried in the least. He had prepared a few hundred cavalry, a few score chariots and a couple thousand foot soldiers and now waited for word from Susharma. Only four days were left for the Pandavas' agyaatvaas to end, and this worried Duryodhana and Shakuni.

While they were brooding, the rider from Susharma arrived in Hastinapur, tired and out of breath, his horse foaming at the mouth and nearly dead with exhaustion. They had ridden at top speed for a whole day, hardly

[51]Dronacharya's son

stopping for water or nature's call, and were nearly collapsing when they were ushered inside the palace.

'King Susharma has camped two days' ride away from Matsya, Prince Duryodhana. He also wanted me to tell you that he ensured that the Matsya spies saw him and they fled in alarm to inform their king. He is expecting the attack anytime tomorrow,' the messenger told Duryodhana.

'Excellent,' beamed Duryodhana. 'Take care of this messenger. See to it that he and his horse are well cared for. He must rest and then return to his master after he has been amply rewarded in proportion to the stature of the Kuru Empire.' Duryodhana barked orders to his attendants, 'Inform all the elders, and sound the alert that the army will leave for Matsya within a *muhurta*.'[52]

As per orders, a general alarm was sounded and messengers were rushed to the residences of the Kuru elders, Bhishma, Drona and Kripa. Presently, a small raid party was ready to proceed for Matsya.

Back in Matsya, Uttar Kumar presided over the safety arrangements of the walled city. He went from gate to gate, from turret to turret. He checked the recesses of the fortifications and the back alleys. He checked the secret passageways and secured the causeways. He made sure

[52]A *muhurta* is an Indian unit of measurement of time, corresponding roughly to forty-eight minutes. The muhurta was the Vedic 'hour' before the sixty-minute hour was adopted, probably due to Mesopotamian influence. A 'half hour' was a *ghatika,* that is twenty-four minutes, and the Vedic day had thirty muhurtas. The terminology continues to be used in common parlance in India, although not in terms of measurement of time.

the moats were filled with water, the drawbridges were secured and the *shataghnis*[53] mounted on the walls of the fort. There was no room for error, the whole city had been left in his charge with only a handful of soldiers. He set up a patrol party to check the ramparts and sent scouts to scour the areas around the fort for enemy activity. After he had checked every inch of the insides of the walled city, he retired to the general assembly room with a few soldiers of the royal guard. The room was situated at an elevation and had a great view of the ramparts of the fort and the fields beyond from its window. The prince sat down on the couch at the end of the hall and mentally went over his preparations. It had been almost a day since the king had left the fort to face the forces of Susharma. They must have reached the enemy camp by now and the battle may have started. Uttar Kumar wondered what was happening there.

His reverie was broken by the clatter of footsteps. As he looked towards the source of the sound, a messenger came running into the room, out of breath, his clothes disheveled, his eyes staring, rivulets of sweat pouring down his forehead. He staggered to a stop near the couch, steadying himself with difficulty, trying to catch his breath.

'What is the matter, soldier?' Uttar barked.

'Sir—sir—sir…' the soldier stammered.

'What? Spit it out,' Uttar said impatiently.

'The Kuru forces are stationed a few hours ride from the fort. They have unfurled their banners and

---

[53] *Shataghni* is a machine which can kill a hundred people at once. The term tells us that the use of machines in warfare is not a recent concept but has existed since pre-historical times.

have assumed battle formation. The army is only a few thousand soldiers, but all the Kuru elders are with them—Bhishma, Drona, Kripa, Ashwatthama, Duryodhana and Karna…' the soldier blurted out.

Uttar stared at him, taken aback by the sudden barrage of information. Then he saw that the soldier had more to say.

'Is there more?' Uttar asked.

'Yes sir,' the soldier was almost in tears now.

'They have raided the adjoining villages, rounded up all their cattle and gold, and are currently holding them captive in their camp,' the soldier looked relieved after spewing out all the bad news at once. He now waited for instructions from his prince.

Uttar paused, thinking and weighing his options. Then he smiled, this was a god-sent opportunity for him to show his skills. How better to do it than to defeat the world-famous Kuru warriors all at one go and secure Matsya's cattle and gold? He beamed and sprang up from his seat, surprising all the attendants in the room and the messenger who staggered back, almost falling over.

'I shall go out to fight the Kuru forces and bring back our cattle and gold which they have unfairly snatched from the villagers. Go and inform the royal guards to prepare my chariot. No one else needs to come with me. The rest of the soldiers must stay back and guard the palace. I alone am sufficient to defeat these people and bring back our cattle,' the prince said.

The messenger's jaw dropped open. He took a moment to comprehend what Uttar was saying and ensure that he had heard it right. Then the truth dawned on him and he did not know whether to be happy or scared. Finally, he decided to run along and carry out his errand instead of troubling himself by thinking too much; thinking was someone else's job!

An alarm was sounded in the palace. The royal guards ran hither and thither to yoke the prince's chariot and assemble his weapons, while the prince put on his body armour and chainmail. The royal priest was called to offer prayers to the gods and to mark the prince's chariot and weapons with auspicious marks to ensure his success in battle.

The news spread rapidly in the ladies' quarters and Uttara and Queen Sudeshana came running to Uttar. They were concerned for his safety and fussed over how he can possibly fight the mighty Kuru warriors alone.

'This is the moment I have waited for all my life, mother. Don't worry, I shall return soon after defeating these raiders and securing the cattle and wealth of Matsya,' Uttar said.

The queen was happy to see her son's confidence and prayed for his wellbeing. She brought out the golden tray with the lamps, marked his forehead with vermilion and kissed his head.

'May you be victorious, son, and bring greater fame to the royal house of the Matsya people than anyone has ever done before,' the queen blessed her son, handing him the royal sword.

'Please take Brihannala with you,' Uttara requested her brother, pressing his hands with hers and peering into his eyes. 'She was Arjun's charioteer and may be able to help you.'

'Alright. Let Brihannala come and drive my chariot,'

Uttar said. 'I will show her how real warriors fight. Maybe she will learn a trick or two from me and let me know if I am better than Arjun.'

All this time, Brihannala was standing behind the queen and the princess, chewing her lips and saying nothing. Now she chimed in happily, 'Yes, my prince, it will be an honour to see you fight. I am a very good charioteer and I used to work for Arjun. I shall be honoured if you will accept my services and let me be your charioteer. When you have won the war, I will help you round up all the cattle. I will also collect the *angavastram* (upper garment) of all the Kuru warriors and bring them for Uttara. This will teach them a lesson and will be an appropriate gift for the princess.'[54]

'Ha ha! Yes, that should teach the old men a lesson,' Uttar laughed at the idea of Brihannala disrobing Bhishma, Drona, Karna and Duryodhana. 'Go Brihannala, mount the chariot and wait for me.'

With Brihannala seated in the charioteer's place, Uttar mounted it and ordered her to drive out of the walled city. As the chariot started to move, the queen and the other ladies of the palace sang benedictions and sprinkled rice grains, holy water and flower petals on the chariot. It rolled towards the exit gate and was soon out of the fort. The drawbridge was raised and the gates of the fort were closed once the chariot drove out. The soldiers stood on the ramparts and the ladies gathered in the general assembly hall to see Uttar trundle down

---

[54]Disrobing someone during a skirmish or a war was considered a great dishonour and a sign of defeat, and the one who was able to do so was considered victorious.

the dirt path from the castle towards the plain fields, where the Kuru forces waited.

Meanwhile, after a day of fighting, King Virat had quickly routed the forces of Susharma and the remaining Trigarta soldiers had retreated. Kanka, Ballabh, Granthika and Tantipala had shown exemplary courage and fought like seasoned warriors in the battle. Virat was very happy and made a mental note to reward their valour once they returned to Matsya. Kanka had not been wrong, Virat thought, when he had promised that the one akshuhini forces of Trigarta would be defeated easily.

Thus, the victorious Matsya army marched back to the fortified city where they received a hero's welcome. The remaining palace guards as well as the citizens, women and children alike, all cheered and showered them with petals. As the procession entered the palace gates, Virat could see the queen and the royal priest at the entrance with the flowers and the auspicious lamps, but he could not see Uttar. Was he ill? Why had he not come out to welcome his father?

Once he was inside the palace and alone with his courtiers, Kanka and the ladies of the royal household, Virat asked the queen, 'Where is Uttar Kumar?'

'A day after you left, Maharaj, we got word that the Kuru forces had raided the villages outside the city and rounded up all the cattle and gold they could find. Uttar Kumar went to retrieve our cattle and gold. We are yet to receive any word from him,' the queen informed Virat with a heavy heart.

'Uttar went to fight the Kurus?' Virat exclaimed.

'Yes. And he went alone in his chariot, driven by Brihannala,' the queen said.

'Brihannala? The eunuch?' Virat was getting more and more confused. 'Wasn't there a single soldier left in the palace who could drive his chariot?'

'I suggested that he take Brihannala, father,' Princess Uttara spoke up. 'Brihannala had served as the charioteer of the great Pandava warrior Arjun. She herself told me about it so I recommended to the prince that he take her as his charioteer.'

Virat was suddenly very worried. It wasn't only that Uttar was very young and inexperienced, but also the fact that his first battle would be with the vastly superior Kuru forces and he had no other help except a eunuch who taught dance to his daughter. Virat's forehead was creased with worry.

Kanka understood what was going on in Virat's mind and he approached the king, his hands folded, saying, 'I can see that your majesty is worried about the prince and his safety while fighting the Kuru forces. Let me assure you, Maharaj, that with Brihannala by his side, the prince cannot but be victorious. Brihannala is not only a good charioteer, but she can also wield weapons if it comes to that. She has never been to a war where she has not been victorious.'

Virat was puzzled, but recent events had proved that Kanka knew what he was saying and his prophecies did turn out to be true.

'Kanka,' the king said, 'If you say that Uttar is in safe hands, I will believe you. I will retire to my chambers to bathe and then pray while I await news of Uttar. Please send a few scouts to bring news of the battle between Uttar and the Kurus.'

Saying so, the king walked off into his chambers and the assembly dispersed. Only Kanka remained with Ballabh, Granthika and Tantipala. Uttara also stayed back, standing some distance away, hidden from view, observing the four men. As she stood watching, the other three folded their hands, got down on their knees and bowed low in front of Kanka.

'*Bhratashree* (Elder brother),' the three said in unison.

'Please get up. We still have some time to go before we can reveal ourselves,' Kanka said, 'We must also wait for Brihannala and see what developments happen there before we decide on our next move. This is Duryodhana's doing. It is a deliberate move to spot us during our agyaatvaas. Unfortunately, I had not anticipated this pincer attack when I got the intelligence that they were planning an assault.'

'These people are hiding something,' Uttara thought. 'But they seem to be nice people and have so far helped father in his battle against the Trigarta forces. Who are they?'

Ballabh, Granthika and Tantipala had risen and were standing close to Kanka, talking to each other in hushed tones. Uttara started to retreat quietly when Kanka spotted her. He wasn't alarmed, angry or annoyed. He only smiled at her gently and whispered, 'Don't tell your father anything, not right away. For his own good. Everything will be clear tomorrow. Uttar Kumar is safe with Arjun—er—Brihannala. Go prepare for the prince's welcome.'

Uttara's eyes twinkled. She had had her suspicions,

but now it looked like she knew who they were. Kanka was right about this not being the right time and she would wait for them to reveal themselves.

3

Uttar Kumar's chariot went down the dirt road leading up to the field where he knew the Kuru forces were stationed. He held a bow in his left hand and had strapped a quiver full of arrows to his back. His sword was sheathed in its golden scabbard and strapped to his waist. His banner fluttered majestically in the wind. Uttar felt confident; his day had come!

He noticed that Brihannala had commandeered his chariot's horses very skilfully. The horses obeyed her commands as if they had been trained under her guidance. They understood every flick of her wrist, every jolt to the reins. Impressed with Brihannala, Uttar Kumar looked at her closely; maybe there was more to her than met the eye. She was well-dressed, her lower limbs covered with a dhoti[55] that looked more masculine than feminine. Her torso was covered with a *kanchuki*[56] and over that she had slung an angvastram.[57] Whatever portion of her torso was visible looked well-toned and muscular. Her forearm rippled with

[55]A generic term for a wraparound garment worn in rural India; usually worn by men, it is also used by women in several parts of India with an additional garment for the upper half of the body.

[56]Classically, a wrap-around blouse which is tied behind the back, worn by Indian women

[57]*Angavastram* literally means 'body cloth'. It is a form of a stole used by both men and women to cover the upper part of the body either in a wraparound fashion or slung over the shoulder.

muscles as she flipped the reins of the horses and Uttar Kumar noticed that her hands were calloused. These callouses were in a peculiar pattern. It was not the hand of a mridangam[58] player or even that of a manual worker; these were the hands of a warrior. These callouses were earned by years of handling the sword and, what was stranger, by the repeated friction with the string of a bow. Her face, though feminine in its beauty with its arched eyebrows and long eyelashes could easily be that of a handsome man.

Uttar's train of thought was disturbed by the sound of Brihannala challenging the horses to slow down. Her voice rang out clearly, addressing the prince now.

'We are almost there, prince. I can see the flags that adorn the chariots of Bhishma Pitamah, Acharya Drona and Kripacharya. Karna, Duryodhana and Shakuni are also here. Behold them standing in a beautiful formation, their bows in hand, their masts fluttering majestically in the wind. Look carefully! Behind them, the elephants, the cavalry and the foot soldiers of the mighty Kuru army are arrayed in formation too. Stand guard!'

There was a rasping quality to Brihannala's voice that made Uttar's hair stand on end. Pulled back to attention, he looked around him as Brihannala started to move the chariot slowly in a wide semicircle so that Uttar could get a good view of his adversaries.

Fear touched his heart lightly with its cold fingers. Something fluttered in his stomach and his innards cringed with a deep-seated cramp rising from inside his pelvis. His tongue suddenly went dry as Uttar Kumar

[58]Indian percussion instrument played with both hands

looked around him to assess the enemy.

In the centre of the Kuru formation stood Bhishma, taller than the other warriors who surrounded him, built like an aged bull and battle-scarred from the decades of wars he had seen. His clothes were white, as were his long beard and hair, which he had tied neatly behind his head. His creased and handsome face seemed set in stone as he stood erect, his divine bow in his left hand. Bhishma was the picture of divine valour as well as penance personified.

Flanking Bhishma stood Dronacharya, the warrior sage, teacher of martial arts to both the Kauravas and Pandavas. His dress was saffron, the colour of renunciation, his beard greying, and his hair tied neatly in a braid. He was of medium height, stockily built and dark-skinned. His jet-black eyes looked piercingly around, striking the fear of God into men.

Adjacent to Drona was Kripacharya, wearing red-coloured clothes and carrying his mighty weapons with such ease as if he was born with them.

On the other side of Drona was Ashwatthama, his son, taller than his father, dusky and clean-shaven, his curly hair tied in a knot behind his head. He was heftily built and had an expressionless face. On his forehead shone the jewel which he was born with and which, people said, made him immortal.

Also present was Karna, shining like the sun in his golden *kavach-kundala,*[59] which he was born with.

---

[59] *Kavach* means armour, and *kundala* means earrings. Legend has it that Karna was born wearing the armour and the earrings which were a part of his body and were impenetrable, thus making him unassailable in war.

Rumour had it that Karna was a child of the Sun god and was unassailable till he wore his armour.

Accompanying Karna was Duryodhana, the Kuru prince and heir-apparent, dressed in a black dress and black armour. He also had jet-black hair and bushy eyebrows. His well-muscled arm was twice the size of Uttar's thighs. He was world-famous for his skill with the mace and for his cruelty.

As if this was not enough, there were also Dushasana, the evil brother of Duryodhana who had tried to disrobe Draupadi, and Shakuni, Duryodhana's maternal uncle who had plotted the gambling match that had led to the Pandavas' exile as well as the usurping of their empire.

As Uttar Kumar looked at these warriors, dreaded throughout the land for their martial prowess, his confidence started to ebb. He realized, albeit a little late, that he had taken things a little too lightly. Maybe now wasn't the time to prove his valour. While he was still trying to decide what to say to Brihannala, she spoke up.

'Get ready, O Prince, to redeem the pledge of valour that you have taken. Stand fast, keep your arms ready! I shall drive the chariot closer for combat.'

'NO!' Uttar Kumar shouted a little too loudly, for the sound carried across the plains and reached the ears of the Kurus. Suddenly, Bhishma and the others started to look in their direction!

'No…' Uttar Kumar repeated, albeit a little softly this time. 'I cannot fight these legendary warriors. What was I thinking? How can I, a mere scrawny youth, presume to even face these giants in the battlefield?' He started to hit his head with the flat of his hand as if to wake himself up from a nightmare.

'Brihannala, my dear Brihannala. How can I fight them? You know how valiant and seasoned they are. And I am a child in front of these people,' Uttar almost started pleading now. 'Please take me away from here, I cannot fight. I want to go back to the fort and think over this.'

'No, my Prince,' Brihannala thundered. 'For the Kshatriya there is no going back from the battlefield. You will fight and I know you will win this war. Don't be afraid.'

When Brihannala refused to obey Uttar's request he panicked. Fear-stricken he said, 'Brihannala, please. I must go back. I cannot stay here. I will die. Please take me away from here. I am not prepared to fight these people. I was a fool. Please forgive my mistake. Take me away from here.'

Uttar Kumar kept saying the same things repeatedly in his panic, his eyes wide now, his forehead clammy, his clothes drenched with sweat. But Brihannala did not budge.

'I will help you. You cannot lose. Don't be a coward. Fight. Redeem your pledge, fight for your honour; don't spoil the name of your family!'

But Uttar Kumar was approaching hysteria in his fear. He jumped down from the chariot, stumbled, and started to run towards the fort, not looking back even once. 'If you will not drive me back, I will run back to the fort. I am not staying here to die,' the prince said, running for his life, crying openly.

As the Kurus watched amusedly from a distance, Brihannala also got down from the chariot and started to run after the prince, calling for him to stop. It was a comic sight, Uttar Kumar running like a madman with Brihannala following him like a person deranged, her hair flying in the air, her clothes disheveled. The Kuru warriors broke out in raucous laughter that flowed across the plains like a tidal wave, reaching Uttar Kumar and Brihannala. Only Bhishma did not laugh. He stood very still and watched Brihannala closely, his eyebrows twitching, his old eyes staring unblinkingly, and then, he smiled wryly.

Finally, Brihannala caught up with Uttar Kumar. With much effort she was able to hold him still and speak a few words to him.

'Stop. Wait. I am ready to take you back to the palace. Please come back with me.'

At the mention of the word 'palace', Uttar Kumar paused and looked at Brihannala. 'You will take me back to the palace Brihannala? Yes? Promise me please that you will?' he pleaded.

'Yes, I will. Now please come back with me to the chariot and do as I say. If you listen to me very carefully and follow everything I say, not only will you live and go back to the palace, but you will also be hailed as the victor,' Brihannala said.

Uttar Kumar stared at her like a man who had lost his mind and nodded. Brihannala gripped the prince's left arm firmly, and guided him to the chariot like a parent helps a child to walk. Once the prince was inside the chariot, Brihannala whipped the horses and they took off. Away from the battlefield they went but not in the direction of the fort. Brihannala was going somewhere else!

'This is not the way to the palace, Brihannala,'

the prince squealed, still not entirely assured of her intentions.

'Yes, I know,' Brihannala said firmly, the tone of her voice commanding. 'Be patient a little longer.'

On and on they rode, away from the palace and towards the common cremation ground of Matsya.

'Why are we going towards the *shmashaan* (cremation ground)?' Uttar asked, whimpering like a child now, tears flowing down his cheeks.

'I need to retrieve something from the old banyan tree there,' Brihannala said, her voice fired with new urgency and purpose.

'But that tree is haunted. The dead body of an old hag hangs there by a leather strap. We should not go there.'

'I know that story. I was the one who planted it amongst the people of Matsya,' Brihannala said.

'Why? If it is not a dead body, what is it then?' Uttar asked, his curiosity getting the better of him, the tremor gone from his voice.

'You will know soon enough,' Brihannala said, the authority and command in her voice becoming increasingly clear to Uttar Kumar.

Presently, the chariot stopped under a huge banyan tree and Brihannala got down from the charioteer's seat, beckoning Uttar to follow her. Gingerly, he also got down and stood looking at Brihannala perplexed, anxious and curious.

'Please climb up the tree. There is a large leather bag tied to the branches high up in the tree. Cut its fastenings and bring it down.'

Uttar Kumar followed the order obediently, feeling

better that he was no longer in command. While he climbed up the tree to look for the leather bag, Brihannala adjusted her clothes. She rearranged her hair, removed the face paint and the kohl from her eyes, removed her kanchuki, and redraped the angvastram in a different way. She tightened the dhoti she was wearing, making it look more masculine. She removed her ornaments and threw them casually in the chariot; gone were the bangles, the nose pin, the ear drops and the *chhoramani*, the hair pin. After she was done, she stood waiting for Uttar.

When Uttar descended from the haunted tree carrying the huge sack of leather, he was surprised by who he found standing there. Brihannala was gone and in her place stood a middle-aged man, well-built and handsome, his hair tied neatly behind his head. Uttar's mouth dropped open as he wordlessly put the leather bag down on the ground and stood looking at the warrior who stood before him. The man smiled gently, amused by Uttar's bafflement, and retrieved a dagger from the folds of his garments, bent down and cut the leather string holding the bag together.

The bag opened, revealing a plethora of weapons inside. Beautiful, divine weapons. They shone with an aura of their own. The exquisite artwork on their metal and the lustre on their surfaces were other-worldly. Looking at them, Uttar felt himself brimming with confidence. He looked at the man who was Brihannala some time ago and saw his eyes shining. The man bent down, picked up a sword and strapped it to his waist. Then he bent down again, picked up an exquisitely carved, extremely beautiful, divine bow. He held it in his hand, caressing it, and strung it gently, slowly strumming the string of the bow as if it was a musical instrument and he a musician. After this, he strapped a quiver full of arrows on his back and wrapped the remaining weapons again in the leather bagand put them in the chariot. All this while, Uttar Kumar watched him in awe, kneeling on the ground, immobilized by what he was witnessing. When the man paused, Uttar found his voice.

He brought his palms together, bowed his head and knelt in front of this warrior. 'Please forgive me for whatever mistakes I may have committed unknowingly, sir, when I thought you were Brihannala. But now I see that you have been living among us in disguise for a reason. Please do tell me who you are and for what purpose you are here? I am your servant and shall do as you instruct.'

'Rise, O Prince. I am Arjun, son of Kunti. We have been living here for the last one year to spend our period of agyaatvaas. Brother Yudhishthira is Kanka, Bheem is Ballabh, Nakula and Sahadev are Granthika and Tantipala, and Draupadi is Sairandhri. This period of our incognito existence is now over. Please rise and honour me by being my charioteer so that I can teach Duryodhana and his raiding party a lesson,' Arjun said.

Uttar's face shone with a new light as the full import of Arjun's words struck him. Overwhelmed, he said, 'I shall be honoured to be your *saarthi*,[60] O Parth.'[61]

Following this exchange, the two mounted the

[60]Charioteer

[61]Another of Arjun's names. Arjun's mother was Kunti, the daughter of king Kuntibhoj. She was also called Pritha. Hence Arjun, her son, was also known as Parth.

chariot with their positions reversed. Arjun was now the rider and Uttar Kumar was the charioteer. The chariot sped towards the ground where the Kuru forces waited, its leaders still perplexed about what they had just witnessed.

Arjun's chariot raced towards the battlefield, his *dhwaja*[62] sporting the figure of Hanuman[63] fluttering in the wind. As the Kuru army came in sight, Arjun slipped leather finger guards on his hands.

'Steady,' he warned his charioteer, who nodded, realizing that the time for action had come.

Arjun held the Gandiva[64] high over his head, pulled its string back right up to his ear without mounting an arrow on it, then pulled it a little more before letting it string go. A deafening twang echoed across the ground, booming like the sound of the sea, threatening like a war drum, crashing like a percussion wave over the ear drums of the Kuru soldiers standing far away. Their attention was suddenly drawn to the sound, all jokes ceased and the warriors gripped their weapons tightly, uneasy, unsure of where this sound came from or what it signified!

'This is the Gandiva!' Bhishma said calmly as if talking about the weather, drawing the attention of all the Kuru royalty standing on their chariots.[65]

---

[62]Flag atop the chariot

[63]The monkey god in Ramayana, another Hindu epic

[64]Arjun's bow was named Gandiva. In the epics, the weapons and accessories like conches, etc., all have names. Every warrior also had his own dhwaja which could be used to identify him from a distance.

[65]In the epics, all the named, divine bows and conches had their characteristic sounds. An astute warrior may decipher another warrior's

'Gandiva?' everyone parroted in reflex, like children repeating after their teacher, their voices laced with doubt, disbelief and more than a little fear. They were still coming to terms with this new piece of information when another sound boomed across the ground. It sounded like a wail—low, rumbling, deep-throated, ululating, full of foreboding and warning the Devdutt, Arjun's conch, had been blown to announce the beginning of hostilities and warn the adversary. It was unmistakable this time. Bhishma suppressed a knowing smile as he recognized the sound, while Shakuni looked confused. Was it Arjun? How? Where?

They found their answer soon enough as the chariot sporting the Hanuman dhwaja came into view, cruising down the dirt path and started to swerve into an arc. Arjun stood erect on the chariot—handsome, valiant, his white clothes fluttering in the wind. Uttar Kumar was the charioteer now, and sat with a renewed confidence. A temporary paralysis came over the Kuru camp as they saw the chariot approaching. They could neither move nor raise their weapons; they even forgot to shout orders to the soldiers standing behind them. Their expressions frozen on their faces by the suddenness of the event, the surprise that Arjun had sprung on them, the Kuru elders failed to respond in time as Arjun loaded arrows on his Gandiva and shot them towards the place where the Kuru forces stood.

Six arrows, in three pairs, zipped through the air and thudded into the ground in front of the chariots of

---

location on the battlefield simply by listening for the sound of their weapons or the blast from their conch shells.

Bhishma, Drona and Kripacharya, making Bhishma smile involuntarily. This was Arjun's way of paying his respects to his elders. Always the ideal student and the perfect archer, it was only Arjun who could have conveyed his respect in this way, warrior to warrior. While the three elders stared at the white-tufted arrows embedded in the ground in front of their chariots, Arjun quickly shot several arrows from his bow at the speed of light. They whizzed past everyone and before anyone could even hear the twang from the Gandiva; the masts bearing the flags of Duryodhana, Karna, Ashwatthama and Shakuni were cut down from their chariots. It was a sign; the first round had been won by Arjun!

Before the masts of the Kuru warriors could touch the ground, Arjun released another barrage of arrows towards Duryodhana with unimaginable agility. Duryodhana's canopy was shot down, the bow that he held in his hand was cut into two pieces and his crown, toppled by an arrow from the Gandiva, flew and dropped to the ground several paces away from the chariot. Arjun was not trying to kill Duryodhana; that would have been easy had he wanted to do it. He was scaring the Kauravas, teasing them, showing them their place and driving home a point. Panic gripped the elders and sudden pandemonium broke out in the Kuru forces as they realized that Arjun had taken them on single-handedly and was pressing his advantage.

'Take care of Duryodhana. Surround him. Arjun is targeting him,' Bhishma shouted to all the leaders of the army, giving some direction to their confusion.

Jolted into attention, everyone swung quickly into action. Drona, Kripa and Bhishma started targeting their attack towards Arjun, but he cut down their arrows as easily as if he was humouring children and then kept pressing towards the Kuru prince. He was not concerned with others and did not pay them attention. He directed all his fury towards Duryodhana, putting the Kauravas on the defense.

'Karna, defend Duryodhana. Take him away from the battlefield. If Arjun reaches him, we will have lost even before the skirmish begins,' Bhishma shouted to Karna.

Duryodhana's charioteer had taken the cue and quickly turned his chariot around. He whipped his horses to move away from the thick of action. Duryodhana did not protest. Such was the fury of Arjun's attack that even Karna meekly followed Bhishma's command, unable to think and react quickly on his own. He tried his best to save Duryodhana but his best was not enough. Arjun's speed, skill and ferocity surprised everyone. It had been thirteen long years and they had forgotten why Arjun was still the world's unbeaten archer. Arjun was just reminding them of this fact.

Shakuni, Karna and Ashwatthama surrounded Duryodhana's fleeing chariot and tried to block Arjun from pursuing him. On the other hand, Bhishma, Drona and Kripa kept attacking Arjun from behind, trying to divert his attention from the party that was defending Duryodhana. But it was not easy to overpower Arjun. For thirteen years, he had buried his emotions, his anger and his frustration, deep inside his heart. They had kept simmering and smouldering, reaching a flash point. Now, when he saw Duryodhana, all his pent-up emotions boiled over like a volcano erupting after a period of forced quiescence. It was impossible to stem this barrage of emotions. His armamentarium now included divine weapons which he had earned through penance during his exile in the forest. He had returned from exile stronger, better, faster and angrier!

The Kuru forces, the warriors and the elders realized this and fought evasively, trying to save their prince and get away from the battlefield with their lives and their honour intact. They attacked Arjun only to draw his attention and waste his time so that he would not pursue Duryodhana, who had now realized that it was time to flee if he wanted to live to fight another day.

Anyone who came in front of Arjun was overwhelmed by a shower of arrows and had to flee to save their life. When Shakuni tried to stop him, Arjun broke his armour, cut his bow, and damaged his chariot so badly that he had to jump down and flee on foot to seek shelter behind an elephant. Ashwatthama tried to save Shakuni and was similarly rewarded. His charioteer was killed, his bow cut down and his armour impaled by Arjun's arrows. If it were not for Karna he would have lost his life, even though Arjun wasn't keen on killing anyone. While Karna intervened, he was still unable to do anything in the face of Arjun's sharp arrowheads which seemed to rain like hail, spewing fire. When his quiver ran out of arrows, Karna had to flee too, his ego humbled.

The small contingent of soldiers following him felt the heat of Arjun's archery when he let loose the Agneyastra and it started to burn through the rank and file of the Kaurava army. They fled for their lives, leaving their weapons and animals behind; seeing this, the other soldiers also broke rank and scattered, as did the animals of the small force. The elephants ran trumpeting, the horses scattered whinnying and the men ran for dear life, screaming. The morale of the foot soldiers and cavalry, already sagging after encountering Arjun unexpectedly, was completely shattered and they dispersed like clouds hit by a gust of wind.

Seeing the Kuru warriors harassed by Arjun, Bhishma sent Drona and Kripa to defend the group surrounding Duryodhana and he himself confronted Arjun. For every arrow that Bhishma shot, Arjun shot two. It had been a long time since the grandfather and the grandson, the teacher and the disciple, had parried thus. Bhishma was enjoying it, as was Arjun. But Arjun knew that this was not the time for enjoyment, so he shot a smokescreen in front of Bhishma and kept pursuing the fleeing forces.

However, Bhishma's intervention had given the others sufficient time to rally and organize themselves. While Duryodhana stood back, protected by an arc of warriors, the others attacked Arjuna together. They formed a semicircle in front of Duryodhana and rained arrows on Arjun.

This went on for some time till Arjun decided that, it was time to end the skirmish and send the Kurus home shamefaced. Arjun retrieved the Sammohanastra[66] from his divine quiver and, summoning all the gods who controlled this weapon, shot it in the sky towards the center of the arc that the Kuru warriors had formed. The weapon exploded in the air in the middle of all the chariots and quickly released a gas that paralyzed them all.

---

[66]Weapon of mass hypnosis

As the Kuru warriors stood still, albeit awake, their remaining foot soldiers, cavalry and elephants fled the scene, leaving their bounty of cattle and gold unprotected.

There was a sudden lull in the fight as Arjuna requested Uttar to stop the chariot right in front of the chariots of the Kuru warriors.

'Go get their angavastram. I promised them to Uttara. Collect the sacks of gold and set the animals free,' Arjun commanded Uttar Kumar, who quickly carried out the orders. He then trotted back to his chariot, lugging the sacks of gold onto the chariot.

'Let's go,' Arjun said, and they were off, pursuing and guiding the horde of cows, which also fled back to their homes after being released from captivity. As the chariot sped back to the Matsya palace, the Kuru warriors stirred and realized what had just happened. Arjun had single-handedly defeated and insulted them by collecting their clothes, seizing their gold and leaving them standing helpless, like statues in their chariots. They had not achieved anything and had instead been disgraced.

Bhishma stirred first and addressed the others just waking up from their hypnotic sleep, 'Let's go back to Hastinapur and rethink what needs to be done. The Pandavas' agyaatvaas is over and we will need to discuss when we can call them over for parley.' The others, still too groggy from the gas released from the weapon, nodded absent-mindedly, turned their chariots, and followed Bhishma towards the Kuru capital, still smarting from the smacking Arjun had given them.

Author's Note

The story of the Pandavas' agyaatvaas, killing of Keechak and defeat of the Kuru forces at the hands of Brihannala appears in the 'Virat Parva' of the Mahabharata. This rendition is neither a complete nor and accurate and unabridged translation of the mentioned portion of the epic. However, it does attempt to give a quick look into what forms an important portion of the Mahabharata. After this, the parleys for avoiding the war started, with Krishna serving as one of the messengers. These ultimately failed, leading to the great fratricidal war of the Mahabharata, in Kurukshetra, a city situated in the present-day Indian state of Haryana.

PART TWO

DWITIYAH: SHIVA

The Cosmic Dance: *Rudra*

As the colour of the sky brightened in the east, the sun rose languidly, full of guilt and shame at the great horrors of the day before. Its first rays fell on the ash-smeared yogi[67] who wandered the lands of Bharata, the land of the gods. But this was no ordinary ascetic; he was the 'Swayambho',[68] the self-born, the celestial ascetic. Tall, fair[69] and well built, his head framed by matted locks, he was dressed in a loincloth made from the skin of dead animals· The trident he carried glimmered in the morning light, but the yogi seemed unaware of the world around him as he walked slowly, aimlessly, in a trance. His half-closed eyes were bloodshot and his face was streaked with tears. As he moved, he sometimes jerked his head, his locks flying around like angry serpents, a ferocious energy coursing through his limbs, barely under control like a wild animal straining at its leash. He would often open his eyes, look around in surprise

---

[67]One who practices yoga and meditation. Yoga literally translates to addition or joining; hence yoga helps a person join one's inner self to the supreme cosmic consciousness.

[68]'Swayambho' mean self-born. The eternal cosmic deities like Shiva and Vishnu or Hari, are Swayambho, self-born or self-created.

[69]Contrary to the popular depiction, sometimes, of Shiva or Shankar as dark or 'blue', he is known to have been fair. He has been described in various *stutis* or devotional hymns, as 'Karpurgauram'—fair like camphor.

and then, looking at the form he carried in his arms, burst into tears. Sadness would give way to anger, his eyes would roll upwards and a spot on his forehead between his eyes would start glowing. He had wandered this way the whole night, crazed with anger and sorrow.

There were those that followed him, keeping their distance and scurrying away to take shelter amongst the trees and shrubs when he had his bouts of anger. They couldn't muster the courage to walk up and console him, or stop him from the course he had set himself on. Anger had blinded him the previous night, and almost as a reflex, the yogi had entered the meditative state in which he had spent decades in a secluded cave high up in the mountains. Scores of years the yogi had meditated, unravelling the mysteries of the world to whoever came seeking it from him—the devas, the asuras, the mortals and the ascetics; he refused help to no one. He had taught his followers yoga and aarogya,[70] natya[71] and tantra[72]. He had existed like this since times immemorial, since before time itself, and would have continued to do so had he not consented to marry Sati.

The memory of the name brought him to his senses; as if he awoke from some deep sleep. Looking at the form he carried in his arms, charred beyond recognition now, he convulsed with rage. Nandi and the others following him fell to the ground in fear. The more he looked at her body, the more the convulsions grew. It was easy to see what he carried in his arms was once

---

[70]Health science
[71]Art of theatrics, or dance
[72]Occult sciences

the beautiful woman he had loved and married. He had carried the body through a long night of horror that the world would never forget. His convulsions grew more rhythmic as his body and limbs moved with an energy his followers had never seen before. Even as he carried her, with one hand he used the *damroo,* his one-handed drum, to time his movements. Its ominous boom sent shivers down the spines of the people watching him. Was this what they feared it to be? The rhythm was getting increasingly clear to everyone; its sound primal, threatening! The yogi danced his dance with the body slung in his arms. The two forms looked grotesque dancing together and every so often the lines separating their bodies blurred and the two coalesced into one.

The celestial beings watching him from a distance, fearing the worst, had rushed to inform the only person who could stop him. While the yogi continued his gyrations, the crimson spot on his forehead pulsated and throbbed, and grew ever brighter. The heavens were crowded with all the celestials, watching in awe and fear, whispering prayers. The animals of the forest scurried away from the place knowing in their guts what was happening. The end was near. The yogi kept dancing faster and faster, beating the damroo and looking at the form in his arms; his semi-trance did not allow him to see the object that approached him from the sky in the east. Moving fast and glowing brightly like a comet, the Sudarshan, the celestial missile, had been let loose by Hari, the Padmanabha.[73] While Shiva danced immersed

[73]Padmanabha: one who has a lotus sprouting from his navel. Brahma, the creator, sits on that *padma* (lotus) and creates the universe.

in his thoughts, the missile approached him, aimed at the form in his arms.

Shiva had never been on good terms with his father-in-law Daksha Prajapati.[74] Brahma, Daksha's father, had once been chastised by Shiva[75] and thus Daksha had always nursed a grudge against him—a grudge which had amplified with time. Unfortunately for Daksha, his daughter Sati had taken to worshipping Shiva and had performed severe austerities to please him. She wanted him as her husband and her penance had borne fruit. The Bholenaath[76] had consented to lead his marriage procession to Daksha's capital to wed Sati.

Daksha, who never regarded Shiva as anything more than a homeless ascetic, grudgingly approved of the match because his counsellors and other prominent sages and devas had persuaded him; but he had not been happy. Sati was after all a princess, a Prajapati's daughter! Daksha believed his daughter had brought insult and ignominy to her royal house by marrying Shiva and his anger had turned upon Sati for betraying him. Even during the wedding, Daksha had been civil only for the sake of appearances. He had sulked throughout and had rushed through the auspicious ceremonies, inviting great consternation from the priests. His insulting behaviour

[74]Prajapati is a generic term, a title which simply means 'a leader of men'. This can also be used for a king or an emperor, as it has been used here.
[75]Brahma was born with five heads, one of which was ripped off by Rudra or Shiva when Brahma had lied to him at the beginning of creation.
[76]Bholenaath: *bhole*—simple, gullible, one with unblemished mind; *nath*—lord, master

had not escaped the Mahadev's notice, but Shiva had borne all the insults patiently so that Sati would not feel bad. However, after the wedding Shiva had conveyed to Sati his resolve to never visit Daksha's kingdom again since Daksha obviously did not want anything to do with the two of them any longer.

Sati consented happily, trusting Shiva to know better and had been content living with him high in the Kailash mountains[77] until she heard of a great sacrificial feast being organized by her father. Daksha had invited all the sages, kings and other leaders of men but had deliberately omitted Shiva. This did not matter to the Mahadev for he was content living in Kailash but Sati wanted to go to her father's place for the feast, to meet her family and enjoy the festivities. Shiva tried to convince her otherwise but she went anyway.

Accompanied by Nandi and Shiva's other followers, his *ganas*,[78] she visited her father's place only to be given the cold shoulder in the beginning and public humiliation later. Daksha had been looking for an opportunity to vent his anger against Shiva and Sati's visit had given him just that. He made it a point to bring to everyone's notice that though Shiva had not been invited to his festivities, he had still sent his wife

---

[77]Mount Kailash is Shiva's mountain abode and lies in present-day Tibet, beyond the Himalayas. The area has great religious significance for several Asian religions like Hinduism, Buddhism and Jainism. Mount Kailash has a lake, Manasa or Manasarovar, which is a place of pilgrimage for devout Hindus, Buddhists and Jains. This region is also the fountainhead, the source, of several large river systems of South Asia like the Indus or the Sindhu, the Brahmaputra or the Tsangpo, and the Ghaghara or the Saryu, a tributary of the Ganga.

[78]The word *gana* literally translates to 'people'

Sati to represent him and maybe collect some gifts. Shiva was after all an ascetic with no worldly possessions and was dependent on donations from royal houses such as his for his sustenance! But Shiva did not even have the honour to come and do the begging himself and had sent his wife. What sort of a man would do so, Daksha had taunted publicly.

Some of the guests had laughed at Sati, making fun of her discomfiture, while others had made snide remarks about her husband. All this was done in public view and in Sati's presence. She had borne the insults heaped on her quietly but had lost her composure when Daksha dragged Shiva into it. Disgusted and angry at her father and his guests, she entered the sacrificial fire to end her life, but not before warning those present there of the fate about to befall them. She told them in clear words that all the sages, gods and devas of this world would not be able to save themselves from Shiva's wrath.

When she entered the sacrificial altar, offering herself to the great Mother Shakti and asking her to shelter her spirit, a wave of terror had swept across the palace premises; everyone shuddered visibly at the thought of the impending doom. As the flames licked her fragile frame, Sati's spirit had risen from the pyre, as luminous as the fire, and had united with that of the Universal Mother. She had absorbed Sati's spirit and, laughing raucously, had disappeared, leaving everyone wondering what they had just witnessed.

The entourage that Shiva had sent to accompany Sati fled in panic and, shivering to their bones, prostrated themselves at his feet. As they narrated the story, Shiva's rage knew no bounds. He immediately rushed to Daksha's capital and stormed into the sacrificial grounds, his ganas following close behind. Tears flowed like streams, searing his eyes and streaking his cheeks. He had sat down in the *padmaasana*[79] at the altar near Sati's charred remains and, laying Sati down on his lap, had howled in pain. His curses had rent the sky and made everyone tremble. Birds of prey started cawing, wolves howled in unison, hyenas laughed and elephants trumpeted, driven mad by an unknown fear clutching at their hearts. The sky became overcast with clouds and the earth trembled. All the divine guests and members of Daksha's royal household quaked with fear.

Daksha fell upon the ground trembling, begging for mercy, realizing too late that doom was imminent. Shiva did not hear anyone, did not see anything. He was already deep in a meditative trance! He jerked his head back, and in a blind rage pulled out two locks of his matted hair, smashing them to the ground and murmuring ancient invocations. The ground trembled under the weight of his locks and a cloud of dust arose which soon cleared to reveal Veer Bhadra and Bhadra Kaali, Shiva's alter egos, the personifications of his yogic self. Fiery-eyed and armed with all sorts of weapons that dripped warm blood, the duo knelt by the feet of their master like tame beasts. Shiva was still in a deep trance, his body glowing with energy, his face contorted in anger. He had become Rudra—the angry one. He opened his crimson eyes slowly, rising from the lotus posture with Sati's body in his arms. As he turned to walk away from the altar, he commanded the duo to destroy

---

[79]The lotus posture used by yogis

everything in sight, speaking in an ancient tongue that no one understood. Thus it began!

Veer Bhadra and Bhadra Kaali laid waste to anything they set their eyes on. They assumed huge, demonic proportions and, baring their fangs and shrieking like sirens, the two horrific beasts fell upon their prey. The twin messengers of death tread the sacrificial grounds of Dakhsa like giants let loose in a world of lilliputs. Doors were smashed, windows broken, and pillars and pavilions pulled down. Any living being in their path was decapitated and disemboweled. Kaali snatched everyone's heads and drank their blood, while Bhadra sought out Daksha and pinning him under his feet cut his head off with the trident he carried. Howling like a hungry beast, Bhadra tossed Daksha's head into the sacrificial fire which had consumed Sati and kicked his lifeless torso around for pleasure till he found someone else to prey on. Men, women and animals fled the scene, howling and crying, while the carcass-eaters waited in the shadows for their turn. Day turned to night, wild animals howled and shrieked, but the twin harbingers of death continued to wreak havoc upon mortals and gods alike, pursuing them into the nearby woods where they had sought refuge.

Rudra meanwhile had walked away from the palace, unmindful of the ongoing bloodbath. His eyes half closed, he carried Sati's charred body out of the impure premises. The faithful ganas followed him, painting a strange sight.

Down the mountains he went, into the forests and over the water; he knew not what came his way and it didn't matter anyway for his heart was broken. Sati's charred remains hung limp in his strong, ash-smeared arms, bobbing up and down as he walked. He was mindful of only one emotion—rage: blinding, searing rage obliterating all other emotions. He wanted to end the world; he had resolved that this was what the people deserved—those who had let his beloved down and let her die while they watched and laughed.

His eyes blazing with fire, the Virupaaksha[80] roamed the earth while the gods huddled together in guilt, shame and fear, wondering how to stop him from destroying everything. They knew what was coming; the Tandav, the 'cosmic dance', would soon begin!

This dance was Rudra's way of venting his immense yogic energies; to cure or to curse, he had used the Tandav in different ways with devastating effect.

As he walked the earth through the night, plants wilted, rivers and streams stopped flowing and the moon shone no more. Occasionally, some part of the carcass he carried would fall off and drop to the ground. As it struck the earth, Rudra would shudder and gnash his teeth, his body convulsing with the pain of separation, his limbs flying wild. After some time, the activity would cease and Rudra would continue his aimless wander while another one remained in his place. Bhairav stood guard where Sati's body parts fell.[81] The ganas hurried to cover the part with fresh earth, pay obeisance, do *prana pratishtha*[82] to consecrate the place and name it

---

[80]Literally: ugly-eyed one, or angry-eyed one

[81]Traditionally, it is believed that Bhairav guards all the Shaktipeethas, and one cannot enter the Shaktipeetha if Bhairav doesn't allow it

[82]Literally: infusing life into the deity. After *prana pratishtha*, the deity is living and is regarded as a person. He or she is woken up daily, and is

after the part that fell. Thus, Rudra kept walking and his followers kept creating Shaktipeethas or 'houses of Shakti', another name for Sati, the divine Mother. Thus came Bimala, Tara Tarini, Kamakhya, Vishalakshi, Manikarnika, Kapalini, and on and on. The madness seemed unending until, at the very crack of dawn, Rudra seemed to slow down.

Nandi and the others thought his anger had abated but they were wrong. This was just the lull before the storm broke. Meditating and contemplating, wavering between anger, guilt, sorrow, pity and rage through the night, the Mahayogi had finally arrived at a conclusion. The world had to be destroyed for it to be cleansed of its sins. The gods, devas and the sages had erred in letting Sati die in the *yagya* fire. They had to atone and needed to shoulder the blame for causing the end of the world!

As the first rays of the sun hit him, he slowly began his dance with Sati still in his arms. His bodily eyes were almost closed, but the Trinetra or 'third eye'[83] was turning red, ready to open and destroy the world with the Kaalagni, or the fire of dissolution, that would spew forth from it. His body glowed brighter and brighter, and soon it was impossible to look at him. He danced in a deep trance far away from the world, while Sati was

---

lulled to sleep at night, is served food and offered clothes. This deity holds rights over property.

[83]Shiva, and sometimes Kali, is depicted as having a third eye in the center of his/her forehead. The third eye marks the *aagya chakra*, one of the 'nodes' of the body used in tantra or yoga. The two bodily eyes are used for seeing the mortal world while the third eye is a window into the subconscious. In Indian tantric traditions, the aagya chakra is represented by a lotus with two petals representing Shiva and Shakti.

cradled close to his bosom, her touch reminding him why the world needed to be destroyed.

❧

Shiva was so absorbed in his trance that he did not notice the missile that Vishnu had let loose in his direction. All the celestial beings had fled in terror to Hari, seeking his intervention to stop Rudra. They appealed to him to remove the burnt and dismembered body of Sati which was not allowing Rudra to cool down and become Shiva again.

It was for this reason that Hari, the lotus-eyed god, decided to destroy Sati's body with his Sudarshan Chakra (the divine discus). It would leave Rudra unharmed due to his yogic trance which had created an energy shield around him, radiant and powerful. It was the only safe way to end this vicious cycle and stop Rudra's Tandav from reaching its climax.

So he had let loose the deadly missile which now flew towards Rudra like a flash of lightning, hardly visible as it approached its mark. Rudra had nearly completed his dance, his body glowing, the crimson light from his Trinetra splitting the orb of light which surrounded him, growing stronger and beginning to sear everything in its vicinity; the Trinetra or the third eye was opening! It was then that the missile hit him.

There was a huge explosion—a surge of energy and light—and a boom that threatened to level the ancient mountains. Everyone was momentarily blinded. Then the light subsided, the noise died down and the earth ceased to tremble. Finally, when his ganas could look up, they saw Shiva standing poised in the abhaya mudra[84] or the 'benevolent pose'. Sati's body was gone, dismembered by the Sudarshan Chakra, and Shiva had slipped back into the deepest meditative slumber.

His followers scurried hither and thither, looking for the parts of Sati's mortal shell which had been scattered all over Bharatavarsha. Everywhere they went they found some piece of their divine Mother and along with that they found Bhairav standing guard. They buried the piece, consecrated the grounds and left Bhairav guarding the Shaktipeetha.

After some time, Rudra stirred and woke up from his trance, his anger receding, the benevolence in him taking over his rage and turning him back to Shiva. The world needed healing, the ageless one knew this. He had been rendered mortal by his love for Sati and had given in to mortal feelings of love, anger and sadness. This would not happen again. He knew his anger had wreaked enough havoc the previous night. There had been enough violence and mindless slaughter. Veer Bhadra and Bhadra Kaali still roamed the mountain ranges in the vicinity of Daksha's capital, quenching their bloodlust, seeking the royals and the devas, plucking off their heads and entrails, and drinking their blood from headless torsos. They needed to be placated, the dead needed to be roused and made whole again. The world needed continuity; it was not time yet for the do its work.

Shiva resolved to fix what had been done the previous night knowing full well that not everything could be changed. He would bring to life those whom Bhadra

---

[84] *Abhaya* literally means without fear

and Kaali had slaughtered but he could not bring his Sati back. She had been charred, turned to ashes and then dismembered by the Sudarshan Chakra. He saw that it was *vidhi*, natural law. This had to happen; they had to be separated before they could meet again, finally and forever. Him and Shakti, Prakriti and Purusha,[85] two halves of an eternal whole, they were meant to be together. But not yet. The world wasn't ready. He saw it now, looking beyond time, beyond what even the gods could see.

As he walked back towards Daksha's capital, the devas who had escaped slaughter came in hordes and prostrated themselves before Shankara. Brahma, the grandsire of all creation, and Vishnu, the dark-skinned god who lies on the infinite ocean of milk, also came. They approached as supplicants, as mendicants even, to please and placate him. Shiva looked at them with indifference; they did not matter. The one who mattered was gone but he knew she would come back again. Till then Shiva had some healing to do, for himself and the world.

His gaze seared their very souls. They knew their sins were far too heavy but Shiva was gracious and generous; he would forgive! While they lay at his feet, Shiva blessed them all. As they sang praises of the timeless and ageless Shiva, Veer Bhadra and Bhadra Kaali came too. Beckoned by their master, the duo came as tame animals, their fangs still dripping blood, pieces of raw flesh sticking between them. Hideous and terrifying, the two came and

---

[85]The male and female energies of the universe; the active and passive halves of creation; yin and yang

knelt in front of Shiva, grunting and belching, smelling of carcass and death, their hair disheveled, their eyes red with wine, meat and the flesh of men and gods. They came with their terrible weapons and laid them at the feet of the ascetic with three eyes. They lay their heads upon his feet in respect! The devas gasped in fear, still quavering at the sight of the twin personifications of death.

'You can go now. It is done!' Shiva said, and his ganas were gone in a cloud of smoke like they never existed, their howling and their raucous laughter echoing across the valleys. The Mahadev then went around the devastated premises and stood in the centre of the sacrificial ground that ran red with the blood of the devas. He made an occult *mudra* with his hands, whispered ancient mantras to the winds and breathed an 'Aum'. Miraculously, all the dead stood up as if from slumber. All except Daksha were revived from the dead since his head had been thrown into the fire by Bhadra and could not be found. The others, back from the dead, prostrated themselves at the feet of the Mahayogi and chanted his thousand names, calling him Shiva, the auspicious one! Shiva blessed them all, instructing his ganas to go into the forests and bring the head of the first living creature they found. Daksha needed to live again!

The ganas scampered away and returned swiftly with the head of a wild goat that Shiva installed upon Daksha's torso, bringing him back to life. Thus, Daksha became a lifelong devotee of Shiva and, renouncing his kingdom, went away to Kashi to spend his old age chanting his name.

Shiva, on the other hand, walked back to his cave high on Mount Kailash to continue his meditation, not to be disturbed till another maiden would take it upon herself to win his heart.

The Cosmic Dance: *Sunartaka*

1

The news spread like a forest fire enveloping the Himalayas and reached Aushadhipuram[86] carrying a wave of happiness. Himavan, ruler of the Himalayas, was ecstatic with joy; his wife Mena, the queen, almost swooned with happiness. Tears running down their faces, they ordered huge festivities across the whole kingdom. Alms were distributed to the needy, food was served to all and all the priests were honoured with *dakshina.*[87] Uma was returning home after her penance and she had been able convince Shankara, the Aadi Yogi,[88] to marry her!

Himavan was the king of the Himalayas with his capital at Aushadhipuram, the abode of all the medicinal herbs known to man. Even the divine physicians,

---

[86]*Aushadhi* means medicine, *pura* or *puram* means city or abode; hence, 'Aushadhipuram' literally translates to 'abode of medicines'. Traditionally the *Himalayas* have been considered the repository of all the medicinal herbs described in Ayurveda, the Vedic treatise on health, or 'disease-less-ness'—*ayur.*

[87]*Dakshina* means donation to the priests, teachers, or sages. It is not the same as alms, which are given to the needy.

[88]*Aadi* means original; Aadi Yogi thus refers to the 'original' yogi, or one who was there at the beginning of this world.

Dhanvantari,[89] Ashvini Kumars[90] and Guru Brihaspati[91] used to come to the valley to collect the herbs and other medicinal plants. He and his wife Menaka or Mena were a pious couple who looked after the people of their kingdom like doting parents. Their glory and fame had spread far and wide and they had won acclaim from the devas as well as the divine sages. They were ardent devotees of Shiva, the Aadi Yogi, and maybe this was the reason that the 'Mother'[92] had chosen them to be the parents of her mortal incarnation. In her previous birth as Sati, her father Daksha had been disrespectful towards her and Shiva. Unable to bear the pain of being the daughter of someone as obnoxious and sinful as Daksha, she had given up her mortal body in the flames of the yagya her father had organized just to insult Shiva.

All hell had broken loose after Sati's death. Shiva had destroyed Daksha's yagya and beheaded him through his servants Veer Bhadra and Bhadra Kaali. He had almost destroyed the world in his uncontrollable anger but had been stopped from doing so by the timely intervention of Hari.

After this, Shiva had become a recluse again. However, the devas had gone in supplication to the divine Mother, Shakti, pleading her to be born as the daughter of the pious Himavan and Mena and to marry Shiva so that the divine duo could be brought together once again. Their pleas had not been without a selfish purpose. Tarakasura, the asura (demon) king, had been

---

[89]Physician of the gods and source of the science of Ayurveda
[90]Twins, divine physicians, also known for their physical beauty
[91]Physician priest of the devas
[92]Shakti or the female half of Shiva

troubling them after obtaining a boon of conditional immortality; he could only be killed by a son of Shiva.

The divine beings had conspired and appealed to the Mother, their tears washing the ground beneath her feet, singing hymns to her in their sweet voices. The Mother had consented, knowing what was inevitable. She and Shiva were two halves of the same whole; they could not stay apart for long and were meant to be together. Only when they were united would the world become whole again. The devas' plea was only an excuse to do what had to be done anyway. The Mother knew this, as did the timeless yogi who sat in recluse in a cave and meditated, seeing the world with closed eyes.

Himavan and Mena had prayed too, performing austerities, yagyas and penance to have the Mother as their daughter. She had granted them their wish.

When Mena was pregnant, everyone remarked how radiant she looked and how she emanated peace and tranquility through the ten months that she carried Uma. The pregnancy had passed quickly, with the queen growing in splendour each day.

When the time was right and the planetary bodies were in the right conjunction, the Mother had appeared in the form of a baby from Mena's womb. The devas had crowded the heavens for a glimpse of the divine baby and had showered flower petals on her. The gods, the forest spirits and the deities who ruled the hills had all come in attendance, their hands folded and heads bowed in reverence to the Mother. Himavan and Mena had held the young infant, dark as the night, in their arms and had named her Kaali.[93] She would later also come to be known as Uma, or Parvati.

Uma quickly blossomed into a precocious young girl. From a very young age she would draw the likeness of Shiva in the sand and would fast to have him as her husband. How this divine love had blossomed in her young heart no one knew, for strange are the ways of *vidhi* (fate).

One day when the itinerant monk Narada visited the king's court, Uma greeted the saint with *arghya* and *padya*.[94] Being very pleased with her services, Narada told her to ask for a boon.

'Sir, please guide me on how to obtain the realm of Shiva,' Uma said.

'Why do you want to do that, child? This is not an easy task. Not even the yogis, meditating, fasting and doing penance for scores of years, can hope to see Shiva,' Narada said, trying to test Uma's resolve.

'You know Shiva lives high up in the mountains in a cave and sometimes he lives in the shmashaan.[95] He has ghouls and goblins[96] and all sorts of ugly creatures as his

---

[93]Shiva Purana tells us that Uma was dark-complexioned. Tradition shows her as both dark and fair. The complexion of the 'Mother' is immaterial and hence, it is up to the reader how they would like to imagine Mother Uma. She can be both Gauri (fair) and Kaali (dark) and is worshipped in both forms.

[94]Vedic rituals prescribe four things which must be offered to any guest visiting one's house. *Arghya*: any gift—a flower, some fruit, a sweet, a sprig of the holy darbha grass, etc.; *padya*: water to wash the feet; *aachamaniya*: water to drink or wash one's face; and *aasana*: a place to sit.

[95]Cremation ground

[96]Shiva's followers are the *bhutas* and the *pretas*, misconstrued as ghouls and goblins, or evil spirits. In my understanding however, they are just a

friends. He wears snakes as ornaments,[97] has ferocious locks of hair that can scare a girl like you and his ancestry is unknown,' Narada continued.

'Look what happened the last time a princess tried to attain him. Don't try to do something which is neither good for you nor easy to attain. Live here in Himavan's palace and enjoy your life with your friends and other royals. Why do you want to choose a life of hardship when you can easily live a life of comfort?' Narada quizzed her, looking at her obliquely and waiting to hear what she had to say.

She smiled and replied, 'It may be as you say it is, O Rishi! But I still want to attain only Shiva and nothing else. My only goal in life, the only reason I have been born and am alive today, is to attain Shiva. His snakes will be my garlands, his ghouls and goblins shall be my apsaras, his ash-smeared form will be lovelier to me than the flower-draped body of Kandarpa.[98] But without him, this luxurious palace is also like a prison to me. Please do guide me sir, and help me attain my objective.'

Narada laughed heartily, pleased at Uma's single-minded devotion.

'I am pleased to see your resolve, Uma,' he said. 'May you be successful. I will teach you the correct ways of worshipping Shiva so that he will grant your wish.' Narada then instructed Uma in the methods of Rudra-stuti. He

---

type of 'people', like the *yaksha, kinnar, gandharva,* etc. The bhutas and the pretas do not conform to the rules or norms of civil society, live like free spirits, roam around endlessly, are ferociously dressed and look 'ugly'.

[97]Shiva is described in various stutis or prayers as 'Pannagabhushanam' which means one who has snakes as ornaments.

[98]Another name for Kamadeva, the god of love

also taught her how to chant the thousand names of the yogi who has no beginning and no end. She listened with rapt attention and absorbed everything like a sponge.

The following day, after Vaamadeva[99] had left Aushadhipuram, Uma went to her father and told him of her resolve to do penance in the forests. Himavan was crestfallen and Mena cried and pleaded with Uma to change her mind but she was completely focused on Shankara.

'I live only for Shankara,' Uma said. 'If I cannot attain him, I might as well enter the fire like Sati did.'

Faced with Uma's relentless resolve, Himavan and Mena had to accede to her wishes. They let her go with great difficulty, following her till the very gates of Aushadhipuram where they said their goodbyes as Uma proceeded towards the jungle for her penance, wearing the colour of renunciation and chanting the names of Shiva.

Up the mountains and into the verdant forests she went, seeking the right place for her penance. She chose a spot sanctified by the presence of tall devadaru trees with all the auspicious signs on them. A mountain stream gurgled nearby which would provide water for her daily needs and the forest would give her fruits for sustenance as well as flowers to offer to Shiva.

She tied her hair in a bun, spread a mat of kusha grass and, facing east, sat down in the lotus-posture to meditate in front of a *paarthiv linga*[100] which she had

---

[99]Another name for Narada, owing to his contrarian views on everything; *vaama* means 'left'

[100]*Paarthiv* made from natural non-living objects, mostly mud; *linga*: spirit or emblem. Shiva is worshipped as *murti*, sculpture and linga, a symbolic or

made from mud. Every day she immersed the previous day's linga in the adjacent stream and made a new one. Then she would devotedly worship it, offering it flowers and the *bilva patra* or *belpatra.*[101]

With time, the fervour of her prayers progressively increased and she ate and drank less and less. Instead of sitting and meditating upon Shiva, she stood up and started to pray to him. Later, she stood on one leg and stopped eating anything except fruits. Shiva still evaded her. Then she quit eating fruits and ate only herbs while continuing to pray. Finally, she ate only leaves and continued her mortification. The intensity of her penance started burning up the worlds and the gods of the elements ran hither and thither, seeking respite from the heat. They went to the grandfather (Brahma) in supplication.

'O Pitamah![102] Uma's penance is burning up all ten directions. Agni, Vayu and Varun are finding it difficult to continue their work. Surya (Sun) and Chandra (Moon) are finding it difficult to go around the earth. Uma is unsettling everyone. Please plead to the Mahadev to appear before her and accede to her wishes or we shall all perish in the heat of her desire.'

Brahma agreed to try to persuade the Aadi Yogi to

---

representative mound of mud. Contrary to the popular, and popularized, belief of the linga being a phallic symbol, the linga also means 'symbolic' or 'representative'. In tantric traditions, the human body is said to exist in two distinct forms—the *sthool sharira* or the physical body, and the *linga sharira* or the non-physical/spiritual body. In this context the 'Shiva Linga' refers to 'the spirit of Shiva'.

[101]Leaves of the bel tree or the wood apple tree, which are dear to Shiva.

[102]Grandfather

appear before Uma and accept her prayers.

Meanwhile the intensity of Uma's penance kept on increasing. By now, she had also stopped consuming the leaves and stood on one leg without food or water, immersed in thoughts of Shiva. This finally woke the Mahadev up from his meditative trance and he smiled when he saw Brahma standing before him, hands joined in supplication. 'I know why you have come, O Learned One. The time has arrived. I shall visit Uma,' the yogi said to Brahma, sending waves of joy among the devas.

Thus it was that Shiva, pleased at Uma's penance, appeared before her and roused her from her meditation by placing a finger on her forehead, between her eyebrows, awakening her third eye—her aagya chakra.

'I am pleased with your penance, Aparna,'[103] Shiva said. 'Ask for any *vara*[104] and it will be granted.'

'O Mahadev. If you are pleased with me, grant that I may have you as my vara,' Uma said hesitatingly, her hands folded and head bent.

Shiva's carefree laughter rang loudly across the jungle and reverberated back from the mountain peaks, filling the valleys with happiness. It was an auspicious laughter, pleasing even to the ears of the gods.

'So be it. I shall marry you, Uma,' he said smiling.

Uma was overcome with emotion, tears flowing from her eyes as she laid her head on Shiva's feet.

'Arise, Uma. Go and inform your parents that I am

---

[103]One of the meanings of *parna* is leaf. Aparna is another name for Uma because she meditated on Shiva without eating a single leaf.

[104]*Vara* can mean both a benediction/boon as well as a spouse; here it is used as a double entendre

willing to be their son-in-law if they will have me,' Shiva said, still smiling.

As he smiled, nature smiled too. Flowers blossomed across the valleys, spreading their fragrance far and wide, and birds chirped happily, not knowing what it was that filled their hearts with such unbound joy. A strange bliss enveloped the divine beings in the heavens and the mortals on earth. However, ill omens were seen in the court of Tarakasura, upsetting the asuras.

Shiva was almost deliriously happy. He had waited so long for this; only he knew how he had ached for his Sati. He had wanted desperately to meet this Uma when he learned that she was doing penance for him. He wanted to see for himself if Uma was his Sati. He had come with great trepidation.

His heart beat faster as Uma raised her head from his feet and looked up at him. Their eyes met and Shiva felt weak with delight. Yes, it was her! She was his Sati, his Uma, his Aparna, his Parvati, his Kaali, his Durga, his Gauri. She had the same eyes, the same voice, the same dusky colour of the starry skies above Kailash. Shiva beamed longer than he should have, frozen in the moment looking at Uma. Could she look into his heart and know who he was, who SHE was? Did she know about them? Did she know they were two parts of one entity?

In his love for Uma, the ageless yogi had suddenly become an ordinary man, a mortal. He was happy, confused, weak, strong, afraid and bold—all at once. He wanted to touch her to make sure she was who he thought she was. He would know her by her touch, for how can one half not recognize the other? He knew it was her and knowing this, Shiva was suddenly as impatient as a child. With great difficulty, he pulled his gaze away from Uma and blessed her, letting her go on her way to Aushadhipuram.

'Go home, Parvati,' he said. 'Tell your parents the news that I shall come and meet them when the time is appropriate.'

As Uma turned away from Shiva to return to her home, his heart skipped a beat. He resolved he would visit her city soon in a way no one would know so that he could see her again.

2

Shiva's ganas soon learned of their master's promise to Uma. His happiness gave everything away. Then of course, there was Narada, the gossip monger of the gods, the celestial bard, the itinerant monk. He had gone from door to door singing and telling everyone that Shiva had agreed to marry Uma and the world had erupted in joy. The devas and the demigods had thronged to Himavan's capital to break the news to him and pay their respects. Brahma, Vishnu and the other gods had made a beeline to Kailash to pay their respects to Shankara and congratulate him for his decision to marry Uma. When they were granted an audience, they could not believe it was the same Shiva they had known from before his meeting with Uma. The Mahayogi could not stop smiling. His right hand was always in the abhaya mudra. Shiva was happy!

The demigods who had rushed to Himavan reached the palace before Uma and Narada. They broke the news of the success of Uma's penance leading to Himavan and

Mena weeping with joy. They declared a whole week of festivities across the kingdom and decreed that the capital was to be decorated to receive Uma upon her return.

Thus, the gates were decked with flowers and the roads sprinkled with perfumed water; so much incense was burnt in every nook and corner that the whole valley smelled like a fragrant flower. Lamps were lit in all the homes, in doorways, in windows, by the side of the roads, in fields, in orchards and in pots hanging from the trees. The whole city looked like a bride at a wedding. Dancers and damsels were invited, music played and people danced in the streets, delirious with joy and the *sura*[105] that flowed from the royal stores.

The mountain people also came when they heard the news, descending from their dwellings up in the heights. They came with their young and their old, women and children, and danced and sang in the streets. The *yakshas* came as did the gandharvas and the *kinnaras.*[106] The atmosphere was so infectious that Narada also danced, beating his castanets and twirling his *shikha.*[107] The gods and the devas also came, some openly while others in disguise, and danced in the streets. The whole world was overjoyed!

Himavan and Mena waited at the city's gates to receive Uma, and when she came, embraced her and wept with joy. Uma rode a chariot through the streets on her way

[105]Liquor
[106]Semi-divine species who sing and dance for the gods/devas
[107]Braid

to the royal residence as people clamoured for a glimpse. Rosewater and incense were sprinkled on her from turrets and balconies, benedictions were pronounced and she was showered with flowers.

Once the royal entourage reached the palace, the king and the queen accompanied Uma to her chambers where servants waited to give her a bath and rub aromatic oils on her body. Her hair was washed and perfumed, her nails colourfully painted, her eyes lined with kohl and her limbs tattooed with henna. Her hair was braided with flowers and pinned with a *chooramani*.[108]

When they had decorated Uma like the goddess she was, the ushers brought her out onto the balcony of the palace to greet her people and look upon the festivities going on in the streets just beyond the porch. The mother-daughter duo sat on an elevated platform and chatted happily while Himavan attended to the guests and the affairs of the state.

From where they sat, Uma and Mena could see the procession right where it started at the gates of Aushadhipuram. They could see the different groups of people dancing, singing and playing different instruments along the serpentine road to the palace. Everyone was present there, from the short *bheels* to the tall yakshas, and the hefty gandharvas to the pretty apsaras. There were even contingents of the asuras,[109] daityas[110] and *danavas*.[111] Uma could see the *saptarishis*[112]

---

[108]Hairpin

[109]Demons, or adversaries of the *suras* or devas

[110]Sons of Diti and cousins to the devas but always at war with them

[111]Sons of Danu; cousins to the devas but always at odds with them

[112]The seven primordial sages, sometimes interpreted as the

at a distance, walking sedately but enjoying the lilting music and buoyant atmosphere. Some groups of revelers had camped by the side of the royal highway and were drinking, eating and feeding children. Otherwise, the roadside was crowded with bystanders and ordinary citizens of Aushadhipuram who wanted to see the merry procession. Some citizens had even climbed up the trees and perched at the very top to be able to see the parade. It looked like a single living organism, writhing along, moving happily towards the palace.

As Uma and Mena sat looking at the procession, the fragrant mountain breeze fluttering their perfumed hair, they could see some commotion in the distance near the gates of the city. It seemed to be a happy commotion, otherwise the guards would have been alerted and there would be warning shouts. As the duo peered into the distance, they could see the crowd part and form a semicircle.

'What is going on?' Uma thought. 'What was pulling the attention of the mortals, the demigods and the devas towards it?'

Uma and Mena looked intently towards the far end of the dancing serpent to try and locate the source of the sudden interest.

At first only a tiny speck in the distance, the stranger who was pulling all the attention of the crowd towards himself slowly came into view. As they stared unblinkingly, the crowd seemed to pick up his rhythm and soon he had a following that was dancing around him. The musicians were drawn towards him, the apsaras flanked him and

---

anthropomorphic representation of Ursa Major.

even the asuras followed his lead. Some mountain people, with matted hair and wearing animal skins, followed this man into the procession, surrounding him and dancing along. The dancing serpent had acquired a new rhythm and pulsated with a new energy.

Slowly the person in question came into view. He was tall, fair and well-built. His handsome face was framed by long, thick hair that flowed right down to his waist and was decorated with wildflowers. His supple limbs were decorated with pearls and rudraksha. He wore twin anklets on both his feet which tinkled as he walked and danced. He was wearing clothes made of fine silk, and was carrying a flower in one hand and a one-handed drum—the damroo—in the other. His neck was painted with vermilion and his limbs were marked with sandalwood paste. When he smiled, his teeth shone like pearls and the happy effulgence that exuded from his smile infected everyone. He danced with a carefree abandon that people had not seen before. His limbs moved around with the sophistry of an apsara while his eyes held the mischief of an imp. It seemed as if this *nartaka*[113] had hypnotized everyone. Mesmerized, the people had eyes only for him—they sang and danced only for him, forgetting themselves, their families and the reason they had come out in the first place. The dancing serpent momentarily paused its journey to the palace and inverted upon itself. Those who had overtaken this nartaka and were near the palace also paused, waiting for him to catch up so that they could get a glimpse of him.

---

[113]Dancer

Uma and Mena saw all this from their perch on the balcony and smiled in wonder. They waited expectantly for the dancer to reach the palace gates so that they could enjoy his performance up close.

It seemed like an interminable wait as the nartaka slowly made his way through the crowd, urging everyone to dance. He seemed to be enjoying himself thoroughly and was in no hurry to reach the palace. As he got closer to the gates the tempo of his dance and the music which accompanied him increased. Even Uma was tapping her feet in time with the music, feeling strangely exhilarated at the sight of this man. The music and the dance were infectious, overpowering and extremely stimulating. The nartaka finally entered the compound followed by the delirious crowd. He stopped just short of the balcony and continued his performance for Mena and Uma. He looked directly at them, knowing that they were enjoying his dance and laughed loudly.

'I will expect a reward, O Queen, if you like my performance,' he said, addressing Mena directly.

'And you will have it, Sunartaka,[114] if you can please my daughter here with your dance,' Mena said.

'That is exactly why I have come here, my Queen,' Sunartaka said meaningfully. 'To please Uma and be rewarded in return.'

A mischievous smile played on his lips, making him look even more attractive. Uma looked at him unblinkingly… Could he be…? She was not sure.

'What is your dance called, Sunartaka?' Uma asked the dancer.

---

[114]Literally: skilled dancer

'It is the Ananda Tandava,[115] my lady,' Sunartaka said, his voice suffused with happiness.

'It is him!' Uma thought and suddenly she was delirious with excitement.

'No wonder everyone is so drawn towards him when he dances. Who wouldn't be wonderstruck by Shiva's dance?' she thought and smiled to herself, amused at the piquant situation of Shiva dancing in front of her to please her. 'Mother and the other people do not even realize what a great scene they are witnessing.'

'Show us your dance, Sunartaka,' Uma said to the dancer, playing along with Shiva's mischief.

'As you command, my lady,' Shiva said with a flourish and started beating his damroo.

As the beat of his drum started to pick up, the other musicians joined him. The gandharvas played their instruments, the apsaras danced, and Shiva started to sway to the rhythm. His anklets tinkled as his feet moved, his hair flowing like the Ganga which normally adorned his *jata*.[116] His eyes twinkled playfully as he danced.

Shiva lost himself to his emotions. Different people saw him dancing differently. He was one person and then suddenly he was many, dancing separate dances for everyone. It was His doing, His maya. He showed people what they needed to see, what they needed to know, what they expected to see, what their minds were ready to see. The common man saw an itinerant dancer dancing to his drums, Mena saw a divine dancer, Sunartaka's followers saw their Mahadev, and Uma saw her Shiva.

---

[115] *Ananda* means happiness, and Tandava is Shiva's dance

[116] Matted locks

Uma sat spellbound as Shiva danced in front of her, only for her. This performance was Shiva's way of showing his love. Uma did not know that Shiva danced for more than just her pleasure. Shiva danced to show her who he was, who she was and what the eternal entity, the eternal truth was. She also did not know yet that Shiva's dance kept the world going; it created, it sustained, it destroyed. She would learn soon though; Shiva would show her how his dance was the dance of the galaxies, the dance of creation, of the universe, and the *anu* or the sub-atomic particles. Shiva would show her how his dance was everywhere, how the universe was manifested in his dance, how the gods which the world prayed to were born and were later assimilated into him.

Shiva slowly started to show her things meant for her eyes only. He showed her the fifty-three mudras (the *sanyukta* and the *asanyukta*[117]) with his hands.

Uma felt as if she was in a trance watching Shiva dance. He showed her the birth of Sati, her penance, his marriage to her and her final immolation. He showed her the destruction of Daksha's ceremony by Veer Bhadra and Bhadra Kaali, all the blood that was spilt that night, and all the carrion eaters who had their fill, He showed her how he had danced with Sati in his arms and had wanted to destroy the world. He showed her his Trinetra, which had nearly opened and let the Kaalagni loose upon the world. He showed her Hari, the Padmanabha, and how he had stopped Shiva.

---

[117]Mudras are the gestures of the hand used during Indian classical dances, esp. Bharatnatyam, to express emotions. The *sanyukta mudras* are gestures which need both hands and *asanyukta mudras* use a single hand.

All this and more played in front of Uma's eyes. She saw Sati's spirit merging with Shakti and Shakti merging with Shiva; the devas pleading with Shiva; her parents praying to the Aadi Shakti,[118] and herself being born and raised by Himavan. She saw her *tapasya,* her penance, and witnessed Shiva appear before her to grant her wish. She saw how all of this had been pre-ordained, and how she belonged to Shiva forever, since the beginning of time.

Then she saw herself dancing beside Shiva in tandem, separate but one. Then she was Shiva and Shiva was her, the lines separating them blurred. Shiva stood poised before her as the Ardhnaarishwara, half man/half woman. The right half was Shiva, the left half was Uma. The right had matted locks, the left had flowing hair; the right wore tiger skin, the left wore silk; the right had a garland of skulls, the left had a string of flowers. Ardhnaarishwara danced in front of Uma, showing her the oneness of all creation, the falsehood behind any kind of division. It showed the unity of the *atman*, the soul, and the Brahman, or the supreme consciousness.

The Ardhnaarishwara danced and Uma saw the beginning, the middle and the end. It showed her the primordial pillar of fire which was at the beginning when he was called Rudra and the gods worshipped him. It showed her the fire of destruction which was the medium through which everything was assimilated within Shiva. The third eye was wide open now, but it was shared by both Shiva and Uma. She found herself looking into the fire, into the Kaalagni, watching the fire of destruction

---

[118]Another name of the Mother

eat the world and then create a new one from its ashes, everything happening simultaneously.

Then the vision changed and Shiva was not Ardhnaarishwara anymore. In a flash of light he was the Narteshwara or the Nataraja, the Lord of dance, the Lord of knowledge and learning, the dispeller of darkness, the provider of abhaya. He stood poised within the fire of creation, the Prabhamandala. His right knee was flexed, his left leg raised and pointing to the right. He suddenly had four arms. The left upper arm carried the fire of creation and destruction, the left lower pointed towards the right, the palm facing down and back. The right upper arm carried the damroo[119] while the right lower had a serpent coiled around it and showed the abhaya mudra.

The demon of ignorance, Apsmara, lay trampled under his feet as Shiva danced as the Nataraja, quelling ignorance and spreading the light of knowledge.

It was all too much for Uma to bear. Though she was Sati's reincarnation, her intellect had been clouded by maya, the illusion of this world. Shiva was trying to rid her of this illusion; he had kindled her aagya chakra. But her strength gave way and she swooned. Suddenly, there was a commotion in the palace as Mena and her attendants rushed to help Uma. Some sprinkled water on her, some brought smelling salts. Uma was revived and sat up.

'O my child,' Mena said, 'you must be too weak from your long penance. You must rest. We can always have the revelry later.'

---

[119]The pose is called the *damroo hasta*: the hand carrying the damroo.

'No Mother. I am alright, just a little weak. Please do not stop the people from expressing their joy on my account. I shall be better soon. Please enjoy the festivities and reward this Sunartaka well. I shall go inside and rest,' Uma said, her eyes twinkling again, amused at the knowledge Shiva had shared with her. She was also tickled that the Mahadev had danced for her in public and no one had known.

As Uma turned to go, she secretly winked at Shiva. Their secret was safe with her!

Mena turned to Sunartaka and said, 'You danced beautifully, Sunartaka. I am pleased with your skills. Name your reward and you shall have it.'

Sunartaka's laugh was full of mischief as he said, 'If you are pleased, O Queen, let me have the hand of your daughter in marriage.'

There was a shocked silence all around and everyone breathed a collective sigh.

'What do you say, you fool?' Mena reprimanded the audacious dancer. 'You have the cheek to ask for the hand of my daughter in marriage? You presume to think you can be a match for her?'

'But I heard she has consented to wed Shankara, the lonely ascetic who lives up in the mountains,' Shiva quipped, jesting with Mena. 'Shankara is ugly, naked and ash-smeared. He lives with ghouls and goblins in a cave. He has serpents coiling all over his body. His body is as rough and hard as the bark of the devadaru tree. When you have consented to give the hand of your daughter in marriage to a person as ugly as him, what is wrong with me?' Shiva persisted, gesturing towards his well-clad, bejewelled body.

'I am better looking than him. I have ancestry which Shankara doesn't. I can dance and please your daughter in a way Shankara cannot. I am a much better match for her than Shankara.'

The crowd was shocked at the unknown dancer's ignorant banter. 'He is either drunk or plain mad to talk to the queen like this,' they whispered amongst themselves.

'The queen is going to have his head for this mistake,' others said.

They were right since Mena was overwhelmed with anger.

'Arrest him,' she shouted, hysterical.

Mena stormed inside the palace while the royal guards advanced towards Sunartaka menacingly. Suddenly everyone saw that a few of Sunartaka's friends formed a protective circle around him. They wore animal skins and carried an assortment of weapons, looking more ferocious than the palace guards.

In the middle of all this commotion, Sunartaka still stood smiling as if nothing had happened. In fact, his smile was so radiant that it was becoming difficult to look at him. As the palace guards strode towards him with their weapons brandished, a commotion broke out in the crowd.

'Everyone stay put. No one else will be harmed. Only the Sunartaka will be apprehended.' the palace guards shouted, trying to calm the people down. But it was already too late.

The procession broke up and the people started

to run helter-skelter. In the ongoing commotion only Sunartaka stood quietly, encircled by his people, his ganas, shining brightly like the sun. By the time the soldiers reached the spot where he stood, they were all gone—the errant dancer and his friends. They had disappeared without a trace. The soldiers returned to the palace empty-handed and reported to the king and queen.

In the meantime, Mena told Himavan and Uma everything, and while Himavan turned red in anger, Uma burst out laughing, surprising her parents.

'Don't take me otherwise, Father,' Uma said apologetically, 'this whole charade by the Sunartaka and your response to his seemingly audacious demand makes me laugh.'

'Charade, you say? Charade? Is there something here we do not understand, Uma? Do you know who he is?' Himavan said as Mena looked on with interest.

'Yes Father, I know him and so do you both. It's just that you and Mother did not recognize him. Even I found it difficult to recognize him in this disguise,' Uma responded.

'Who is he?' Mena asked curiously.

'O Mother. He is the one whose hair the Chandra and the Ganga adorn and hence he is called Chandrashekhar and Gangadhar. He is the one who was there in the beginning and hence he is called the Aadi Yogi. He is the one who will assimilate the world within him with the Kaalagni[120] from his Trinetra. He is the one who will remain when even the universe is destroyed and when

[120]Fire of destruction

Vishnu has gone to sleep.[121] He is the one whose locks gave birth to Veer Bhadra and Bhadra Kaali. He is the one who dances the Rudra Tandava and the Ananda Tandava. He is the one whom even the gods pray to. He is the beginning, the middle and the end. He is the Pashupati, he is Ishaan, he is Ishvara,[122] he is Nataraja[123] and he is the Ardhnaarishwara,' Uma answered.

'O Father, you do not know who he was? He was Shiva, my Shankara. He had come to our city to see me, to please me and to meet you.' Uma fell silent, out of breath and overcome by emotion.

Himavan and Mena stared at Uma in consternation. They could not believe their ears. Shiva had come to Aushadhipuram? And they could not recognize the Mahadev nor welcome him properly? Together they huddled and consulted each other on what to do next.

Finally, they turned towards their daughter and said, 'How can we make up for this great mistake, Uma? We should have welcomed him to our city and offered him arghya and padya. He went away without even a word with us. How can we send a message to him?'

'I do not know who would be the appropriate messenger to send to Shiva. If you intend to give my hand in marriage to him, you will need to inform him of your intention and offer to host him for the ceremony.

---

[121]According to Hindu beliefs the world is created by Brahma when Vishnu, the Padmanabha, awakens; and is destroyed in the primordial fire when he goes back to sleep on the Ananta Shesha, the infinite serpent

[122]Pashupati, Ishaan and Ishwara are all Shiva's names

[123]Nataraja or Nateshwar or Narteshwara are all Shiva's names as he is the source of all dance forms. Sanskrit root *Nritya* or *Nartya* means dance or performing arts.

We will need a learned person to carry out this great task,' Uma said.

'I don't think we will find a better person to convey our apologies and invitation than the celestial purohit,[124] the itinerant brahmana, son of Brahma, Narada. What do you say, Mena?' Himavan said.

'I think you are right. Rishi Narada is the right person to act as the messenger as well as the purohit at Shiva and Parvati's wedding ceremony,' Mena agreed.

Uma sat smiling on the couch while the palace suddenly burst into activity as Himavan summoned his courtiers and packed them off to look for Narada. Mena started preparing for the ceremony that would unite Shiva with Parvati in holy matrimony.

Meanwhile, Shiva sat in his cave on Kailash, surrounded by his ganas. He knew the inevitable and waited impatiently for the invitation that he knew would arrive soon enough. This time there would be no mistakes. The omissions of the last time would have to be rectified and everything would have to be planned perfectly. The fate of the universe depended on the marriage of Shiva and Parvati.

---

[124]A purohit is the priest who presides over auspicious ceremonies

PART THREE

TRITIYAH: VISHNU

Narasingha: The Manticore

1

'Where is Vishnu?' Hiranyakashyap,[125] the daitya king growled, his baritone shaking the very pillars of the royal court where he stood confronting his son Prahlad. His hands gripped his mace, his face was taut and his eyes were bloodshot with anger. The pillared hall had fallen silent. The musicians had stopped singing and playing their instruments. The prince faced his imminent death at the hands of his father.

Despite the dire threat, Prahlad stood quietly, his serene face devoid of any emotion except the tranquility which comes from pure wisdom and divine grace. He stood with his *yagyopaveetam*, the sacred thread, slung over his left shoulder, his forehead marked with the *tilaka* and his lips murmuring the thousand names of Vishnu—the 'Vishnu Sahasranamam'.[126]

'Where is Vishnu? That cheat. The one you people call Narayana. He is nothing but a charlatan. Where is he? You say he is everywhere? Is he here?'

---

[125]Daityas are descended from Diti and Rishi Kashyap. Hiranyakashyap and his elder brother Hiranyaksha were the first daityas. The name of the lineage was derived from the name of their mother.

[126]*Sahasra* in Sanskrit means 'thousand'. 'Vishnu Sahasranamam' thus translates to 'the thousand names of Vishnu'.

Hiranyakashyap thundered again, his muscular frame towering menacingly over Prahlad.

'Yes, Father, he is everywhere,' Prahlad replied humbly. 'He pervades all matter and dwells in all animate and inanimate objects; he is inside me *and* you.'

Listening to Prahlad teach him the tenets of bhakti, or devotion towards the lord, Hiranyakashyap's anger flared even more as if someone had poured butter into fire. His eyes smouldered, his nostrils flared and his limbs trembled.

'Let us put your Vishnu to the test,' he growled. 'Call upon him to save you. If he is here, in this hall, he will come to save you, right? You say he is here so let me see if that is true. Is he in this pillar?'

'Yes Father, he is in the pillar too,' Prahlad said quietly, retreating a little as his father advanced menacingly. His arm which held the mace was raised high over his head, ready to strike.

'Tell him to come out and save you from my anger,' shouted Hiranyakashyap as he swung his mace and hit the stone pillar. There was an ear-shattering sound as the pillar broke into a thousand pieces and crumbled to the ground, raising a huge cloud of dust.

Hiranyaksha and Hiranyakashyap were the sons of Diti and Rishi Kashyap.[127] The boys grew up to be powerful young men; tall, muscular, adept at all forms of warfare

---

[127] *Hiranya* means gold and *aksha* means eye. Hiranyaksha was also known as 'Hiranyanetra' (*netra* also meaning eye in Sanskrit). Hiranyakashyap was sometimes known as 'Hiranyakashipu', both of which can roughly be translated to 'golden clothes' or 'golden throne'.

and exceedingly cruel. They had realized early on that asceticism or even adherence to civic rules was for the weak; it was not a life they wanted. They refused to follow in the footsteps of their illustrious father and decided to carve out their own destiny by conquering the whole world and subjugating it with brute force and bringing it under their feet. They called themselves daityas, after their mother Diti.

The two brothers left home early and formed a mercenary band of their own. They started small, overpowering small groups, villages and communities. Soon their group grew, held together by a lust for power, money and abominable cruelty as well as a common dislike of authority. They openly flaunted the laws set by the kingdoms of that time and refused to honour the prevalent gods. Those who opposed them were either captured or killed. Several years of conquering and plundering later, they had their army and kingdom—the daitya kingdom. Its capital was a beautiful city set within a valley surrounded by snow-capped mountains. All the surrounding kings feared them; they had fought with and defeated all the *manavas*, danavas, yakshas, gandharvas, kinnaras and *kiratas* to the northeast[128].

Though they had subjugated almost all these groups, they could not conquer the powerful *adityas*, also known

---

[128]The *manavas* are the descendants of Rishi Manu, incorrectly understood as men or humans. The danavas are the sons of Danu, and foster brothers of the *daityas.* The yakshas, gandharvas and kinnaras or kimpurushas are different 'people' or 'janas' sometimes described as semi-divine species. As mentioned before, jana in Sanskrit simply means 'people' or community and does not imply race or caste. The Mahabharata, mentions more than 360 types of janas.

as the devas or the gods. To do this, something more than just brute force was required, since the adityas were skilled warriors, had the support of powerful friends and the knowledge of divine weapons which the daitya brothers lacked. Resolving to learn the use of divine weapons and forge new alliances, Hiranyaksha put his brother Hiranyakashyap in charge of the kingdom and set out for the Himalayas to do penance.

For several years he performed *tapa*,[129] pleasing Mahadev Shiva and Pitamah Brahma. From them, he learned the use of divine weapons and earned their blessings. Armed with their good wishes and his newly-earned knowledge of divine weapons, he returned to his kingdom, collected his army and marched on Amravati, the capital of the devas, intending to attack it. Hiranyakashyap stayed back to defend the kingdom and consolidate their position. He kept hearing news of the devasur sangram[130] from his spies and the horse riders dispatched by his elder brother.

The adityas were difficult to defeat but Hiranyaksha persisted. The war went on and on. Sometimes the devas would suffer while sometimes the daitya forces would scatter. Hiranyaksha would gather them again, change tact and attack deva allies to weaken them, while preparing for the final assault. This went on for a long time and the devas started to get weary of the war. The two sides were locked in a stalemate with no one able to rout the other force completely. The devas realized

---

[129] *Tapa* (roughly translated) refers to the mortification of self. It can also be construed to mean pushing oneself to the limit to achieve some difficult aim.

[130] War between gods and demons

that there was no way they could defend themselves from Hiranyaksha without divine intervention. Thus, they went to seek help—hands folded, heads bowed and their egos humbled—to the only person who could take their side unabashedly in this crisis, and save them and their world from Hiranyaksha's madness. They went to Mahavishnu, the dark-skinned god who lies upon the infinite ocean of milk, the Ksheer Saagara. Vishnu agreed to help them.

Meanwhile, Hiranyaksha turned his attention to the other allies of the devas. He tried to conquer the 'earth people', and abduct their princess Bhudevi, who was renowned for her beauty and revered as the worldly incarnation of Mother Earth. Bhudevi fled when her people were defeated and sought shelter with the *saagaras*, the 'ocean people'.[131] The saagaras hid her in a subterranean cave deep inside the ocean to keep her safe from the reach of the daityas. But Hiranyaksha was relentless. He pursued Bhudevi into the ocean, beneath the waves where she hid, looking for her in all the regions where the saagaras could have hidden her. The prize was too great and Hiranyaksha was too greedy to see that Bhudevi was the one who would lead him to his impending doom.

When Hiranyakashyap heard about the attack on kingdom of Bhudevi, even he thought maybe Hiranyaksha had gone too far. Bhudevi was untouchable since she was considered to be the earth incarnate. Lusting after her could be the undoing of his valiant brother and could tip the scales against the daityas. He tried to warn his brother to be more tactful but Hiranyaksha did not listen.

---

[131] *Saagara* means ocean

Then Hiranyakashyap learned what he had feared all along had come to pass. All the forces of the devas and their allies had united against Hiranyaksha to save Bhudevi. When Hiranyaksha pursued her into the waters of the ocean, trying to find her hiding place, he had been confronted by a mighty boar the size of a mammoth. His hide was made of metal and studded with spikes, rough, strong and impenetrable. He had huge tusks like thunderbolts and his eyes had rained fire. He had spoken in several tongues at the same time which could be understood by all. He had roared so loudly that the earth shook and the mountains trembled. All the devas, the 'earth people' and the 'ocean people', had bowed down in respect, fear and reverence to the divine beast.

This mighty boar, or *varaha*, had risen from the depths of the ocean at the speed of light, carrying Bhudevi with him, promising to protect her. When he saw that Bhudevi was mortally afraid of Hiranyaksha, he had challenged the daitya to a duel. The two of them fought like monsters, a celestial battle witnessed by all the gods and goddesses. The earth quaked under their combined weight as they fought and threw each others' gigantic bodies around. Hiranyaksha fought with his sword and shield; the boar fought with his hooves and tusks. The boar's hooves churned the ocean to a froth and his tusks dug the earth up, making valleys out of mountains. Never had anyone witnessed a battle as fierce and between two evenly matched opponents since the creation of the world by Brahma. They had fought on and on and on—for what seemed like an eternity—until Hiranyaksha started getting tired. He had summoned his divine weapons and had used them all against the varaha one by one. But all the divine weapons had been useless against the monstrous beast, falling off his metallic hide like water off the petals of a lotus plant. The boar had scoffed at Hiranyaksha, laughing his guttural, primitive laughter which had echoed across the earth and resounded in the heavens. When he ran out of divine weapons and could not fight the magical beast anymore, Hiranyaksha had eventually been gored to his death by the varaha.[132]

People later whispered that it was Vishnu who had taken the form of the boar to save the earth goddess and slay the daitya king Hiranyaksha. They started singing his lore and calling him the Supreme God but Hiranyakashyap did not believe this. He was a man of the world and did not trust this superstitious mumbo-jumbo. He relied on the strength of his arms and the metal of his sword. He believed that anything that lives and moves could be fought, hurt and killed. There had to be something more to the story than what the people had started singing in the Puranas.[133]

Though he was angry at his brother for being so reckless, he was angrier still at the dicey devas. They had resorted to trickery to kill his valiant brother when they could not defeat him upfront in a battle, for the boar had to be *mayavi,* a trick with which they had trapped and killed his brother. He swore to avenge Hiranyaksha and re-establish the dominion of the daityas all over the world. Even though the army had scattered after

---

[132]This legendary battle between the daitya king and the divine boar or *varaha* is said to have occurred in present day Kashmir at a place now known as Baramulla—*varaha* + *mulah*—origin of the boar.

[133]*Puranas* literally means tales of yore, or fables or legends.

his brother's death, a small force still loyal to their cause remained. This was the contingent of faithful soldiers he had deputed to guard his capital city and his royal palace as he went to practice penance.

'I will acquire what even my brother could not acquire, something more powerful than any divine weapon. I will acquire immortality,' he promised himself as he left his family and his expectant wife behind.

He went to the Tapovan[134] and started meditating upon Brahma. For scores of years he meditated, burning up all the directions with the power of his penance. His focus was so strong, his tapa so fierce, that Brahma appeared before him, pleased with his devotion.

'Arise, son,' Brahma said. 'I am pleased to see your single-minded devotion. What do you want?'

Hiranyakashyap's eyes twinkled. His moment had come.

'I want to be immortal, Pitamah,' he said.

'Alas, that is not in my hands, son,' Brahma replied. 'Even I cannot bend or break the laws of nature. I must act within their purview. Whoever is born must die. I cannot grant immortality. However, you may choose the manner of your death. I will grant that.'

Hiranyakashyap had thought hard. If he could choose the manner of his death, he had to make conditions so strong that his death became nearly impossible. That would make him immortal—or nearly so.

After a moment, he smiled.

'If you so wish, father,' he said. 'Please grant that I may not be killed by either man or beast, deva or asura,

---

[134]The forest of penance (*tapa*: penance; *vana*: forest)

astra or *shastra*,[135] neither during the day nor at night, neither inside the house nor outside it, neither on earth nor in sky or water. O Father! Grant that I may only die when these conditions are met.'

'Tathastu!'[136] Brahma said, smiling, and went back to his abode, knowing what demonic forces were about to be unleashed upon the world.

Meanwhile, the adityas had gathered their forces again after Hiranyaksha was killed by the varaha. The morale of the daitya forces was low, and when Indra rode out on his majestic elephant leading the army of the devas, the daitya army was routed and fled to save their lives. A few returned to the daitya capital to seek shelter and to reassemble under Hiranyakashyap, only to find that the daitya prince had gone for his penance. The deva army pursued the retreating daitya army, and finding their capital leaderless and undefended, fell upon the city. The remaining army, leaderless in Hiranyakashyap's absence, was no match for the aditya forces and the city fell after the army surrendered. As the deva army entered the daitya city, people ran hither and tither to save their lives. The city capitulated in a matter of hours; the royal palace was soon overrun by the deva forces.

Indra, the leader of the devas, instructed that none other than those who wielded arms was to be harmed. Women were to be respected and the royal family

---

[135] *Astra*: weapons that are thrown from the hand; *shastra*: weapons which are held in hand while fighting

[136] So be it

shown due courtesy. The deva soldiers were disciplined and fearful of Indra's wrath and thus, abiding by his instructions, the unarmed daityas were saved from a being massacred.

Hiranyakashyap's wife, Kayadhu, was expecting around this time and was left unattended since most of her servants, attendants and royal physicians had fled from the city. She sorely needed help. Her dire circumstances were duly conveyed to Indra who consulted Narada Muni, the celestial itinerant sage. Narada Muni took it upon himself to look after the daitya queen and escorted her and her maids to his ashram or hermitage. While the city recovered from the deva attack, Kayadhu spent her days in the tender care of the womenfolk of Narada Muni's hermitage. She enjoyed the pristine environment, the beautiful groves, the freshwater springs and the simple, spiritual lifestyle. Narada Muni saw to it that she was well looked after.

In time, Queen Kayadhu gave birth to a beautiful baby boy. The queen named him Prahlad, since he was the reason she was finally happy after a long time.[137] Prahlad grew up in the spiritual environment of the hermitage of Narada Muni, who performed all the ceremonies that should be performed for a child, like *chudakarma* and *yagyopaveetam.*[138]

---

[137] *Prahlad* means one who gives joy, or brings joy

[138] *Chudakarma* is the compulsory tonsuring of the head that is done for every Hindu child when they are one or two years old, irrespective of the sex of the child. *Yagyopaveetam* is the sacred thread ceremony that is performed when the child is ready to go to the *gurukul,* the teacher's family. The thread is an indicator that the person wearing it is a student or has been instructed in the shastras by a teacher.

No one knows how a deep devotion for Lord Vishnu sprouted in young Prahlad's tender heart. Everyone noticed that the Lord's name was always on his lips. The other sages and hermits were astonished when they saw such maturity in one so young. Prahlad was mature beyond his years and he learned the scriptures quickly. He was thirsty for stories of the Lord. He learnt the Vedanga, the Veda and the Vedanta while other children were busy playing games.[139] Thus, Kayadhu and Prahlad spent their days happily in the ashram, listening to the chants and the vedic mantras of the sages and waiting for the day when Hiranyakashyap would be back from his penance.

2

Hiranyakashyap returned from his penance to find his capital starkly different from how he had left it. Here was a city that was sombre, almost afraid to be happy and nearly devoid of life. The palace was populated by only a few loyal servants who had remained for its upkeep. Most of the soldiers, except those who had surrendered and sought mercy from the devas, were gone. His bodyguards remained, but were a dispirited lot. Their happiness, vitality and energy seemed to have left them; they were

[139]The Vedangas are the tenets of basic learning, like pronunciation and etymology, and are six in number—*shiksha, chhanda, vyakarana, nirukta, jyotish* and *kalpa.* They are required for correctly learning the Vedas, which are, literally translated, 'revealed knowledge'. Vedanta are, as the name suggests, the end of the Vedas. They are commentaries, philosophical extrapolations, enunciations and explanations of all the knowledge that is inherent in the Vedas. The Vedanta are, in effect, the very gist of all philosophical knowledge that can be found in Hindu dharma.

just living ghosts of their past selves.

Hiranyakashyap was shocked to see this. When he walked into the palace and into his royal court, the eyes of those who recognized him lit up. It seemed as if his sight had given them a new lease of life. He had kindled hope in them again—hope and confidence—their mighty king was back!

After putting his house in order, Hiranyakashyap enquired about what had happened in his absence. The more they told him, the more his anger grew at the treachery of the devas.

'Striking at a defenseless city! What else could one expect from the two-faced devas,' Hiranyakashyap seethed with anger.

'Where is the queen?' he asked his attendants.

An elderly chambermaid who could not go with the queen stepped forward—hands folded, head bent—and said, 'If the great king promises to spare my life, I shall speak the truth.'

'Speak. I grant you abhaya,' the daitya king replied.

'When the city fell, my Lord, all the queens's servants and handmaidens fled for their lives. She was in the family way and needed ministration,' the elderly woman said. 'The kind Narada Muni took pity on her and took her with him to his hermitage so that she could be cared for. I have heard from my sources that she has given birth to our prince there.'

Hiranyakashyap did not know whether to be happy or angry. He was happy that his wife was alive and had delivered him an heir. But he would have been happier still if she had been here, in the daitya capital, instead of with Narada Muni. He was contemplating sending emissaries to the hermitage to summon his family back when an usher entered the court and bowed low.

'What is it?' barked the king.

'My Lord, Narada Muni is standing outside and seeks your audience,' the usher replied.

'Bring him in,' Hiranyakashyap said, and got up to greet the celestial sage as he entered the court.

'Narayana, Narayana,' Narada Muni said as he entered the court of Hiranyakashyap, followed closely by the daitya queen and Prahlad.

'My King,' Narada Muni said. 'Please accept my apologies for hosting Queen Kayadhu in my ashram without your permission. It seemed the best thing to do at the time since she needed assistance and care. What better place than the hermitage of a monk in the lap of nature for the queen to spend her time?'

Narada smiled impishly. It was known all over the world that he was the celestial mischief monger. He would pit one deva against another or the devas against the asuras but his motives were never evil. He only considered himself a medium for achieving greater purposes. He was always cheerful, often sang and danced, and was a fount of knowledge. He never directly antagonized anyone and thus had no enemies.

Hiranyakashyap was also trapped in Narada Muni's guile. Instead of being angry with the sage, the daitya king found himself smiling and thanking him.

'Thank you for taking care of my family, O Great Sage. I shall forever be in your debt', the king said.

'There are no debts, son. Whatever we do is not because of our own volition; it is because He wills it,' and he pointed upwards.

'He means Vishnu,' Hiranyakashyap thought, but let the bait pass; he would not be found wanting in his manners.

The king thanked the sage for his benevolence and motioned the courtiers to lead the queen and the prince to their chambers inside. As the trio bid goodbye to each other, Hiranyakashyap noticed that Prahlad had applied the Vaishnav tilak on his forehead.[140] He frowned and made a mental note of it. He would have to take this up with his son later. Vishnu would not be worshipped in his kingdom. Never.

Slowly, Hiranyakashyap started reconstructing the daitya kingdom. He renovated and bolstered its defences. He sent word out to all his followers and people that he was back. They started to trickle back into the kingdom. The royal guards were strengthened and the army reconstituted from scratch. He let his courtiers know that he had earned 'immortality' from Brahma, telling them to spread the tale around and beyond the city. He hired bards to travel the land, singing of his prowess and newly-achieved immortality—he was the new god now! He forbade the worship of the old gods, of nature, earth or the sky—from now on, everyone would worship only Hiranyakashyap. He made his own reverence compulsory throughout the kingdom and this was to be followed even in the royal household. This was how he ensured complete devotion and compliance towards his order throughout the lands he ruled. Those who resisted

[140]Vaishnav means belonging to Vishnu or 'of Vishnu'. Tilak is the mark that many Hindus wear on their foreheads. The Vaishnav tilak is a vertical mark made in the middle of the forehead, signifying that the wearer is a Vishnu devotee.

giving up their ancient gods were swiftly, mercilessly and publicly punished in the most horrific of ways to make others capitulate. Temples were erected in the honour of the new deity Hiranyakashyap. Royal spies, soldiers and guards ensured that his idol was present in every household as well as in all public places and the citizens were seen paying their respects publicly. Order, under the shade of a sword, returned to the daitya capital.

The former vassal states were sent warnings reminding them of the taxes owed to the daitya king. While some of them capitulated easily; others did not. Hiranyakashyap made an example of those who dared defy him. The treatment meted out to the first rebellious kingdom was the most brutal—the city was sacked like no other in living memory. The sands of the rebellious kingdoms ran red with the blood of their occupants and their royalty. After the first few kingdoms were brutally crushed, the others conceded defeat.

Word of Hiranyakashyap's boon of immortality soon spread far and wide causing great unrest even in the heavens. The devas knew that the story of the daitya brothers was far from over and prepared for the assault they knew would come. Representatives were also dispatched to Vaikunth, the abode of Narayana, the one who had slaughtered Hiranyaksha in his varaha incarnation. The devas, together with Brahma, made a beeline to Sridhar's abode to petition him for his help again. Hiranyakashyap, with his boon of immortality, would be impossible to kill by any other means but divine intervention.

Hiranyakashyap led his armies on a conquering campaign throughout the land, from the Mahendra Giri[141] through the Vindhyas,[142] to the land which the Vedic people called the Sapt Sindhava.[143] All the kingdoms buckled under the force of his brute power. Daitya power soon became unchallenged all across the land, from the Himalayas in the north to the sea in the south, their supremacy firmly established and their fame rivalling that of the devas. Finally, when he had subdued all the manavas, gandharvas, yakshas and *nagas*, Hiranyakashyap turned his sights towards Amravati, the city of Indra, the leader of the devas.

The two armies met in the rocky grasslands at the foothills of the Himalayas. The sun, the moon and the *nakshatras* (constellations) were all arrayed in the heavens to witness this legendary battle of the deva and daitya forces. Both armies had innumerable soldiers in formation as far as the eye could see. Standards, flags and battle insignia were everywhere, hoisted up by foot soldiers and war animals. The dust raised by the feet of the soldiers and animals, blotted out the light of the sun, making day seem like twilight. The earth quivered, the mountains trembled and the waters of the rivers stopped flowing since the element gods, the vasus, had come out in force to support the devas.

---

[141]Mountain range in southern India, part of the Eastern Ghats

[142]Mountain range in Central India separating the northern plains from the southern plateau

[143]Sapt Sindhava: the land of the seven rivers. The seven rivers, enumerated from east to west, were the Saraswati, Shutudri or Sutlej, Vipasha or Beas, Parsuhni or Ravi, Asikini or Chenab, Vitasta or Jhelum, also known as Hydaspes by the Greek, and Sindhu or Indus.

The devas had brought out their chaturanga army. It had four separate classes of warriors—the elephant riders, the charioteers, the cavalry and the foot soldiers or infantry. In the centre of the army, right in the front and interspersed between others in the front row were the war elephants wearing armour plating on their forehead, their tusks gilded with bronze. Each war elephant was manned by a *mahavat*, the rider who guided it with a goad in his hand, for the elephant was a dangerous animal. Used tactfully, it could rout the enemy in a matter of a few hours; used foolishly, it could trample its own people. Behind the mahavat sat the warrior who would lead the unit which comprised one elephant, one chariot, three horses and five foot soldiers. The whole army was built on this ratio of 1:1:3:5.

The chariots usually flanked the elephants but maintained a safe distance, for who could know the mind of the beast. The chariot was driven by a charioteer or saarthi and the warrior stood behind *in the car* under the canopy. The outcome of the war depended as much on the skills of the warriors as on the expertise of the elephant drivers and the charioteers in manoeuvring their respective vehicles.

The horsemen surrounded the chariot and the elephant, flanking them and standing a step behind. The horses were the finest steeds, some white and some tawny in colour, pure-bred and rigorously trained over generations for warfare. Last of all came the foot soldiers, wearing armour, carrying shields and long spears or long swords. This was the way the deva army was structured, for this was the conventional wisdom taught in the shastras.

At the head of this army was Devaraj[144] Indra, mounted on a war elephant. He was tall, well-built and battle-scarred, wearing white clothes. He carried several divine weapons atop his elephant but his favourite was the Vajrayudha or Vajra in short[145]. It was an indestructible and infallible weapon. It was imbued with divine powers The weapon adorned Indra's side like the Pinaka adorns Shiva's or the Saranga adorns Vishnu's.[146] It shone like the thunderbolt itself, blinding the casual observer, and instilled confidence in whoever looked at it. Looking at Indra wielding the Vajra mounted on his war elephant, the army of the devas was filled with confidence. Flanking Indra stood Mitra, Varun and Agni, his fellow devas. Behind him were the *marut*s, the gods of wind and storm, fiery-eyed, with sharp teeth, long tails and voices like that of thunder and lightning.[147]

The daitya army, on the other hand, did not look anything like the deva army. Hiranyakashyap had

---

[144]A title which literally means 'king of the devas'

[145]*Vajra* in Sanskrit literally means 'hard like diamond' or 'indestructible' and, by extension, 'a weapon which does not fail'. Over the years the Vajra, as wielded by Indra and several other deities in Indian, Greek and Norse mythologies, has come to mean the thunderbolt. The Vajra which Indra wields is probably a club with ribs and a sharp piercing point, or a mallet with a spear or blade like extension, something like a battle-axe.

[146]Pinaka is the name of the celestial bow which Shiva wields. It is one of his lesser-known weapons and was used by him to destroy the indestructible trio of the sister cities of Tripura. Saranga is the name of Vishnu's bow, and thus Vishnu is also known as 'Sarangapani'—one who holds the Saranga in his hands.

[147]The *marut*s are companion gods of Indra. They have variously been described as either seven, forty nine or sixty seven in number in different legends. They are the reigning deities of wind and storm and are ferocious fighters.

harnessed wild animals to serve as his soldiers' mounts. Thus his army had wild elephants, dark horses with flowing manes, mules, wolves, jackals, hyenas, bears and tigers. His soldiers were dressed in fearful costumes, had applied frightening face-paint and held dreadful, unconventional weapons in their hands—clubs, machetes, battle-axes, mallets, double-edged swords, slingshots and long spears. Their headgear consisted of the filleted-out heads of dead animals with their horns intact, giving the daitya soldiers the look of chimeras. Their rank and file did not stand in formation but buzzed around the field like a group of flies hovering over a dead body. Their strength was in their numbers. The daitya army stretched as far as the eye could see and it heaved, moved, pulsated and shouted like a single fearsome beast—one called death.

Looking at the unimaginably huge daitya army would've sent shivers down the spine of any casual observer. They looked like the *kalakeya*s that came out from the oceans to wreak havoc upon the earthlings.[148] The eyes of the daityas were red with rage or the sura (alcohol) that they ritually consumed before war to make them fearless. They held their weapons high, shaking them, bared their fangs and ululated in high-pitched voices like the guardian spirits of the underworld, calling their opponents to their gruesome ends.

---

[148]The *kalakeya*s were a group of very ferocious, and abominably cruel danavas who had fought on the side of Vritra, an asura whom Indra later slayed. After Vritra's defeat at the hands of Indra, the kalakeyas had hidden in the depths of the sea and came out only at night to wreak havoc upon the earth by their mindless slaughter of defenseless hermits, till they were finally killed by the devas with the help of the sage Agastya.

However, the devas were confident of their victory because, even though their numbers were smaller, *yet*, they were a well-trained and a cohesive force. Successive wars had shown that tactics and strategy always won over merely numbers.

As the opposing armies faced each other, thirsting for blood, there was a momentary pause before the start of the hostilities. Everyone stopped in their tracks, waiting for a signal, their hearts beating with anxiety and anticipation. Indra and Hiranyakashyap surveyed their armies one last time before finally letting them go into the skirmish; the moment was at hand! Hiranyakashyap raised his mace, studded with nails the size of a man's hand, and Indra raised his arm holding the Vajra, shining like the lightning bolt that seared the bosom of the skies upon his command. This was the indication. War bugles and conch shells were blown, trumpets were sounded and the standards and signal flags were waved—it was a go!

The two armies rushed towards each other, hungry beasts galloping towards their game, colliding into each other with a force that moved the heavens. They looked like two tidal waves crashing into each other. Their dominant colours were distinctive, silver and gold, and thus their commingle looked like the mingling of the waters of the Alaknanda and the Mandakini at Devprayag.[149]

The earth trembled under the combined weight of the two mighty armies. The noise of swords clashing

---

[149]Devprayag literally means union of the gods or goddesses. Devprayag is a hill town in North India where the two tributaries of Ganga—Mandakini and Alaknanda—meet to form the Ganges River.

against swords, crashing on shields and piercing armour, rent the air. Arrows swished across the landscape, spears flew like missiles and found their mark, clubs and mallets thudded with deadly accuracy into their intended destinations, producing sickening sounds as flesh and bones were crushed. The twang of divine bows was heard across the battlefield, with the boom of divine astras finding their mark and landing on their targets becoming a familiar sound. The devas wielded divyastras or divine weapons, which could kill hundreds and thousands of foes at one time with sickening accuracy. The cries of daityas and devas, challenging, attacking, groaning, shouting, yelling, crying, howling in pain, filled the air and invited the carrion eaters to the field. Blood flowed from dead and dying bodies and mixed with the earth so that the field was soon covered in a red sludge, a quagmire made from the entrails of men. The field was littered with severed limbs, decapitated heads and mauled and mutilated corpses of the devas as well as the daityas.

Agni, Varun and Mitra led their battalions and fanned out in a radiating fashion from where Indra mauled the enemy with his divine weapons.

Agni, the fire god, the one with the complexion of burnished copper, was known as the mouth of the devas since his fire devoured everything in its path and delivered the souls of the devoured beings to Yama, the god of death. Wherever Agni went, he was surrounded by flames, engulfing his enemies, swallowing them up and cooking them with heavenly fire. Men yelled and screamed as they were burnt alive by Agni. But the numbers were too many to handle. The daityas kept coming like a deluge without end, like a swarm of locusts and even though Agni unleashed the heavenly fire of destruction, they would not stop. Agni looked around for help from other devas but they were similarly occupied. The daitya army had overwhelming numbers and if Indra did not think of something soon, the devas would have to retreat.

Varun and Mitra were in a similar situation, as was Yama, the god of death. He was there collecting souls and using his infinite, luminescent noose to drag the enemy soldiers to their death. He wore black clothes and rode a demonic bull with huge horns gilded with gold and hooves like monstrous ploughs. His eyes were red with rage as he egged his bull on, breathing fire, whipping his paash, his noose.

All the devas fought valiantly but were no match for the demonic forces of the daityas. The devas knew and Indra realized this. He directed his elephant towards the spot where Hiranyakashyap stood amidst all the chaos and the bloodshed, silent and majestic, like a mountain unmoved by the little winds that buffet its peaks. His forehead shone with the brilliance of his penances, his mighty arms looked like tree trunks, his battle-scarred torso a testimony to the many wars he had waged. His long, dark hair was tied neatly and curled into a bun on his crowned head; the diadem in his crown sparkled. He stood in his golden chariot, driven by another fearsome asura and pulled by eight ferocious lions, filling others with fear. Looking at him, it did not seem like he was in the least bit worried about the outcome of the war. He was confident of his victory and the smug look on his face worried Devaraj Indra. This was not good!

Following Indra's cue, Varun, Mitra, Agni and Yama directed their forces at Hiranyakashyap. If they could capture or kill him the war would be won. Even he could not be able to withstand their combined onslaught; *could* he? A small, nagging doubt assailed their hearts. Hiranyakashyap, after all was immortal due to the boon that Brahma himself gave him. How was he to be killed? The devas looked at Indra who had no idea either. Even Yama, the god of death, did not know the way forward. This was an unprecedented situation; they had never killed an immortal before!

No one could've foreseen what happened next. The devas attacked Hiranyakashyap with all their combined might, hurling their divine weapons at him. Arrows, spears and mallets flew in the air towards the daitya king. He countered all the weapons with a long *danda*, a staff, which he held in his hands. It was spiked with nails, bulbous at one end and pointed at the tip, thus capable of being used either as a club or a spear. It was a ferocious instrument which he wielded with ease and deadly accuracy. It was this shaft he used to deflect all the weapons hurled at him, swinging it so fast that it became almost impossible to see him. A few arrows flew past his danda and found their mark. Some thudded into his armour, some pierced it, but he kept standing, kept fighting. His armour and his black and gold dress was streaked with dark blood but still the daitya king fought. He battled energetically and mercilessly, as if nothing had happened, for he knew that these mere arrows could do him no harm; he had the boon of immortality. The devas were perplexed and the daitya army roared in exultation watching these weapons fail against their king.

Varun and Mitra together hurled their divine spears at Hiranyakashyap and both found their mark. They thudded with sickening force into the body armour of the tall daitya leader but Hiranyakashyap looked at them as if they were toothpicks, broke them in two, extracted them from his flesh and continued fighting. The twin gods were crestfallen—this had never happened before. How could any mortal survive after being impaled by their spears imbued with infallible ancient mantras. They were surprised and awe-struck by Hiranyakashyap's valour. While his soldiers fought around him, slaying and devouring the deva army, Hiranyakashyap stood and faced the combined onslaught of all the principal devas himself.

When everything else seemed to be useless, Indra used his vajra.

Invoking the ancient forces of the universe which ruled gods and men alike, chanting arcane mantras to infuse the deadly weapon with all the powers at his command, Indra held his divine astra aloft for all to see. The ancient gods thundered in the skies, flashing their bolt of lightning, agreeing to lend their might to the Vajra. Indra held it aloft; it seemed to shine like the very thunderbolt which flashed in the skies above and hurled it towards Hiranyakashyap. The mighty thunderbolt was shining, sparkling and throwing sparks of fire followed by celestial lightning. The weapon flew towards the daitya king who waited to effortlessly catch it in his hands, smiling all the while.

A collective gasp escaped the lips of all those present on the battlefield when Hiranyakashyap caught Indra's magical weapon and holding it in both hands broke it into two. It shattered with a thunderous sound, a doomsday bugle, and sent sparks flying as the 'indestructible' metal collapsed. The broken shaft lay useless in the hands of the daitya king, who held the now useless Vajra aloft for everyone to see. The might of Indra had been broken as was the myth of his invincibility. This was a sign that Hiranyakashyap was the new ruler of the world: the new God.

The devas took their cue and retreated hastily. Defeated and shamefaced, they trudged back home to Amravati, which the daitya king, in his generosity, had spared. Indra hung his head in shame. His glory, the divine light that shone through him, was gone. He looked lustreless. The other devas—Agni, Mitra, Varun and Yama—followed him, looking as crestfallen as their king. The deva army, battered and bruised after having lost many men, trudged into their capital. They were ordered to disband and go to their homes till such a time that the principal devas could find a solution to this problem.

The solution was clear to everyone—they would have to go to the Mahavishnu in supplication once more and seek his divine intervention. Only he could help them now!

3

The daitya army returned to their capital triumphant! Hiranyakashyap was now the undefeated ruler of all land. He was the new divinity, the new God. As he rode into his kingdom, little did he realize that the seeds of his destruction had already been sown and that his downfall had already been planned. It would be executed shortly and the medium for that downfall would be none other than his own son!

Meanwhile, Prahlad had learnt all that he had been taught and had excelled at everything but he had consistently refused to worship his father Hiranyakashyap as a deity. His teachers knew that this self-deification was a sticking point with their king and as far as this was concerned he would not listen to anyone. This was non-negotiable! It did not matter who the defaulter was—the penalty for this mistake was death. Thus, they tried to convince, cajole and blackmail him; but Prahlad would not be moved. He was firm in his devotion to Vishnu, the almighty god of all creation.

Then the fateful day came when Hiranyakashyap, established on his throne again after his victory over the devas, summoned Prahlad's teachers to ask them about his progress. Trembling and fearing for their lives, they entered the courtroom—hands folded, heads bowed—tears running down their cheeks.

'Forgive us, Lord,' they said in one voice. 'Prince Prahlad does not agree to our requests to accept you as the One True God. We have tried everything, but he will not worship you. We do not know what to do. We seek your protection. Please do not punish us.'

Hiranyakashyap was taken aback. His own son worshipping Vishnu, that dicey deva, the killer of his brother Hiranyaksha? Maybe it was time he summoned the errant prince and talked to him.

Prahlad was called to court to answer for his actions and beliefs.

He walked in calmly and greeted his father, the mighty Hiranyakashyap, the daitya king who ruled over the entire world, who had defeated Indra, Agni, Varun, and even Yama, the god of death himself.

'Pranam *taat,*' Prahlad said.[150] 'You summoned me?'

'Yes,' thundered Hiranyakashyap, shaking the court with his deep voice. 'You must answer for your actions, Prince Prahlad. You refuse to worship me? Is this true or are my servants lying? Tell me the truth.'

'I always speak the truth, Father. Never in my conscious memory have I swerved from the path of the truth, nor will I now,' Prahlad paused, then continued. 'Yes, the accusation is true. I refuse to worship any mortal.' His words rang out clearly in the silent court hall.

The courtiers could not believe what they were hearing. How could anyone have the courage to talk to Hiranyakashyap this way? Did Prahlad not value his life? Was he not afraid of bodily harm, and a slow and painful death? Was he insane? Even the insane usually come to their senses in front of the great daitya king. Even death trembled in front of this killer of death. They bit their lips in angst and waited to see what would happen.

'You refuse to worship any mortal?' Hiranyakashyap repeated and then burst into demonic laughter.

The hall echoed with the raucous sound of his mirth.

'But I am not mortal, dear Prince,' Hiranyakashyap said, still smiling. 'Do you not know? Or maybe you do not believe this?'

'Everyone born in this mortal world is mortal, Father,' Prahlad said respectfully. 'Immortality is not possible. It

[150] Pranam is a respectful salutation usually used to greet elders; *taat* is a term of respect and can be used for any senior or junior. Here, it means father.

is against the natural law, against vidhi. Not even the gods can defy these laws for they have been written by Narayana himself. Only He, who sleeps on the infinite ocean of milk, on the serpent that the wise call Shesha, only He is immortal.'

The court was deathly quiet. No one had ever dared to speak to Hiranyakashyap this way before. As the courtiers watched, trembling inside, they saw his temper rising. His bushy eyebrows were knotted in the centre of his forehead, his arms twitched and his eyes turned crimson as he boomed, 'Who is this Vishnu? Where does he live?'

'He is everywhere he wishes to be, Father. He can be anywhere,' Prahlad answered humbly.

'Oh, he is everywhere, is he? Is he in this hall? Why doesn't he come and face me? Why doesn't he come and stop me? Why doesn't he fight me? Is he afraid of me?' Hiranyakashyap asked, enraged and impatient.

'Why should he be afraid of anyone? He is the lord of all creation. He appears and disappears as per his wishes and the needs of his devotees. If one calls out to him with devotion, he always responds.'

'Then call him. Call him and tell him to save you. Call him with all the devotion at your command. If he is here, he will appear and save your life, won't he?'

By this time Hiranyakashyap had lost his temper and his inhibitions. He forgot that it was his son that stood before him. His hand involuntarily clutched the handle of the mace with which he had killed huge elephants in one stroke.

'Call him,' Hiranyakashyap repeated, maddened with rage.

'Ask him to come and save you from my mace. Where is he? Is he here beneath my throne, is he here behind the curtains? Is he in this pillar? Then let him come out and save you or you die at my hands today,' Hiranyakashyap roared, his mace held high in the air.

Prahlad stood with his hands folded and his eyes closed, murmuring his prayers. As the arm holding the mace descended, everyone flinched.

At that moment, There was an ear-shattering sound like a thunderclap as the pillar broke into a thousand pieces and crumbled to the ground raising a huge cloud of dust. Hiranyakashyap had hit the pillar instead of Prahlad!

While the cloud of dust stood suspended in the air, Hiranyakashyap paused, his mace still gripped in his hands, his huge frame quivering with uncontrollable anger.

Through the doors and windows of the grand hall, the light of the setting sun fell on the cloud of dust which had risen when the pillar had shattered, making it look luminous and infusing it with a light of its own. The light inside the palace had started to diminish since it was early evening and the attendants rushed around to light the lamps—it was going to be nightfall soon. The assembly was tense with anticipation and fear.

Hiranyakashyap waited with the mace in his hand, squinting at the luminous cloud of dust which was beginning to settle. Prahlad stood with his hands folded—eyes closed, head bowed—murmuring the 'Vishnu Sahasranamam'.

In the relative darkness of the court hall, the cloud of dust which had glowed with a heavenly light now seemed to increase in luminosity for a moment. Slowly the dust settled and everyone's eyes adjusted to the divine 'glow' emanating from the place. Hiranyakashyap was staring at the orb of light in front of him curiously, when he thought he heard a growl like that of a lion.

'What is this? Where did this sound come from?' he said.

No one knew, though they had heard it too.

Then it came again, louder this time—the unearthly growl of a lion, loud and clear, shaking the hall, striking fear in hearts of the daityas there. Hiranyakashyap looked around for the source of the sound when he saw Prahlad kneeling, his head on the floor, bowing to someone or something.

'What is it? What are you bowing to?' he shouted, angry and perplexed, the shadow of a doubt creeping across his mind.

Stepping out from the orb of light and dust that emanated from the destroyed pillar was a huge figure, unearthly in its proportions, inspiring awe and striking fear into the hearts of even the most valiant. Silhouetted by the divine glow which still crested his frame, the entity stepped forward. He was tall, taller than the daitya king by an arm's length, making Hiranyakashyap look puny. The figure stepped out from the shattered pillar and growled again, his voice shaking the very earth on which Hiranyakashyap stood, resounding through the royal hall.

Hiranyakashyap noticed that the figure had golden hair like a mane which flowed down to his strong shoulders; large bushy eyebrows; prominent cheekbones; huge protuberant jaws like that a beast; and large fangs like that of a lion. It looked like the head of a lion on the torso of a man. His long, muscular arms ended in huge hands which looked more like paws with long and sharp talons. His hide shimmered with a divine aura and his forehead was marked with a Vaishnava tilaka, not dissimilar to what Prahlad himself wore, which glowed. He wore a *pitambar*, or garment of yellow silk,[151] and upon his chest was the ancient symbol of the Shrivatsam.[152]

This Narasingha, or man-lion, stepped out from the pillar growling loudly and ferociously, making the courtiers quiver! Hiranyakashyap was taken aback, his mouth open, his eyes staring; he was frozen into inaction. He had not expected this unearthly beast to emerge from the pillar, the very one that he had shattered to prove Vishnu's nonexistence! The daitya king had never experienced fear like he did now, raw and primal. He had never known fear even when fighting the mighty devas in the battlefield. He knew he was invincible and immortal. So why was he afraid now? Hiranyakashyap could not understand why he felt weak and feared for his life when he looked at this magical beast shimmering in the evening light, baring its fangs and advancing towards him.

He stepped back defensively and instinctively gripped

---

[151] *Pitambar* is the yellow garment Vishnu or Krishna is often described as wearing

[152] The Shrivatsam is a holy symbol in ancient Hindu iconography, much like the Swastika, it's better known and much-abused cousin. Literally translated it means 'beloved of Shri', the goddess of wealth and prosperity and Vishnu's consort. The Shrivatsam is also known as the 'endless knot', and is one of the ancient iconographic symbols recovered from the sites of the Indus-Saraswati Civilization.

his mace tighter. The hunter had very quickly turned into the hunted.

The Narasingha stepped out from the pillar and walked over to Hiranyakashyap, who retreated in a fearful daze and tried to fend off the beast with his mace. He threw it at the huge man-lion but it glanced off his skin like a drop of water slides off the leaves of the plantain tree. The mighty weapon that had made the devas tremble looked like a toy bouncing off the hide of the brute. Although the weapon could not harm him Narasingha grew angrier and roared loudly once more, his voice reaching the heavens above and warning the devas about what was happening below. They hurried to catch a glimpse of this divine incarnation of Vishnu, the Narasingha: the manticore. They crowded the heavens and sang hymns praising the lord of all creation who had agreed to descend upon the earth to save them from the daitya King.

Inside the hall, Prahlad was sitting on the floor, cross-legged in the lotus posture, his eyes closed, meditating upon the lord and singing. He sang hymns praising the lord in his sweet voice. The Narasingha looked at him, pleased, and then moved on to Hiranyakashyap, ignoring the others.

Hiranyakashyap had faltered and fallen across the steps leading to the throne on which he sat. He stared at this beast moving towards him, paralyzed with fear, and opened his mouth to say something or scream for help but no sound came. His voice and valour had failed him, as had the strength of his arms. His divine weapons were of no use as he lay at the feet of this monstrous beast, crouching like a lowly animal, whimpering with fear. The man-lion walked up to him, lifted him by his neck and turned around to carry his prey outside into the patio, with Prahlad following him, his hands still folded in supplication.

'Pray to him, Father, pray to him,' Prahlad said. 'He is the Lord Vishnu. He is the one you wanted to meet. He has come to meet you himself. Pray to him. Beg his forgiveness and you shall live.'

But Hiranyakashyap couldn't hear what his son said to him. His ears were ringing with the sound of his own fear.

Narasingha carried the daitya emperor out into the patio and sat down on a stone slab there, laying Hiranyakashyap on his lap like a baby or a sacrificial animal. The time was right—it was neither day nor night, it was *gaudhuli.*[153] The place was right—it was neither inside nor outside. The Narasingha was neither man nor beast, nor deva or asura, and when he ripped open the entrails of the daitya king ending his life with his long adamantine nails, the weapon was also right—it was neither astra nor shastra. Thus ended the illustrious but cruel life of the younger of the two daitya brothers, Hiranyakashyap, according to his own wishes. His pious and righteous son, Prahlad earned the favour of the dark-skinned god, Narayana, and ruled his daitya kingdom justly for a long time, bringing prosperity to his people. His name and glory lit up all the ten directions like a star and he came to be known across the world as one of the greatest devotees of Vishnu. In time, his

[153]Dusk; traditionally considered an inauspicious time to be spent in prayers

grandson would also rise to the same fame and cause Vishnu to incarnate once more on the earth as the Vamana, or the midget. This grandson of Prahlad was the illustrious daitya king Bali who also helped the devas in their Samudra Manthan or churning of the ocean.

Author's Note

The story of the Narasingha incarnation of Vishnu ends differently in different scriptures. In most of them, the legends agree that Narasingha was still very angry even after he had slain Hiranyakashyap and threatened to annihilate the world with his anger. All the men, devas and the gods were in mortal fear and decided that Narasingha had to be placated to prevent him from destroying everything in sight. How this was brought about is mentioned differently in different accounts. The legend of Prahlad states that Narasingha was pacified when Prahlad sang to him and he patted the lad, blessed him and went away. However, other scriptures like the Shiva Purana, the Skanda Purana and the Bhagwatam differ. In the Shaiviite lore, it is mentioned that Lord Shiva was requested by the devas to stop Narasingha from further destruction and for this, he incarnated himself as Sharabha, another mythical animal—part-lion, part- elephant, part-bird. The Sharabha captured Narasingha, slayed him and wore his skin as his garments. Thus, Shiva is also worshipped as Mrigadhishcharmambaram—wearing the skin of a lion. The Skanda Purana and other legends, specifically the Vaishnava legends like the Bhagwata Purana, mention that Vishnu, to counteract the Sharabha turned himself into a Bherunda, or Gandabherunda, a mythical bird with two heads and fought with the Sharabha. Legends of Shakti, or the Mother Goddess, state that it is the Goddess Lakshmi, Vishnu's consort, who came to Narasingha as Singhni or Simhika, a lion-woman, and makes him realize who he was, thus putting an end to his rage.

Amrit Kalash: The Pot of Nectar

1

Hiranyakashyap, the mighty daitya king, was dead! Slaughtered by the ferocious manticore that people said was an avatar of Vishnu. Prahlad believed it, for he had seen the beast himself. It had calmed down only when he had chanted the 'Vishnu Sahasranamam'. He had picked up Prahlad like a giant might pick up a puppy and had made him sit on his right thigh and had patted his head affectionately. Prahlad did not feel threatened by Narasingha in any way; while others had cowered around him, including the gods, devas, daityas and danavas, Prahlad had sat happily in his lap and had sung the 'Vishnu Sahasranamam' in his sweet voice. The manticore had listened happily with closed eyes, his anger cooling down and had blessed Prahlad with a long and illustrious life as well as an undying devotion for Vishnu. He had then disappeared from the sight of the mortals. People said that his life force had been absorbed back where it came from—the bosom of Shri Vishnu.

After this calamity, the daitya kingdom had suddenly become leaderless. The elders and the senior-most courtiers consulted the priests and astrologers on who would be the most appropriate person to ascend the throne and lead the daityas.

Hiranyaksha had left behind two sons, Andhak and Kalanemi. Andhak, as the name suggested, was born blind and was thus unfit to rule. Kalanemi was too young and immature and had a dark side which the elders did not approve of and thus, Prahlad, the son of Hiranyakashyap, was the obvious choice. Prahlad was mature beyond his years and was well-versed in statecraft. Everyone agreed that he would be the right choice.

Thus Prahlad had ascended to the daitya throne and had led the kingdom through a golden age of peace and prosperity which they had not known in the past and would not know in the future. Prahlad had grown up to be an able administrator. He had not picked unnecessary fights with people who did not bother him. He had also not spared those who had bothered him. Under his command the prosperity and power of the daitya empire reached its pinnacle. People said it was due to his undying faith and unwavering devotion in Vishnu. He made his peace with the adityas, or devas, and swore not to be the one to break the peace; the daitya people had bled enough.

As time passed, Prahlad married and had a son Virochana, and a daughter Virochanaa, who was later given in marriage to Shukracharya's son Tvashta.[154] In time, Virochanaa gave birth to Vishwarupa or Trishira,[155]

[154]Also known, in some legends, as Vishwakarma

[155]Tvashta and Virochanaa, through their daughter Saranyaa or Sanjana, are the progenitors of the manavas, commonly misunderstood as humans. Saranyaa, through Surya, the sun god, gave birth to Rishi Manu from whom all manavas have descended. She also gave birth to two sets of twins—the

who would later become the preceptor of the devas for a short period of time. Virochana got married too and had a son whom he named Bali. Prahlad married his sister, Simhika, to a pious danava, Viprachitti, the brother of Puloma, whose daughter Paulomi or Shachi was married to Indra, the leader of the devas. Simhika and Viprachitti had a valorous son, Svarabhanu. Thus, Prahlad's family had matrimonial connections to the danavas and the adityas.

'This will be good for prosperity and stability on earth,' Prahlad had thought.

Indeed the daitya royal family was happy and prospering, with relatives in all the major clans of the world. But it would not be this way for long. Even though Prahlad himself was discrete and non-belligerent in his policies and did not unnecessarily court trouble, this was not the same for everyone else. The daityas and the devas, like the opposite poles of a magnet, kept getting pulled into each other's affairs, some of which escalated into confrontations.

Andhak, Prahlad's stepbrother and son of Hiranyaksha, was born blind but he had the flame of divinity within him. He was given to Hiranyaksha as a boon from the immortal sage Shiva. Some people said he was the son of Shiva himself and this was the reason for his later greatness and invincibility. Others did not believe it. Hiranyaksha had gone to do penance to please Shiva and

---

Ashvins, the divine physicians, gods of beauty and health, and Yama-Yami. Yama is the god of death, while Yami is the deified river Yamuna.

Brahma and had come back with the boon of invincibility and with Andhak. Though blind, the greatness shone through him, along with an itinerant instability. He had an impetuous nature and could be very adamant, hot-headed and impervious to reason. He grew up to be a valiant warrior and learned scholar despite his blindness. Though he was older than Prahlad, the daityas did not consider him a candidate for the throne when the two daitya brothers—Hirayanksha and Hiranyakshayap—were killed by Vishnu. Many people cited his blindness as a cause while others said he was not a daitya and hence could not be their king. Prahlad did not believe in all this and had offered the throne to him in all fairness. Andhak however, sensitive to the rumours about him, had not laid claim to the throne and had supported Prahlad's ascent instead. Once Prahlad was firmly enthroned and the kingdom was doing well, he had asked for permission from his brother to proceed for penance to the Himalayas.

In the Himalayas, the daitya prince performed austerities, burning up the directions with his penance. He prayed to the grandfather of all creation, Brahma, for invincibility and for the restoration of his eyesight so that he could attain with his mighty arms, as was his birth-right. In time, he was granted his wishes and he returned triumphant to the daitya capital to everybody's amazement.

When Andhak returned, his eyesight restored, Prahlad had immediately offered him the daitya throne again; and this time he accepted. He had always wanted it but his blindness and the rumours that he wasn't a 'real' daitya had prevented him from claiming it.

'I will show them how much of a daitya I really am,' Andhak thought to himself.

The desire to prove himself had propelled Andhak into making the same mistakes his predecessors did. He set out on a campaign of conquest, upsetting the delicate balance Prahlad had nurtured. The world was plunged into a blind abyss of death, violence and chaos once more. Andhak's secret parentage and his boon of invincibility had made him a force to reckon with. It was true that no one was able to stand before him. He had routed all the powerful kingdoms that stood in his way easily, ruthlessly and mercilessly. Then he had turned to the devas and had routed them just as easily!

Prahlad was sad. He could see the path to destruction on which Andhak had propelled himself and the daitya empire. Prahlad tried to warn Andhak but the king was surrounded by a ring of sycophants he would not listen to anyone else.

'Andhak will also meet his fate someday,' Prahlad thought sadly.

And it wasn't long before Andhak ran into his nemesis.

One day he had been basking in his achievements, surrounded by his usual circle of courtiers, when he remarked, 'Is there anything I haven't achieved? Is there anyone left to defeat? Anything left to acquire?'

'Yes king,' his counsellors had fawned over him. 'You are the greatest daitya king of all time. You have achieved what even the gods, the devas, or their leader Indra, could not achieve. But you do lack an appropriate consort. A mighty king without a beautiful consort is incomplete.'

'Hmmmm...' Andhak thought for a moment.

'Suggest a suitable woman for me. I can have anyone—daitya, deva, yaksha, kinnar, gandharav, danava. I am the king of all. I can have Shachi[156] if I want. Tell me who will be a suitable companion to the king of the world,' Andhak gloated.

Vidhi, or natural law, works in strange ways. It is when we are at our most unassailable that vidhi conspires to brings us down. It is at the pinnacle, the zenith of our lives that we are most vulnerable. The tenets of vidhi are simple yet inscrutable for one blinded by maya, the illusion of this world. The secret to a healthy and happy life lies in balance. Everything must lie in a balance and humility is the only way to bring that balance. Prahlad had realized this noble truth early in his life but other daitya kings, including Andhak, had not. Thus it was when Andhak defeated everyone and won over all the kingdoms that he had become ripe for downfall. It was then that destiny struck.

'My lord,' the courtiers said, 'There is only one woman who is beautiful enough to be at your side. A woman like none in the world. A goddess of beauty. Not even Shachi, Indra's consort, can match her beauty. The apsaras of the heavens are also pale beside her beauty. She is the only one who will be a suitable companion for your majesty.'

'Who is this woman?' Andhak asked.

'She lives high in the Kailash mountains with a lone ascetic with matted hair, one who wears animal skin and smears *shavabhasm*, ashes from the cremation ground, on his body. Her name is Uma.'

Clouds rumbled in the skies outside and the earth

---

[156]Indra's wife

shivered at the mention of the name which the doomed daityas brought to their lips. But Andhak, blind with power and lust, did not pay attention to the divine warning.

Thus Andhak, lulled into a sense of invincibility by vidhi dispatched his generals to the Kailash mountains, the holy grounds where the Mahadev, the God of gods, the primordial ascetic, resided. The devas came to know of it and rejoiced—they knew this would be the end of Andhak. Prahlad also learned of the development and was worried; this would be the end of daitya power, the prosperity of their kingdom, the invincibility of their armies. He knew Shiva was the primordial shaft of fire, the *jyotirlinga,* which had manifested itself in the beginning of time and the end of which even Brahma and Vishnu had not been able to fathom.[157] He also knew about the fate of Tarakasur[158] and Mahishasur[159] and what had happened to them when they had challenged the cosmic duo of Shiva-Uma.

---

[157]This is a legend from the Shiva Purana. In the beginning of time, Rudra or Shiva, manifested himself as a pillar of fire. Vishnu and Brahma, both self-born deities tried to find the ends of this pillar and couldn't. Vishnu was honest enough to accept defeat to Rudra, but Brahma lied and was thus cursed with oblivion by Rudra. It is due to the curse of Rudra that Brahma is not worshipped anywhere, and does not command a respectable place in the Hindu pantheon of deities.

[158]Tarakasur was the son of Vajranga, a sibling of Hiranyaksha and Hiranyakashyap. Tarakasur was slayed by Kartikeya or Kumara, son of Shiva and the general of the deva armies.

[159]Mahishasur or the buffalo demon was a shape-shifting asura, who was slayed by Durga or Uma, in her Mahishasur Mardini form.

Andhak's generals went to Kailash and conveyed the demands of their king—that Devi Uma be surrendered to them or else...

Shiva had merely laughed, amused that someone should have the temerity to think of something as atrocious as this. The Mother had laughed too...but her laughter had echoed that of the god of death, happy to finally get the death-noose around the neck of Andhak! The generals had been chased away by Nandi, Shiva's general, like children chase away mangy street dogs. They escaped with their lives and ran back to the daitya capital beaten, bruised and shamed. They recounted their encounter with the animal skin wearing ascetic to their king. Andhak was furious and declared war on Shiva.

Prahlad tried to sound a word of caution to his brother.

'Don't start this war, brother,' he said. 'Shiva is not your ordinary deva. Do not lead our armies out to destruction. You know what happened to our cousin Tarakasur when he confronted Shiva. He was annihilated along with his invincible armies, and Shiva didn't even fight that war!'

'Tarakasur was a coward,' Andhak said. 'I am not Tarakasur. I will show that ascetic his place. You can come if you want or stay back if you choose to.'

'I will not willingly participate in this war which I know will end in the destruction of our forces. We are not on the side of truth this time, brother,' Prahlad had politely refused to be a part of the war and had even convinced his son, Virochana, not to take part in it. However, Bali, his grandson, had gone to fight with

Andhak. Bali was young and wanted to prove his mettle. Though he was an intelligent daitya and his heart was in the right place, he lacked the experience which brings wisdom to a man. Prahlad's sage advice had not moved him and he had gone with the daitya army to march on Kailash.

Prahlad activated his network of spies to bring news of the war to him while he defended the daitya capital. He knew which way the war would go. He only hoped it would not reach the capital, since most of the army had gone with Andhak and they were nearly defenceless. He sat in the courtroom, dispensing the administration and mundane duties of a regent and praying to Vishnu, so that the daitya kingdom be spared from destruction.

News had reached him bit by bit of what had happened far in the Kailash highlands. The daitya army had been routed mercilessly, unprepared as they were for what lay in store for them. Bali had learned his lesson when he was heavily injured and barely escaped with his life. The other daityas had not been so lucky; they had been slaughtered mercilessly by Kumara, Ganesha and an army of Rudras which had issued forth from Shiva. The lonely ascetic had sat on the mountain while his replicas, his Veerbhadras, Rudras, Kapalikas[160] had roamed the field disemboweling and decapitating everyone they encountered.

Andhak had been especially difficult to kill because of his boon. Wherever a drop of his blood fell, a new demonic form would emerge, more ferocious than the one before, and the fight would go on. Finally, the Mother

[160]Veerbhadra, Rudra and Kapalika are all forms of Shiva

had let the *matrikas* loose upon him.[161] Thus while Rudra impaled him with his trident, the matrikas drank up his blood so that no new demons could arise. Watching their king impaled on Rudra's Trishula, or trident, the daitya army had fled, leaving their commander and their king. For days, Andhak remained impaled upon the Trishula, immobilized, dripping blood. He was reduced to only skin and bones before the truth dawned on him. He accepted defeat and prayed to be let down from the trident. Shiva had consented and Andhak stayed on with him and Uma as their ardent devotee, renouncing the world and his kingdom. His new name, Prahlad's spies informed him, was Bhringi.[162]

The daitya forces now led by Bali had returned to the capital city, beaten, broken, reduced in number and demoralized. Prahlad set about reconstructing and reorganizing the empire again. He paid careful attention to the grooming and training of Virochana, his son, and Bali, his grandson. They were the torch bearers of the daitya family. He was growing old and wanted to hand

---

[161]The *matrikas* are fierce goddesses of war, thunder and lightning. Their numbers have been given in different legends as either six or seven or even up to eighty-one. The Krittikas, who had nurtured Kumara, were also known as matrikas. It is after them that Kumara was named Kartikeya. Literally translated, matrika means mother. In later lore, they have been described as the ones bringing pestilence and death upon children younger than twelve years of age but protecting them once they are older. In rural India, they are still worshipped and propitiated for the safety of children and are called 'Mata' or mother

[162]*Bhringi* means bumblebee. The legend of Bhringi says that Bhringi was such an ardent devotee of Shiva that he kept going round him again and again and thus earned himself the sobriquet of Bhringi, the bumblebee. Some legends identify Bhringi with Andhak, others don't.

the kingdom over to someone capable so he could spend his last days in solitude and meditation in the forest.

Virochana, Bali's father, was pious, well-versed in all arts and sciences and had years of administrative experience. However, the daitya streak sometimes manifested within him and he was prone to vagaries of his temper, taking decisions without resorting to the sane counsel of his advisors. His proximity to Kalanemi was worrying too. Kalanemi was the younger son of Hiranyaksha and was closer in age to Virochana than to his brothers Andhak and Prahlad. Kalanemi was, Prahlad thought, a bad influence on Virochana. He was a typical daitya—volatile, violent, cruel and undisciplined. Virochana and Kalanemi's friendship defied logic since they were the exact opposites. Virochana tried to talk some sense into Kalanemi but was unsuccessful.

Bali, on the other hand—though still very young—showed great promise. He was valiant and the soldiers loved him. He was also learned, pious, generous, and had learned a lot from Andhak's failed expedition. His eyes shone with a maturity beyond his years which his friends said was previously seen in Prahlad's own eyes. He had recently become a father and since then he had spent more and more time with his son, Bana, looking after his instruction and training.

Prahlad hoped he would have enough time to tutor both his son and his grandson before he himself retired from active life. Ever since he was a young boy, even before the unearthly beast had appeared from inside the pillar and killed his father, Prahlad had always wanted to be a renunciant. However, his responsibilities had not allowed him to do so. But now, he thought, he was ready. A few years of peace would give him time to groom Virochana and Bali and he could retire to some hermitage, spending spend his days close to his deities and his gods. A few years of peace…

2

Destiny intervened and the daitya kingdom was pulled into war with the devas again. Chandra, the moon god, eloped with Tara, the wife of Brihaspati, the preceptor of the devas, plunging the world into chaos. Brihaspati was angry and the leader of the devas, Indra, warned Chandra to respectfully return Tara or face punishment, but he refused. Instead, he sought refuge with Shukracharya, the preceptor of the daityas, who wilfully obliged, sensing an opportunity to foment disunity amongst the devas. The daityas also came out in support of Chandra and the battle lines were drawn with all the devas, gandharvas, yakshas, nagas and manavas closing ranks in support of Brihaspati.

Prahlad did not want the daityas to support Chandra's immoral act because no shastra could sanction what he had done. He called a meeting of the daitya council to reach a consensus on this issue. He did not want the daityas to go to war with the devas, but he was overruled.

Much arguing and haggling later, the council decided that the daityas would declare war on the devas in support of Chandra. Shukracharya would support the war, Virochana would lead the armies and Kalanemi would accompany them. Prahlad and his grandson, Bali decided to stay back. They would not support this cause.

Thus it began—the most violent war of all the devasura sangrams (war between gods and demons). It was called the Tarakamaya war. On one side were the daityas and danavas, on the other side were the devas supported by all the divine and semi-divine species. The war went on for years. There was no end to the slaughter that was unleashed—the battlefield was filled with the dead and the dying. Rivers of blood flowed. Cut limbs, hacked bodies and severed heads went flying everywhere. Divine astras were used with impunity on both sides with devastating effect. There was fire, wind and the deluge of death everywhere. The daityas brought out their cruelest warriors, their mightiest war animals and their deadliest weapons. Together with the danavas they wanted to finish off this acrimony with the devas once and for all.

The devas, on the other hand, unleashed all their secret weapons on the unsuspecting daitya army, weapons never seen before on any battlefield. These cut the daitya soldiers to pieces, burning, mutilating, hacking and sawing off their limbs. The field was filled with the howls of the dead and the dying.

Prahlad sat on the throne in the daitya court, his forehead creased with worry. The early evening sun had started its slow descent towards the horizon, casting long shadows in the royal hall. The court attendants lit the torches in the hall, fired the incense burners and placed them near the throne, awaiting further instructions. A few courtiers stood around the royal throne, forming a semicircle at one end of the huge, pillared hall. Bali stood beside his grandfather and waited, looking at the old man intently. Prahlad was tall and had been very well-built once upon a time. His wrinkled skin now sagged from his frame and his face had deep furrows etched into them. His long, grey hair was neatly tied in a loose bundle at the back of his head. His bushy eyebrows almost met in the centre of his broad forehead, which he had marked with the vertical mark of Vishnu, the tilakam, which glowed in the evening light.

Ever since the daitya army had gone to war, Bali had helped Prahlad with the affairs of the kingdom. This had allowed him to learn statecraft directly from the great man himself. He had also come to understand his grandfather better. They had long talks, for there was nothing else to do except wait for news of the war. They discussed a wide variety of subjects which included administration, war strategy, history, philosophy, religion, psychology and future strategies. Bali had come to understand why so many people, including the devas, regarded his grandfather as the greatest daitya ever, perhaps the greatest mortal ever! His clarity of thought was amazing. It was as if he had a divine sight which helped him see things in a light no one else could see. He had a kind of balanced personality that Bali had not seen in anyone in his immediate or larger daitya family. He had grown close to his grandfather and had started to admire him, looking up to him as an ideal to be emulated.

Now as he stood close to Prahlad, Bali could see that something weighed on his grandfather's mind. He could see that Prahlad was inwardly debating something. His shoulders slouched and his eyes were nearly closed as if from excessive sleep but Bali knew that his grandfather wasn't dozing; he was in deep thought and in this state he was more awake to the realities facing the daitya family than any other man alive.

'Pitamah,' Bali called softly.

Prahlad stirred and fixed his aging eyes on Bali's tall muscular frame. His old eyes twinkled with a divine spark as they met Bali's gaze.

'What is it, Pitamah?' Bali continued. 'I can see you have something on your mind. You have that faraway look in your eyes which I have seen when you are contemplating something serious.'

Prahlad smiled gently and then turned to look at the courtiers still present in the courtroom. He nodded at them and the courtiers, taking the cue, bowed low and excused themselves. Presently, Prahlad and Bali were alone in the assembly hall.

'Sit down here near me, so that I can look at you closely. I must talk to you about something,' Prahlad said, pointing to a seat close to him.

Bali obeyed and sat down next to Prahlad, looking up at him expectantly, worried.

'I am getting really old now, Bali,' Prahlad began. 'I want to relinquish the responsibilities of the kingdom and proceed for *vanvaas*.'

Bali's mouth fell open.

'Taat...' he could not complete the sentence; he was overwhelmed with emotion.

'No, no. Don't say anything, just listen. Our time may be running out,' Prahlad said meaningfully, worrying Bali even more.

'My race is run, son. I have fulfilled my purpose here on this earth. I must now prepare for the transition that comes for all mortal beings. I will leave this kingdom in your capable hands and devote my time to meditation,' Prahlad paused, thinking again. He talked slowly as if he was tired of it all, or as if he was in deep thought and had difficulty articulating exactly what he wanted to say.

'I know which way the war will go, son, and that is why I am warning you that the responsibility of the kingdom will fall on your shoulders. But before I leave the kingdom in your hands, and I know they are capable hands, I want to tell you some things.'

Bali listened attentively as Prahlad went on speaking, not wanting to spoil the moment by saying anything.

'You do know about the story of the manticore, son?'

Bali nodded, recalling the legend that the whole world seemed to know, that the Puranas sang of.

'When the manticore touched me, put me in his lap and stroked my head, something miraculous happened. I have not been able to tell anyone this till now; there was no need. But now I must tell you this because you have to believe the advice I am going to give to you,' Prahlad paused, catching his breath, and looked up at Bali, meeting his eyes squarely.

'When the manticore touched me, son, he passed on the spark of divinity, the seed of the cosmic consciousness, the fire of eternal knowledge to me. You see Bali, God is not a person as we imagine Him to be. He, or She, if you may, is pure consciousness, an impersonal source of energy, vitality and knowledge. Though this energy manifests sometimes in ways which are beyond our material understanding, it really is beyond the definitions of materialism or even of existence and thus, is beyond human articulation. This pure consciousness does not know the barriers of time and space, person and material universe. This primal energy, this consciousness, cannot be shown or given; it can be felt. One may feel it when one is in deep meditation, in the *susupti* state.[163] You may have felt it yourself during your meditation.'

Bali nodded, not sure where this was going.

'The state that you reach in meditation is a temporary one. One must always come back to *jagrat*, the conscious state, when the dhyanam, the meditation, ends,' Prahlad continued[164]. 'However, what the manticore gave to me is permanent. It has been with me since then, like a continuous, waking meditative state. It is like a light which moves inside me all the time; like a voice which counsels me, guides me; like a vision which lets me see what others cannot. But this comes at a price, son. I cannot share or make others believe the knowledge or vision I have. Thus, I am all alone in this world since only I can see the truth. I am cursed to see everyone wallowing in maya, the illusion of this world, and even though I know the way out, I cannot help them. Cannot even help my family, my loved ones, my son or my daughter.'

'Son, I am telling you this since I see the divine spark in you as well and I know maybe you will understand when I tell you that immortality is not for us daityas,'

---

[163]*Susupti* literally means dreamless sleep and is a state of consciousness described in Hindu philosophy. This dreamless consciousness may be achieved in higher states of meditation.

[164]There are four states of consciousness as alluded to earlier, described in the Hindu philosophy. They are: *jagrat*—waking state; *svapna*—dreaming mind; *susupti*—dreamless state reached in deep meditation, also known as *samadhi*; and *turiya*—pure consciousness, when the knowledge of self, the distinction of matter and energy, cease to exist and the yogi or individual is absorbed into the universal whole. It is also described as absolute emptiness.

Prahlad paused, looking closely at Bali.

'I know. I can see that you are confused why I am suddenly talking about immortality,' Prahlad said. Bali nodded absently. 'You will understand when the time comes. Just listen and try to understand what I am saying. When the need arises, you will remember all this,' Prahlad continued.

'You see son, with the spark of divinity, the seed of consciousness, comes a vision which is beyond the fetters of space and time. I can feel and see things others cannot and thus they do not believe what I say. A great calamity is upon us, son. The daitya family is going to see some very challenging times in the future. I am confident that you will be able to steer our great family out of all the troubles that lie ahead.'

'I am not so sure, taat,' Bali said. 'With you gone, who will guide me? How will I know what is the best course of action in a particular situation? How can I not be influenced by my own biases or the actions of others? How will I be able to take a decision free from *raaga* or *dwesha*?'[165]

'The best course of action in any situation, son, is the one which leads to the greater good and the least violence. Dharma is very subtle, child. Everyone must decipher their dharma according to their situation but if you always keep the greater good of the people in your mind, you will never deviate from dharma. Also remember son, intentions will lead to action, action will lead to consequences which will shape the destiny of

---

[165]*Raaga* means love or attachment, *dwesha* means hatred or antagonism; in this context Bali is asking how to take an unbiased decision.

the daitya nation. One always has a choice, so choose wisely. Remember, we are only responsible for our intentions and our actions, not for their consequences. Being mortal, we cannot control everything—the ways of the daiva, the divine, are inscrutable and beyond our understanding. Whenever in doubt, remember to ask yourself what is right for you to do. Your action must result from your thoughts, your volition, your convictions and your beliefs, not as a reaction to someone else's thoughts or actions. What others do is according to their *tatva*, their inherent character. Their character and their decisions must not influence yours; you will answer for your decisions, they will answer for theirs. Your decisions and your actions must be according to what you think is right and what you think is best for everyone who will be influenced by your decisions.'

'But why are you telling me this, Grandfather?' Bali protested, suddenly alarmed at where this conversation was going. 'You should tell this to father when he comes back. Why are you teaching raja dharma to me?'[166]

'Everything has a reason, son, even though it may not be apparent immediately. Learn to be patient and inculcate forbearance and humility. Try to look beyond the present, beyond the confines of time. Widen your gaze and broaden your horizon. Remember that there will be temptations in the future, greater than we have seen in our times. When confronted with temptations, remember that all life is ephemeral and transient and that is how it should be. No one should try to become immortal, even if offered a choice. Immortality is a great

---

[166]Raja dharma is duties and responsibilities of a king

curse, son, only the gods can bear it.'

'There will come a time,' Prahlad continued, 'when your principles, your priorities, your loyalty, everything will be questioned. Stay on the course of dharma, son. Only dharma will guide you through the calamitous times that are in store for us.' Prahlad fell silent after saying this and the faraway look returned in his eyes.

For a moment, the two daityas sat silently in the empty hall alone with their thoughts. Then Prahlad looked up towards the entrance to the hall as if expecting someone to come, as if looking beyond time, into the past and the future, his aged eyes glazed but sparkling with the divine light that shone inside his soul. Bali looked at his grandfather and was wonderstruck at what a remarkable person the old man was, what a remarkable life he had led, and how fortunate Bali himself had been to have Prahlad as his grandparent, to have touched the greatness, the divinity that lay within him!

'What is he waiting for?' Bali wondered.

As if to answer his queries, an usher announced the arrival of a rider.

'Bring him in,' Prahlad said, a look of resolute determination in his eyes. The moment was not lost on Bali.

'Did he know who was coming?' Bali wondered.

A rider wearing the insignia of the daitya army and plastered with dirt from his ride walked in and bowed low.

'My King,' the rider said, and then stood quietly.

'Say what you have come to say,' Prahlad's voice was firm, steely, commanding.

'The Tarakamaya sangram has ended, my King. The

daitya forces have been routed. And...,' the rider paused.

'Go on,' Prahlad said. 'Do not fear.'

'Prince Virochana and Prince Kalanemi are dead.'

Deathly silence hung in the air as the rider finished his pronouncement and stood quietly. Bali felt his world spinning around him. The daitya forces had been decimated and all the royal princes who accompanied them had been killed. Was this what Prahlad had foreseen when he had cautioned against joining this war? No one had listened to him. Is this what his grandfather had meant when he had said that others do not believe him as they cannot see what he can? Could he look into the future and see what was coming? Is this why he had been talking to him about dharma, immortality and other things? Was he preparing him?

Questions knocked around inside Bali's head but he found no answers.

'You are dismissed, rider. Please send the royal usher inside when you leave,' Prahlad said, his voice steady, his tone cold.

'Taat...' Bali said, his voice almost breaking.

'Steel yourself, son. The time we talked about is upon us and worse will be in store. You will need to be very brave. The time for you to take charge has come. I will perform my son's last rites and will relinquish power in your favour,' Prahlad's voice had the finality of death, of fate, and of divine pronouncement in it.

And indeed, that is what Prahlad did.

The next day the last rites of the daitya princes were performed, their remains consigned to flames and to the eternal mercy of God. Prahlad shed no tears; he had been ready. After an appropriate period of mourning,

Bali's ascension to the daitya throne was announced. No one spoke about the Tarakamaya war and what had happened there. Everyone wanted to forget it.

A few days after Bali's coronation, Prahlad donated all his worldly possessions, distributed all his wealth to the needy and the poor and retired to the forest, wearing garments made from the bark of trees. No one heard from him after that day. Legend has it that he went to Vaikuntha, the abode of Vishnu. The story goes that Vishnu sent a divine chariot to bring him to his abode where he would rest with the lord for all eternity.

Bali ruled his kingdom justly, with a strong hand and a kind heart. He did not invite wars, but did not shy away from them either. His fame as a just and valiant king grew. The power and prosperity of the daitya kingdom rivalled that of the devas. His treasury was full, the granaries were full, people had no dearth of milk and honey. Children learnt arts and sciences from the best teachers in the world. Medicine, art and science flourished. Artisans were happy, farmers were happy, the rain god showered the kingdon with rains regularly. The army was stabilized, there were no mercenaries and all the soldiers were paid regular salaries. The capital was fortified, embankments of rivers were repaired, public tanks, parks and orchards were maintained by the state. The taxation system was just, the gurus, the priests and the *vaidyas* (healers) were respected all over the land, their expenses paid by the state. Education and medicine were free. People gave alms freely, no one stole from anyone, no one was needy, no one slept on an empty stomach. Bali's kingdom was an ideal state that even the gods talked about. His fame rivalled that of Indra, causing the leader of the devas sleepless nights.

3

Devaraj Indra was worried. The balance of good and bad in his kingdom was disturbed. The devas, the custodians of virtue in the world, had become weak. A mysterious illness ailed them. They seemed weak in body and spirit, as if the divine food they ate had no more power to sustain them. They were routed by even the weakest of enemies in every war they fought. They had suffered several reverses in the recent past at the hands of the daityas and the danavas. Though Bali, the daitya king, had been generous in his handling of the skirmishes, his soldiers and the daitya people in general had not been so kind. Unknown to Bali, they troubled the devas incessantly and had made life miserable for them. They had teamed up with the danavas, and in small teams, they raided deva territories, looting and sacking the households, carrying away deva women and celestial nymphs, and indulging in wanton slaughter.

The daitya guru, Shukracharya, had made several advances in the field of *ayur*, or life sciences, and had ensured health and healing for the daityas. It was also rumoured that he had discovered and mastered the *sanjeevani*, the art of bringing the dead back to life. Thus any daitya soldiers that the devas killed, were revived by Shukracharya, demoralizing the devas even more. Their own guru, their preceptor, Brihaspati, did not know this art and though the devas had tried to learn sanjeevani secretly, they had been unsuccessful.

All this was causing Indra great distress. The Indras

preceding him had been much more successful in handling this menace.[167] His predecessors had fought and won several wars with the daityas but the devas seemed to have lost their vitality during his reign. 'Maybe this was due to the curse of Rishi Durvasa,' Indra thought.

Rishi Durvasa was the son of the ascetic couple Atri and Anusuya. He was also the brother of Chandra, the deva who had famously eloped with Brihaspati's wife. Durvasa was known all over the world for his short temper and his propensity for pronouncing curses. His temper had earned him a reputation all over the world and wherever he went people, accorded him great respect out of fear.

Once upon a time, right after the Tarakamaya war, Rishi Durvasa was roaming around in a meditative trance when he chanced upon a procession of the devas led by Indra. The war had just ended and Devaraj Indra had decided to lead a procession through their capital to celebrate the occasion. He sat on his war elephant while his mighty devas walked beside him. There was Varun, Vayu, Mitra, Yama and Agni. Guru Brihaspati walked beside them, happily chanting invocations. It was at this point that Durvasa Rishi had chanced upon the procession and hailed Indra. He offered Indra a garland

[167] It is my impression that terms like 'Indra' are generic terms and denote a position rather than a person. Thus, there can be several Indras over a period of time, the same way that several famous gurus, or teachers, are found in every legend, like Vashishtha, Brihaspati and Shukracharya. These are probably common nouns, denoting a designation or a family name, rather than a proper noun, denoting a specific person.

of divine flowers which he himself was wearing. Indra accepted the gift but instead of wearing it himself, he had put it around the head of the elephant he rode. This garland had several divine flowers in bloom, sweet with nectar that had attracted bees and flies. The poor beast on which Indra rode was troubled by the bees and realizing that the garland was the source of all this trouble, he had plucked it off with his trunk, flinging it onto the ground. Indra, wallowing in his pride, had not noticed this omission but it had not escaped the eyes of Durvasa. His temper had been aroused at Indra's arrogance, and he had promptly pronounced a curse upon him and the devas.

'O Indra! You have become drunk with power and cannot discern right from wrong. Your unfettered power has made you so blind that you disrespect my gift and let your beast fling it to the ground and trample upon it. So be it. Your fate and that of your compatriot devas will also be flung down and trampled upon like the garland I offered you!'

The devas' decadence had started almost immediately and had continued, slowly but surely. Their power diminished progressively as if hit by an unknown pestilence. They lost wars, became weak and could not resist the forces of darkness anymore. Their guru, Brihaspati, could not find a reason for this illness that ailed them and together they had gone to the grandsire Brahma, the fount of all knowledge.

'An unknown weakness indeed ails you, O devas,' Brahma said. 'Nothing but the *amrit*, the nectar of life, which lies at the bottom of the infinite ocean will revitalize you and give you vigour and immortality.'

The devas were perplexed. 'How will we get this amrit, O Grandfather, if it lies at the bottom of the infinite ocean?'

'For that, O devas, you have to churn the ocean to bring forth its riches, one of which is the amrit,' Brahma pronounced.

'But we are weak, Grandfather, how will we churn the ocean?' the devas asked.

'Make peace with the daityas and invite them to help you with the churning. This is a mammoth task and cannot be completed without you joining forces with the daityas.'

'But why will the daityas help us?' the devas asked.

'My sons,' the grandfather continued, 'The ocean, when it is churned, will throw up many riches which can be divided amongst the two groups. Only the amrit you must keep to yourself. It should not fall into the wrong hands. If the daityas get the amrit, they would become immeasurably powerful and this would wreak havoc with the universal order.'

'Indra, you must make peace with Bali. He is a benevolent leader and an intelligent and pious person. He will help you. He has the vision of his grandfather, the touch of the divine. He will understand. It is his destiny to get this done,' Brahma explained

Indra hesitated, assailed by a nagging doubt.

'Taat,' he said. 'If we approach the daityas for help and they agree, but then we do not share the amrit with them, would this not be unfair? I will forever be called a cheat for not sharing with them what is fairly the fruit of their labour too.'

'This is true, Indra. You will forever have to bear this

ignominy; it is your burden to carry. But this is necessary and it must be done. To pull your devas out of this decadence that they have sunk into, you must churn the ocean and let them sip the nectar. But the amrit cannot be shared with the daityas, O Devaraj, however unfair it may sound. You see, the daityas are not asuras[168] because they are born in a different family. They are asuras because they choose to be. They can choose to be suras or devas, but they choose violence and lawlessness since the darkness runs within them, deep and uncontrollable. The power of the nectar combined with their inherently dark nature will lead to great chaos. Hence, they cannot be relied upon to taste the amrit. Don't worry, when you send your messengers, Bali will understand,' Brahma assured the devas.

The devas came back to their capital Amravati and started their preparations. They knew churning the ocean would need a long churning rod with a rope that the two groups could pull. But the proportions of the rope and the rod had to be huge to churn the infinite ocean. Where would they get something like this from? After many deliberations it was decided to use a mountain, the divine Mandara, as the churning rod and one of the serpent kings, Vasuki, as the rope.[169]

---

[168]Asuras, as a generic term, is an opposite of suras, was used to denote anyone with demonic tendencies, in the later Vedic literature. Daitya, on the other hand, is more of a family name than a marker of the characteristics of a people.

[169]Vasuki is the serpent that lies coiled around the neck of Shiva. He is also the sibling of Shesha or Adi Shesha, the serpent on whom Vishnu lies.

Messengers were sent to Mount Kailash, abode of Shiva, to ask for his assent and his blessings for the venture. He would also have to let Vasuki, who adorned his neck, be used as a rope for the Manthan. The Aadi Yogi sat on the mountain among the snow-clad peaks and listened to the petition of the devas who crouched near his feet; but they needn't have come for he already knew. He knew because he saw far beyond what the devas had planned, foreseen or even imagined. He knew what was going to happen and what he would have to do for the devas to be able to enjoy the fruits of the Saagara Manthan. He consented and asked his serpent companion, Vasuki, to act as the rope to help the devas and the daityas in their venture.

Indra and the devas also had to secure the blessings of Narayana, the Padmanabha. When they reached Vaikuntha[170] he blessed them and assured them that he would help if and when they needed it. He told Indra to go and talk to Bali in person. Bali was a great devotee of Vishnu and the dark-skinned god wanted to make sure he knew directly from Indra what the proposition was; he should not be kept in the dark. Their individual duties, responsibilities and limitations should be clear to both the leaders. It was only when their interests crossed that there was a skirmish or a war. And that was to no one's benefit. Bali was Vishnu's greatest devotee and his interests would have to be guarded but Indra and the devas were charged with the custody of the heavens and other celestial duties. It was in the interest of the whole world that the devas be allowed to discharge their

[170]Vishnu's abode

duties unhindered. Whenever there was a war, there was a hindrance in the usual order of things; there was chaos and the whole creation suffered. The delicate balance had to be maintained.

As Indra left the daitya capital with his entourage after talking to Bali behind closed doors, the daitya king turned and walked towards the assembly hall where he had summoned all the major groups of daityas to discuss the devas' proposal. The fragile peace he had achieved after the Tarakamaya war had to be maintained at all costs. However, this was getting more difficult every day. He could see that the daityas were getting increasingly belligerent and restive. They were not inherently a peaceful lot. The root of the problem was in the genesis of the daitya people.

His great-grandfathers Hiranyakashyap and Hiranyaksha had started with a band of mercenaries and had promised their followers a life full of conquests, loot, pillage and wanton violence. Maybe the violence was needed to achieve what they had achieved in their lifetimes. But then the violent aspects of their nature had become central to daitya culture. There was no ridding the daityas of their darkness. So the daityas and the danavas had been labelled as asuras and had been cast away from civilized company, unwelcome in deva homes. The devas, due to their adherence to civilizational rules and chivalrous conduct, had become the 'aryas', or the cultured people. Ordinary people worshipped them and offered oblations in the fire in their names. The devas had been entrusted with important tasks since the gods knew they could be relied upon. Bali yearned to earn that status for his own people but he knew this might not be possible in his lifetime. Even in his own family, out of his hundred sons, only Bana showed any traces of the virtuous character that ran in the family from Prahlad downwards.

Bana was a great devotee of Shiva and had carved out a name for himself as a valiant, pious and generous leader of the daitya people. Bana had, after taking his father's consent, established his own state in the eastern hills[171] and his kingdom had prospered under his able guidance. Bali had later divided the land of Jambudwipa amongst his other sons and had asked them to move out from the daitya capital to make a name for themselves and start their own empires. The daitya family was now spread all over the world and along with the danavas formed a formidable force to reckon with. Besides the danavas, the daityas had close alliances with other 'people' like the nagas.

Despite Bali's best efforts and sincere wishes to the contrary, an unholy alliance between the daityas, danavas and nagas had formed based only on their avarice and predilection for useless violence. The gods, Bali knew, were troubled with this alliance of evil states and favoured devas unduly to protect them from this 'alliance of evil'. Bali had tried several times to correct the priorities of this triumvirate of evil. He had tried to guide them, argue with them and even threaten them, but to no avail. In the end he had given up and simply bided his time. He knew a solution would come at some point, if not by his hands then by those more capable than his.

---

[171]Legends point to present day Assam in the northeast of India as having been Banasur's kingdom

As Bali walked towards the assembly hall that afternoon, he resolved to make one more attempt to make the daityas see the light. He knew the Manthan would go on with or without daitya help. But it would be good for the daityas to be a part of the venture and do it in an atmosphere of friendly cooperation. For once, he wanted them to rise above their base instincts, performing a single act without prejudice, greed and avarice. He knew he would not succeed, but still, he had to try.

As he entered the daitya hall in the gathering dusk, the chatter slowly died. Everybody turned to look at him, some stood up out of respect and some, especially the younger daityas, did not. His *kankanam*, the gold and sapphire bracelets he wore, jingled softly as he strode inside the hall, his leather shoes creaking and his yellow silk robe swishing softly in the evening. Bali looked around. All the daityas had assembled, curious, impatient, chattering. Young, old, tall, short, fair, dark, those with shaved heads and those with flowing locks. They carried an assortment of weapons on their person —the straight sword, the double-edged sword, the mace, the mallet, the short spear, the fearful curved dagger, the machete and the bludgeon, all of which made their enemies tremble in the battlefield.

At the end of the apsidal hall was the semicircular enclosure where the majestic golden throne stood— it was the same throne used by Hiranyaksha, Hiranyakashyap and Prahlad when they were kings. On one side of the hall, to the right of the throne was a new stone pillar embellished with gold, a sculpture of Narasingha carved into it; a solemn reminder of the events that had transpired in the hall. Circling the throne sat the elders, senior daityas, counsellors, advisors and *mantris*.[172] Between them, the advisors and counsellors represented the collective wisdom of the daitya people accumulated over generations.

Bali ascended the throne amidst cries of '*Jayam, jayam* (Victory, victory)!' He sat down on the solid gold throne, shaped like the head of a buffalo, and raised his hand to silence the belligerent daitya crowd. On his right-hand side, stood his advisor Sumantram, wisened with age, who bowed low to his king and waited for the sign. Bali nodded and the aged minister began.

'The devas have approached us through their leader Devaraj himself. They want our help in churning the great ocean. It is a massive venture which they think they will not be able to do themselves. They want to churn the ocean to extract the riches buried in its bosom. They are ready to discuss our demands and they offer peace and their hand of friendship in return.'

Sumantram stopped, out of breath with the effort and looked at Bali, who nodded. A murmur went up in the house as several groups started to discuss the implications amongst themselves.

Bali cast a look at the crowd packing the cavernous hall to its capacity and spilling outside through its massive gates, like a hive buzzing with bees. He waited for the murmuring to increase to a crescendo and then die down spontaneously. When the hall was silent again, Bali rose and started to address the gathering.

'My fellow daityas,' he began. 'Devaraj and I have had

---

[172]Minister or advisor

a long talk on this matter of the Samudra Manthan.[173] The devas have been our arch enemies for a very long time and I will not dwell here on who drew the first blood or who is right and who is wrong. The fact remains that we have been at war for as long as the daitya people's collective memory remembers. But,' and Bali paused for effect, 'even before we were enemies, we were brothers.'

'The devas, daityas and danavas are all the sons of the same father from different mothers. How did we end up like this? Some part of what is happening, or has happened and will happen, can be ascribed to daiva,[174] but not all of it. It is our will that drives our destinies, charts our course and carves our futures. So far, we have willed it that we will fight and win over the devas, and they have willed it the other way round. But that has not worked for either of us. I believe it is now time to change track and try something different. How about we stop fighting each other and get something done together?' Bali stated.

The crowd murmured its approval.

'I propose that we help the devas in their venture but do it without any personal interest or demands from them. This will be seen as a gesture which will absolve us of all our demerits, sins and misconduct till date. This will go down in eternity as a magnanimous gesture that the daitya people did for the benefit of everyone, for the benefit of the cosmic balance, for peace and prosperity all around,' Bali continued.

'How can we let them get away with all the riches

---

[173]Samudra is another name for saagara. Samudra Manthan thus also means Saagara Manthan.

[174]Divine intervention, roughly translated as 'destiny'

that they extract from the ocean? After all we will also work for it?' This was Ugra, a young daitya, tall, fair, well-built. He was one of the young guns wanting to make a mark for himself.

'Ugra is right. We need to share their riches equally or we will not work at all,' Ugra's contemporary, Durmukha spoke.

'I disagree,' boomed a loud commanding voice that resonated across the hall.

Heads turned to look at the owner of the voice—it was Bana, Bali's son and ruler of the kingdom of Sonitpura, the land of mountains, snow and water.[175] Bali was happy that his valiant son agreed with him. He expected Bana to take up the mantle of the mighty daitya dynasty after him.

'I think *Pitri* is right.[176] I support his idea that this is the time we can show our character and bury the hatchet forever. This could be a turning point in our combined histories. Think carefully, this could be our chance to make history!' Bana said before falling silent, expecting the daityas to listen to him. He was one of them, he understood their priorities, their exigencies, their impulses, their needs and desires. The daityas should believe he would give them the best advice! Bana realized he was being too optimistic for hardly had he finished that another voice, clear, high-pitched and authoritative, rang out in the hall.

---

[175]Probably present-day Tezpur town, in the district of Sonitpur, in the modern Indian state of Assam.

[176]The Sanskrit root *pitri* is the source of many words in the Indo-European family of languages, which mean 'father'. Its analogue word relating to 'mother' is *matri*.

'You are all being fooled,' this was Svarabhanu, Bali's uncle, and Bana's granduncle. Svarabhanu was the son of Prahlad's sister, Simhika, and the danava, Viprachitti, paternal uncle to Shachi, Indra's wife. Being related to all three families, the adityas, daityas and danavas, Svarabhanu had friends and informers on all sides and thus his information was considered the most authentic.

'The devas are not doing the Saagara Manthan for just any usual treasure. They want the amrit, the nectar of immortality. They want the twelve adityas to become immortal.[177] The rest of the "treasure" is just by-products. We must demand a share in the amrit too!'

The hall suddenly broke into pandemonium. People shouted, gesticulated and created all kinds of ruckus. Bali and Bana eyed the asuras with sadness. Bana looked across the hall towards the throne where his father stood, his eyes downcast and his shoulders slouched. The asuras had let him down again. He could almost read his father's mind. As Bali raised his head to look across the hall, his eyes met Bana's briefly and he saw understanding and sadness.

Bali raised his hands, 'O my mighty daityas. Please listen to me.'

The sound died down just a little. Bali had to shout to make himself heard.

'The devas indeed need the amrit but it is not for everyone. Even all the devas cannot have it. It is strictly decreed that only the twelve gods, the adityas, can partake of the divine drink. The swayambhos have

[177]There are thirty three Vedic gods—twelve adityas, eleven rudras, eight vasus, and two ashvins

willed it thus. It is for everyone's good. Let us not fight over this. Please agree to do this right one time.'

But no one was listening. The word amrit had driven everyone crazy. Looking at the chaotic mass of daityas in the hall below his throne, Bali realized why they were called asuras. There could be no redemption till they mended their ways.

The crowd had broken up in small groups discussing the issue amongst each other, talking to different leaders and trying to come to a consensus. Soon enough, Svarabhanu, Ugra and Durmukha approached the throne. Bowing low, they addressed Bali gently but firmly and confidently, for that was the daitya way.

'The assembly has decided, O King! We will support the devas' efforts. We will also not ask for any treasure voluntarily but we will ask for a share in the amrit. The nectar must be shared amongst all, whatever little quantities we get.'

Bali's hope died. He nodded and said, 'I defer to the will of the general assembly but I do not share this view and neither, I think, does Bana. Thus, while I will permit you all to go and join their efforts, Bana and I will abstain from this. I hope the assembly will not mind and will forgive their king.'

'There is nothing to forgive, O Great King. The daityas and the danavas are yours to command, always,' Svarabhanu said, bowing low.

Bali nodded and the assembly was dismissed. Bana walked over to the throne and stood near his father.

'Go back to your kingdom, Bana. There will be a lot of bad blood now. I want you to stay away from this and work on your empire. I will bide my time; I still have a few things to do before I abdicate the throne and leave for *sanyaas* (renunciation). The daitya family is too big now for me to control it single-handedly; too big for anyone, I think. We have started on our way down!'

Bana nodded and left the assembly hall with a heavy heart after he knelt before his father and put his forehead on Bali's feet. Bali motioned to Sumantram to follow him—he needed to send a message to Devaraj.

4

The ocean roared and strong winds kicked up huge waves as if protesting what was about to happen. The deep mystical ocean, the unexplored storehouse of all jewels and mythical animals, was about to be churned by the devas and the asuras to extract its riches for the benefit of the gods. A posse of deva and asura soldiers laboured along the beach as they dragged the huge Mandar Mountain on a construct of wooden planks, metal rods, logs of woods, gigantic wheels and an intricate system of levers and pulleys that worked with ropes as thick as tree trunks. It looked like an impossible job, dragging a whole mountain out to the sea, erecting it inside the waters and using it as a churning rod, but the twin armies of the devas and the asuras were determined to see it through. Several huge animals, war elephants, horses and even hordes of men were employed to pull the contraption which helped them drag the mountain out to the sea. Miles and miles of ropes had been made, looking like an endless sea of serpents themselves, to pull the machine carrying the mountain.

Once they got near the ocean, the sand on the beach started to slow them down but they still kept going, replacing the tired animals with fresh ones, repairing cracked planks and changing wheels and pulleys. On and on the mammoth machine moved, hauling the gigantic mountain with it. On the beach, riding the waves, waited another giant construction made entirely of tree trunks tied to each other like a raft. The mountain, once it was dragged out to the edge of the water, would have to be loaded on to this, carried out to the sea and then erected or plunged into the water vertically.

On one side of the beach, the nagas waited and bided their time. Their king, Vasuki, the magical serpent, the first of their kind, the one who adorns the neck of Shiva, would serve as the living rope that would churn this ocean. On another side of the beach, the Garuda, the gigantic eagle which serves as the mount of Vishnu, waited. His help might be needed in hoisting the mountain.

Heave and push, heave and push, went the devas and the asuras, toiling to push the mountain. The huge wheels of the machine which had been constructed by maya, the danava known for his construction skills, inexorably creaked and turned like the wheels of time. The devas and the asuras shouted to encourage each other and to warn people to get out of the way of the mammoth construct labouring its way to the sea.

Slowly and painfully, the mountain was brought out to the edge of the water and transferred on to the gigantic rafts which floated on the waters. An army of devas and asuras pushed the mountain from one end while another group held the rafts together and pulled them in the opposite direction so that the mountain could slide on to the rafts. Push, push, push. With loud noises which seemed to herald the end of the world, the mountain was pushed, dragged and pulled on to the rafts. It snapped the ropes, broke the tree trunks with its weight and sent sparks flying wherever its stones brushed against stone or metal.

Once the Mandar Mountain had been slid on to the rafts, the machine which brought it to the edge of the waves was pushed back. The raft creaked, snapped, and laboured under the massive weight but held fast. The naga people were employed to hold the raft while the devas and the asuras pushed the mountain again to the edge of the floating contraption, towards the water. It would have to be dropped vertically in the water and Vasuki would have to coil himself around it to hold it fast. Once it was at the deep edge of the raft, the devas waited for Vasuki to come and take over. But where was Vasuki?

Garuda, the gigantic eagle, cawed suddenly, its shrill sound deafening, and flapped its wings, sending the devas and the asuras flying like dead leaves scatter in a dust storm. The bird was unhappy. It looked angry and ready to pounce. It shifted from one foot to another, ruffled its feathers, opened its gigantic beak wide revealing its huge mouth and dug the earth with its talons the size of ten elephants. Something had disturbed it and made it very, very angry!

The devas looked here and there and found the source of the bird's displeasure. Vasuki, the serpent king, was making his way to the shore. The huge snake looked like a beast out of their collective nightmares. The devas and the asuras were suddenly afraid of the huge snake that slid out of the forests on to the beach and then slithered close to them, hissing. Its huge fangs were longer than several tall trees put together, its forked tongue which flashed from its cavernous mouth looked miles long. Its yellow-black eyes, slit-like and menacing, made the asuras tremble. Its shiny black skin shone in the sunlight, giving the impression of a star-studded sky and flames issued out of its nostrils when it breathed. The gigantic snake, which could have swallowed whole legions of devas and asuras, slithered on to the beach, eyeing the bird cawing its displeasure at the other end.

The serpents, the *sarpas* and the nagas, sons and daughters of Kadru, were sworn enemies of the legendary birds Garuda and Arun, sons of Vinata. They had come together peacefully only because their respective masters had commanded them to work together for this mammoth task. Thus while Vasuki and Garuda eyed each other, sending shivers down the collective spines of the devas and the asuras, they did not do anything which might offend the other.

Vasuki made his way between the deva and asura armies which ran hither and tither in fear, making way for him. He slid on to the raft and then coiled himself around the huge mountain like a rope. Round and round the mountain he went. The two ends of his body, the head and the tail, were still on the beach while the body was coiled around the mountain being held afloat by the magical raft of Maya danava. Once he had coiled himself around the mountain sufficiently tightly, Vasuki gave the sign to the naga people.

'You can now hold his ends. He will push the mountain in the water and you can churn,' the naga people told the mighty devas and asuras, translating for Vasuki. Trembling, the devas held Vasuki's tail, while the asuras held his head. Vasuki stiffened as his two ends were grasped. He gripped the mountain tightly and slowly started to slide it down from the raft into the water.

While the devas and asuras held on, Vasuki pushed the mountain and the nagas and sarpas[178] pulled the raft out of the water. With the raft out of the water, the mountain suddenly plonked into the sea like a ripe apple, making a huge noise and giving rise to huge waves. Presently the mountain could be seen held vertically in the sea by Vasuki, his two ends gripped by hundreds and thousands of devas and asuras. It was a wonderous sight to behold, one that had never been seen, and the celestial beings crowded the heavens to have a glimpse of it.

'Pull,' said the Devaraj. He had stood to one side, watching, directing, instructing, commanding. He knew that Bali, the daitya king, had not come and hence he himself had to coordinate the task of the asuras too; but maybe it was better this way.

'Pull,' he repeated, and the devas pulled.

'Time it,' he shouted again, and the devas shouted, 'Heave.'

Then they let go and the asuras shouted, 'Pull.' Together both the groups pulled, turn by turn. First the devas, then the asuras. Vasuki held the mountain fast and let the twin armies pull him from both ends one by one.

Suddenly the mountain started to slip from Vasuki's

---

[178]Nagas and sarpas are different. While a sarpa can be translated to a snake, a naga or pannaga can refer to mythical, semi-divine, snake people who can change form and have mystical properties.

grip and slide into the water due to its sheer weight. The serpent hissed loudly, baring his fangs and trying hard to grip the mountain, its breath carrying the vapours of a venom so poisonous that the asuras standing near the head were scorched and the others standing father apart started coughing, sputtering and belching. They lost their grip on the serpent's body and the mountain started to slip even faster. The asuras ran to save themselves from being burnt, and suffocated by the fire, the serpent was breathing out due to the pressure on its belly. The harder the serpent tried to hold the mountain, the more venom it spewed and the more devas and asuras fled. Thus the mountain kept slipping in a vicious cycle.

Suddenly, there was a surge in the waters of the ocean as if a tidal wave had hit the mountain. Water splashed all around, soaking the mountain and the snake, cooling it down and extinguishing its fiery venom, washing it away. The serpent looked visibly relaxed; it hissed no more and no fire or sparks exited its cavernous mouth. The devas and the asuras were surprised at what was happening.

The mountain's perilous slide also slowed and then stopped altogether. The Mandar had almost slipped below the surface of the water and only its peak was visible. Now it rose slowly, majestically, arising from the water and into the sky, like the mountains of yore which used to fly around the skies. The Mandar stabilized and maintained its position; it would not sink anymore. The devas and the asuras were surprised. They looked around and then they peered inside the waters of the ocean to see what had happened. What was supporting the heavy mountain and lifting it out of the water like a child's toy?

Inside the pristine blue waters of the ocean just beneath its sparkling surface, supporting the whole Mandar on its back was a huge turtle, bigger than the mountain, bigger than anything the devas and the asuras had seen so far. It spanned the ocean and the mountain sat atop its back like a toy. The magical turtle's shell shimmered with a radiance that seemed to light up the whole ocean from inside and its forehead was marked with a tilaka, which also glowed. The huge paws of this divine beast were treading the waters of the ocean gently, supporting its own weight and that of the mountain. Its gigantic eyes shone like emerald hills. Its cavernous mouth was open and from it came the timeless sound of the *pranav*, the aum! It was his sight, his touch, his presence which had supported the Mandar and had also calmed the divine serpent down. The devas recognized him as the one who sleeps on another serpent, in another ocean, the dark-skinned god of all creation, the one who holds the *shankha*, chakra, *gada* and padma in his four hands.[179] He was Vishnu himself who had come to help the devas in the shape of the *kurma*.[180]

Once more the devasur army picked up the ends of the serpent and started the churning.

'Pull…' the devas shouted. 'Pull…' the asuras repeated. And the serpent went to and fro. The rod twisted and turned, churning the ocean which is the lord of all the rivers, the repository of all the jewels, the home to all aquatic animals. Faster and faster the devas pulled, faster and faster the asuras pulled, till

[179]*Shankha*: conch shell; chakra: discus; *gada*: club/mace; padma: lotus
[180]*Kurma*: turtle; the *kurma* is one of the avatars of Vishnu

the waves started to froth. The water around the rod bubbled, then turned to thick black sludge seething with fiery waste, the toxins and venom of thousands of eons. The sludge condensed around the rotating shaft, churning, bubbling, giving off steam and then sparks, heated by the friction with the stones of the Mandar Mountain. The steam that issued from the Halahal[181] seared everyone's eyes, noses and throats, and scorched their skin, turning it livid, then black, then blistering it. The devas cried, the asuras cried.

'Help, help. *Trahimam, trahimam*!'[182] they said loudly.

The lone ascetic with matted locks, the one who wears the moon as an ornament, heard them. He opened his eyes, for he was deep in meditation and resolved to help them for he was the Aadi Yogi, the turiya, the Mahadev. He knew that only he could help them. Thus, he strode the skies, his form enlarged, and planted his foot in the sea. His universal form, composed of the skies, stars, suns, moons and constellations, stood tall in front of the devas and the asuras. His matted locks were the dark spaces between the galaxies, his fair skin was the Milky Way, his forehead shone red like the fire of the universe and hence he was called the *lohita*. He strode the skies and the oceans in his cosmic form and the stars came out in attendance to pay their respects to him. The earth, skies and oceans seemed small in comparison to his form. He seemed to swallow the skies when he opened his mouth. His eyes shone with the fire

---

[181]Halahal is the primordial venom that issued forth from the churning of the ocean.

[182]*Trahimam* means 'save me'

of creation, the light of the Hiranyagarbh, the primordial cosmic womb, the ball of fire which was at the beginning. He stepped out from the skies and into the ocean to help the devas and asuras and they worshipped him. With their eyes closed and their bodies prostrated before him, they chanted his names. The kurma worshipped him, for the Adi Yogi had come to deliver everyone from the Halahal. Only the yogi who was there before anyone else, before creation began, before the gods were born, would know what to do with the concentrated poison from all the oceans of the world.

The yogi laughed, his voice echoing from the stars and coming back to shake the earth. He bent down, his hands cupped, and scooped up the boiling, writhing, steaming, exploding mass of black curdled Halahal. He picked it all up as if it was the amrit for which the devas had started this Manthan. He scooped it up in his hands and bringing his cupped hands to his lips, swallowed it all up.

'Har, Har,' the devas intoned. 'Har, Har,' the asuras shouted, ecstatic at what they had just witnessed.

The Mahadev swallowed the boiling, burning mass of dark Halahal and with his yogic energy, held it in his throat, not swallowing it nor spitting it out. The Halahal curdled, boiled, raged, fumed and burst into flames. The yogi held it in his throat and the Halahal scorched it, turning it blue. Thus he became the Neelakanth, the one with the blue throat.

'Har Har Mahadev,' the devas and the asuras intoned. They had been saved!

His work done, the kapalika, the ascetic who wears a garland of skulls, disappeared. He went back to his mountain abode and immersed himself in his dhyanam, his meditation.

The churning resumed with a new vigour. To and fro the shaft went, to and fro the mountain followed. Vasuki helped in whatever way he could and the Kurma kept supporting the Mandar. All things being in their favour, the ocean started to churn out its riches. Out they came, the gems, and the jewels and other riches which had lain in the bosom of the ocean since millennia. It belched them out and they were appropriated by either the devas, the asuras or the gandharvas. Sometimes the *ratnams*[183] chose their masters, sometimes the masters chose the ratnams that they wanted. Thus the Airaavata, the milk-white elephant with five heads and ten tusks, was taken by Devaraj as his mount. The Ucchaishrava, the white steed, fast as the wind with flowing manes and celestial wings, was set aside as a gift for the asura king Bali. The Kaustubh, the divine jewel, the devas gifted to Vishnu along with the Saaranga bow. The wish-fulfilling cow, Kamadhenu, was given away to the sages so that they may have an uninterrupted supply of milk, curd and ghee for their sustenance and rituals. Sri[184] emerged from the ocean and she chose Vishnu as her consort. Vaaruni, the goddess of wine and other intoxicating drinks, emerged from the ocean and was taken by the asuras. The divine tree Paarijat was planted in Indra's garden in Amravati. The divine nymphs that emerged from the ocean chose the gandharvas as their consorts. At long last, Dhanvantari, the divine sage, the source of

[183]Jewels or precious objects
[184]Sri or Lakshmi is the goddess of wealth, prosperity and well-being.

Ayurveda or the science of health,[185] emerged with the Amrit Kalash, the pot of nectar, in his hands.

Chaos broke out amongst the devas and the asuras. They left their respective jobs and posts, dropping whatever they were doing and heading towards the pot of nectar. The devas got the better of the asuras, snatched the pot from the hands of the bewildered Dhanvantari and ran for their lives, the asuras following close behind. Hither and tither they ran, up and down, inside the water and out. Over the mountains and behind the clouds the devas ran with the asuras pursuing them. In this pell-mell, the cover of the pot slid open and a few drops of the amrit fell from the pot and landed on the earth where the manavas lived.[186]

There was a lot of fighting, pulling, pushing, cursing, hitting and fisticuffs. Finally, when the devas and the asuras drew their weapons, Indra intervened.

'Stop,' he said. 'Everyone stop. Let us decide this matter peacefully.'

The devas stopped and stood guarding the pot of nectar. The asuras stopped too and formed a circle around the group of devas, ready to pounce on them at any opportunity.

'Let us distribute it amongst ourselves equally,' Devaraj said.

'Who will distribute it?' asked Ugra, nostrils flaring

---

[185]Ayurveda is the traditional Indian system of medicine and healing. Literally translated it means—the knowledge of health.

[186]The four places where the drops of amrit fell are Haridwar, Prayagraj, Nashik and Ujjaini. All these four places are ancient pilgrimages of Hindus, and every twelve years a kumbha mela, a ritual dip or bath, is organized in these places.

and eyes staring due to the exertion of the running and fighting.

'We do not trust you,' asserted Durmukha.

'I will distribute it,' came a voice, sweet like honey, refreshing as the spring breeze, musical in its tone like the chime of little bells on the feet of a dancer.

The devas and the asuras turned to look at the owner of the voice and froze.

A beautiful maiden stood a little away from the horde of panting, sweating, fighting men, and smiled. She was a living embodiment of beauty and sensuality oozed from her very pores. She wore an *antariya*[187] wrapped tightly around her waist and hips that ended just above her knees hugging her ample figure and showing every curve and niche of her body. The antariya was made of fine, yellow silk, the pitambar, and looked like liquid gold when she walked. The upper part of her body was covered with an *uttariya,* which was wrapped tightly across her breasts, accentuating their features even more without restraining their fullness or their freedom of movement. Her midriff was exposed and she wore a jewel in her belly button. Her anklets were made of tiny bells of gold which chimed titillatingly when she walked. Her hair was strung with wildflowers. Her limbs, supple and beautifully formed, were tattooed with henna and her eyes were lined with kohl. Her perfume carried over the wind for a yojana, driving men and gods crazy with lust. When she spoke her ruby lips moved sensuously and trembled suggestively

---

[187]*Antariya* is a piece of cloth wrapped over the lower part of the body and held in place by a *kabandh,* distorted in later usage as a cummerbund. The *antariya* is the predecessor of the modern-day dhoti which many Indian men, and women, still wear.

with emotions which she half hid and half showed, driving the asuras insane with desire. When she talked to them, she batted her long eyelashes, now showing, now hiding her sea-green eyes which already had the asuras drowning in them. Her gentle laughter sent the hormones raging in the men who stood and gazed at her as if the world had nothing else in it but this divine beauty.

Some stood with their mouths open, some stood with their arms raised. Some had frozen mid-stride, some had their clothes in disarray. Their hearts loudly beat as one as the enchantress walked slowly, her hips swaying from side to side captivating them. She walked over and stood close to them, close enough for her perfume to become so overpowering as to preclude any logic or reasoning.

'My name is Mohini,' she said, her lips trembling as she articulated the words, her chest rising and falling with each breath she took.

'Let me distribute the amrit.'

Wordlessly she waded amidst the steaming mass of men, cleaving through the group like a hot knife through butter. Effortlessly she took the pot from the deva who held it, turned and started to walk, her hips swaying to the timing of a tune which she whistled. The groups of devas and asuras followed, totally under her spell.

'Sit here in two lines, devas on one side, asuras on the other. I shall distribute the amrit to everyone one by one,' she said, pointing to an open area.

Wordlessly, they fell in line as requested, sitting down on the ground under her spell, bowls in hand waiting for her to distribute the amrit.

She started from the devas' side. As she went from one deva to another distributing the amrit, she eyed the asuras, playing coquettish games with them; her eyes talking, moving, suggesting. The asuras were in raptures. Promised good times by her eyes, they lost all sense of time and place. They whispered amongst themselves, sniggered, joked and laughed.

Mohini had reached the end of the line of the devas and was pouring the amrit for the last deva when suddenly, Surya, the sun god, and Chandra, the moon god, shouted.

'He is not a deva. He is an asura in disguise.'

They pointed to the last deva sitting in the line. Indeed, he was not a deva but an asura. He was Svarabhanu, son of Viprachitti, the danava.

Before anyone could react, Mohini had disappeared and in her stead stood the four-limbed, dark-skinned form of Mahavishnu, carrying the shankh a (conch), Sudarshan Chakra, Kaumodaki Gada and a lotus. On his chest lay the Kaustubh *mani* (jewel) and the Srivatsa sign. He wore the pitambar and rode Garuda, the mighty eagle. He flung down his chakra and severed the neck of the asura, Svarabhanu, even as the asura gulped the amrit that Mohini had served him.

Their spell broken, the asuras realized they had been taken for a ride and Mohini, the enchantress, had served all the amrit to the devas leaving none for them. The Amrit Kalash, the pot of nectar, lay empty on the ground!

The asuras fought a losing battle for the honour they had already lost. They were disorganized, disoriented, leaderless and dispirited at having been made a fool of. In the skirmish that followed the distribution of the amrit, the asura forces were routed quickly and sent back to where they had come from. They took the Ucchaishrava horse with them, a gift for Bali from Indra.

Indra and the devas went back to Amravati, triumphant at having tasted the nectar.

Back in the daitya capital, Bali heard the whole story with sadness and remorse; the divine horse in his stable a mute testimony to the things that had transpired in his absence. He was unhappy on several counts. He was unhappy that the daityas had not listened to him, that they had behaved in a most reprehensible manner, that they had been led astray only due to their base emotions ruling over their better judgement. He was sad that the daityas would still not learn anything from this episode, they would only nurse grudges and not be able to rise above this, nor make themselves better than the devas, since their actions were merely reactions to what the devas did. Till the daityas thought and acted of their own volition they would merely be underlings and would always be called the asuras!

He could not change their destiny, Bali thought, but he would change his.

To become like Prahlad, he needed the touch of his master, his lord, the god of all creation, one who sleeps in yoga-nidra on the infinite ocean of the cosmos, Hari.

Author's Note

The term asura has been used here in the negative sense, in which it has been used in all the classical literature of India. In Vedic literature, however, and especially the earlier layers of the Vedic texts, the term asura meant demigods or lesser gods. In time, however, asura came to signify 'bad', and deva came to signify 'good'. It is interesting to note that in the old Avestan literature, which is etymologically and linguistically close to the early Vedic literature, asura, or ahura as it is called in the old Avestan language, the Vedic 's' being replaced by the Avestan 'h', means good, and *daeva*, or deva of Sanskrit, means bad. A case in point is the Zoroastrian god of all creation, Ahura Mazda, the god of wisdom. It is also interesting to note that *mazda*, which means wisdom or wellness here, is a cognate word for the Sanskrit term *medha*, which also means wisdom, or knowledge. The linguistic closeness, of course, is due to the Avestan and old Sanskrit's kinship with the Proto-Indo-European ancestor language. The cultural difference, however, can be traced to the possible splitting away of the Arya family during the time of Rig Veda. The 'Battle of Ten Kings' alluded to in the Rig Veda, tells the tale of how Sudas a king of the Bharata family, defeated a confederation of ten kings led by a Puru king. A similar story is found in later Indian texts, referring to the falling out between the sons of King Yayati. One of the sons of King Yayati, Puru, was nominated the successor by King Yayati, and the others were driven out from the kingdom. One of the lines of the Bharata family, descended from Puru's sibling, Druhyu, went west, and are supposedly the carriers of the Vedic culture and language, to Iran. It is also interesting to note that the word Iran itself is supposedly derived from the word arya which, despite its being misinterpreted as denoting a 'race' of people, simply means 'civilized' people or ones who defend the cosmic order, also known as *ritam.*

Disclaimer: This nugget of information is meant to arouse the interest of the reader in exploring more about this topic and is not meant to be an authentic source of data in the field of history, archaeology or linguistics.

Vamana: The Midget

1

Bali roamed the corridors of his huge palace, thinking about the events that had happened recently and wondering if his presence could have helped the daityas. He wondered what Bana was doing and about his opinion regarding this matter? Bana was a valiant and dutiful son and an able leader. The daityas saw their future king in him. Bali would be happy leaving the kingdom in his capable hands. He wished Bana was with him so that he could get some feedback about what was brewing among the daityas. Bana had swiftly risen in popularity among the daitya warlords and had his ear to the ground. Nothing escaped his notice. He was a leader in the making and the daityas knew this, always turning to him for guidance, direction and leadership when they could not approach Bali. On especially ticklish matters, Bana had often displayed great discretion and had facilitated decisions for the daityas, counselling his father regarding their issues and coordinating Bali's directions and decisions with the daitya generals. These were the signs of a leader who had risen from the ranks and had made a place for himself through the confidence and the admiration of his men.

The huge, pillared corridor in front of the main

entrance to Bali's palace ran the whole breadth of the palace and had long windows on both its sides which let in the light from the setting sun as he paced. The entrance to the corridor, positioned exactly opposite the entrance to the main palace, was through an ornate archway which led to a huge, heavy door made of wood from devdaru trees and strengthened by a new, secret metal. The secret of the extraction of this metal from its ore as well as its usage had been kept secret by the devas for millennia and used by them for their weapons till Bana learnt of it from his deity, the Mahadev.

Bana had told Bali that this immortal ascetic, Shiva, and his lore were as old as time itself and his followers called themselves Shaiva. Shiva did not differentiate between the gods, the devas, the daityas, the danavas, yakshas, kinnars, gandharvas, raakshasas, bhutas, pretas… They were all the same to him. He never took sides and was easy to please. Once pleased, there was nothing he would not bestow on his devotees. Bana himself had acquired mighty weapons and secret technologies in metallurgy, medicine and tantra from Shiva, including the secret of this 'new metal'. It was magic, its strength was phenomenal and its knowledge had to be kept safe. It had made their new weapons stronger and deadlier than before. Bali had made Bana in charge of all matters related to this metal and Bana had discharged his duties perfectly. The daitya armoury had been refurbished with new weapons and armours.

Thus thinking about Bana and daitya glory, Mahabali paced the long hall in the gathering dusk when suddenly he spied an usher standing near the main entrance, hands folded, head bowed, waiting for a chance to speak.

'What is it?' Bali asked.

'O Great Daitya King! King Bana is on his way to meet you and has sent an advance party to inform us,' the usher said and stood quietly waiting for instructions.

'He Narayana!' Bali exclaimed. The gods had been kind. This was just what he wanted at this time.

'See to it that Bana is greeted properly and when he has rested show him to the dining area. We shall meet over food,' Bali said as he turned and entered the main palace to get ready for dinner.

The dining area was a huge quadrangular enclosure, open to the sky and paved on its sides where people could sit down on the ground and eat. In the middle, there was a paved path for the cooks to walk around while they served food. The daitya king always sat down on the ground to have his food, usually along with his family, friends, generals and soldiers. In fact, anyone who was free could walk in, sit down and eat with the king. Everyone was exempt from rank-based protocols while eating. Even a lowly soldier could sit adjacent to the emperor and break bread with him. This was a habit which Bali had inculcated early in his life and had religiously adhered to. This fostered a great bond between people.

'People who eat together, stay together,' Bali told everyone.

And it was true. All the daityas respected their king's gesture and were honoured to sit by his side. During dinnertime Bali would also ask them about their families and personal lives, thus giving his relationship with his soldiers a personal touch. All the generals, courtiers and other nobility had learnt this from Bali and had fostered the same practice in their respective spheres. Thus the bond of brotherhood between the daityas had stayed strong even with time.

As Bali entered the dining area, he was greeted by his staff. Bali returned their greeting by raising his hand and proceeded to sit at the appointed place. Bana and a couple of other daityas were already there waiting for him. Bana walked up to his father smiling and Bali opened his arms wide and embraced his son. He then looked closely at him.

'Your hair is greying early, Bana,' Bali said with fatherly affection, holding his son by the shoulders. 'You work too much.'

'Still not as much as you, Father,' Bana quipped and shrugged. He pointed to his other friends who stood behind him, waiting to greet the daitya king.

'This is Ugra, here is Durmukha and this is Vikaraal,' Bana introduced them, though no introduction was necessary. Bali already knew a lot about them. They were the young ones, ambitious, aggressive, impatient, reckless and with little value for tradition. They were in a hurry to get somewhere and were always courting trouble. Bali knew that these were the ones who had started the last war after the Samudra Manthan when the daityas had been convincingly defeated. It was a hasty, unplanned and ill-advised move. Bali did not have a very favourable opinion of them.

Ugra, Durmukha and Vikaraal folded their hands and bowed low to greet their king.

'*Ayushman* (long life),' Bali pronounced the routine benediction, though he did not feel like it. These men and their like were the reason the daityas were unpopular amongst all the 'people' of the three worlds.

'Come sit,' Bali said, talking to all the young men. 'Let's have dinner. Talk can wait!'

They sat down on the paved floor, cross-legged in a row, with Bana sitting next to Bali and the others in a line after Bana. Helpers walked around the floor, barefoot, laying down freshly cut and washed plantain leaves as plates. Though several nobilities ate in silver and gold utensils and even the common daitya ate food in earthen utensils, Bali had persisted with the age-old custom of eating on plantain leaves. Cooks and other kitchen staff were supposed to take a bath and change into a fresh pair of clothes before preparing the food, which was served fresh off the stove from the kitchen. This was adjacent to the open quadrangular area which served as the dining quarters.

A large area had been partitioned off in the huge quadrangle to serve as the dining area for womenfolk. The plantain leaves were later collected, mashed, mixed with manure and used as fertilizer in the royal kitchen garden. This system was an age-old custom and Bali's household was probably the only one that still followed it.

As the daitya men sat down, chatting lightly, several servants rushed to and fro serving rice, lentil soup, curd and cooked vegetables to all of them.

'The food smells delicious, just like it has always been,' Bana said as he started to gulp down all the delicacies served to him. His other daitya friends followed suit, enjoying the food and light banter with the king. Bali smiled, looking at the young daityas wolf the food down.

After dinner, the men reassembled in the king's

chamber where they sat around a rectangular table inlaid with gold. Bali sat at the head of the table, with Bana and his friends further down.

'Yes, Bana,' Bali began. 'You obviously have something on your mind.'

'Yes, Father,' Bana said. 'These men have come to me with their supplication. I have discussed the issue in detail with them and now we seek your opinion and leadership.'

'Go ahead, son. Tell me about it,' Bali said.

'You already know, father, what happened at the Samudra Manthan. Our forces were cheated out of the amrit and then when they protested they were soundly beaten and sent back. The men feel dishonoured and let down. Daitya morale is broken. You know that the daitya values his honour above all else,' Bana said with passion.

'I know that, son. This would not have happened had these men listened to me when I was telling them to forgo their demands. The amrit was not for us. The gods were very clear in this and I agreed. The current Indra had come to me to discuss this matter[188] and I had given him my word that my men would not create any ruckus. The rest of the things extracted from the ocean have been shared with us. I do have the Ucchaishrava horse Indra gifted me,' Bali said.

---

[188]I have mentioned elsewhere in the text that Indra, like few other such common nouns, is the name of a title or a position rather than that of a man. Hence different people have been 'Indra' in different periods of time. Once when the current Indra was tainted with sin due to an impious act, Nahusha, a king of the manavas, was invited to the heavens to take the position.

'We do not need the amrit, son. In this *manvantar*,[189] Manobhuva is the Indra and he and his people require the amrit to be able to discharge their duties properly and fearlessly. We, as civilized people, should help in this matter so that the cosmic order, the ritam, is maintained. Only then will we be able to elevate the position of the daityas in the eyes of the gods. This is what I had thought when I advised the daityas not to ask for the amrit. But alas, this did not happen. The daityas chose to defy my advice and now we have this unnecessary conflict on our hands,' Bali continued.

He paused and looked closely at Bana and the other asuras, trying to see if his reasoning made sense to them. He knew Bana would understand but would the others? Would Bana be able to make them see the light? Bana was thoughtful but resolute. His eyes showed no confusion or indecision. However, the other daityas looked as if Bali's talk had no effect on them, as if Bali had not even been able to scratch the surface of their thick skulls with his impassioned speech.

'I do realize that we have committed a folly, father,' Bana said, looking Bali squarely in the eye. 'I have told them this myself. You know I had agreed with your

[189] *Manvantar* is a period of time in Hindu cosmology during which one person is chosen to lead the manavas, the men, and is called the Manu Prajapati, the leader of men, for that manvantar, and one god or demigod, sura or asura, is chosen to lead the gods, and is called the Indra for that manvantar. Each manavatar has seventy-one *chaturyugas,* or succession of four ages—the Krita Yuga, Treta Yuga, Dwapar Yuga, and Kali Yuga. There are fourteen manvantars in a *kalpa,* which is one day or one night in the life of Brahma, the life of the created universe. This day in the life of Brahma is a little over eight billion years, very near to the modern estimate of the age of the current universe.

stand when you had explained this to the daityas in the great assembly. That is why I also did not participate in the great manthan. I have reprimanded most of my friends, contemporaries and even senior generals for this lapse and they have borne the reprimand with humility. Believe me, father, when I say that they realize that they have erred.' Bana paused for effect, eyeing Bali and then his friends to see their reactions.

Bali was also looking intently at the three other daityas accompanying Bana to assess their response. They had come as representatives of the other daitya generals and warlords and hence their state of mind as well as their willingness to understand had to be assessed. Were they repentant? Would they swear to abide by his commands even if they did not understand the full import of his words? Their complete compliance was necessary if they expected Bali's cooperation and help or guidance.

The three daityas, Ugra, Durmukha and Vikaraal, looked downcast and repentant. They also seemed to be at a loss for words since none of them had spoken anything since the discussion started. They had been very vocal during the great assembly which Bali had called before the Manthan but now they looked rather reticent and thoughtful.

'Very uncharacteristic of them,' Bali thought.

Bana was also looking at his three companions, waiting for someone to say something. After a moment's pause Ugra spoke up.

'We remember our conduct during the great assembly, O King. We are ashamed of the way we behaved. We were impatient, hot-tempered and unwilling to listen to reason. We disobeyed your advice and refused to comply for reasons we didn't understand then. But believe us please, that we have learned our lesson.'

The other two daityas nodded.

'Our shameful defeat at the hands of the deva forces made us realize that one needs more than just brute force to win a war. We realized that without you to guide us, direct us and channel our energies, we will just continue to wander aimlessly and will court defeat after defeat. We need your guidance, O King! Please forgive us for our foolishness and help us regain our honour. We, the daityas, have nothing if we do not have our honour,' Ugra got carried away by emotion by the time he finished his piece. But his words had done their job. They struck a chord inside Bali. The sincerity and earnestness in Ugra's voice convinced Bali that the daityas had learnt their lesson.

Bali looked at Bana and saw him nodding and smiling, satisfied that the daityas had finally shown some much-needed humility.

'I accept your apology, Ugra,' Bali said, and then turning towards Bana remarked, 'What do you have in mind, Bana?'

'The honour that has been lost in the battlefield must be regained in the battlefield. There is no other way, Father. I also know you are reluctant to break the peace but there is no sin in challenging the devas for a war. A challenge is fair practice. They can either choose to keep the peace by accepting asura superiority or they can choose war in which case the onus will lie on them,' Bana said.

'We only want to redeem our self-respect, father. An

honourable challenge and a chance to win it are all the daityas ask. We will not attack Amravati, we will not seize their cities, nor plunder the populations under their control. We will not molest women, nor attack the elderly, the infirm, women, children, the unarmed or one who has surrendered. We will not attack without warning and will not pursue a fleeing foe. I have held council with all the generals, warlords and *adhisha*s of smaller daitya janas.[190] They all agree to abide by all the rules of civilized combat. This is an unconditional acceptance of your terms, father. The daityas will honour their word till their last breath,' he added.

The three daityas sitting with Bana nodded their assent and the four of them looked at Bali expectantly.

Night had descended and though the servants had lit the huge torches in the chamber, their flickering light threw grotesque shadows all around the room. In the semi-darkness and the flickering light of the torches, it was difficult to see what emotions were playing on the daitya king's face. His aged face looked handsome and elegant in its features and intelligent in the lines that creased his forehead and cheeks. It seemed as if the long Vaishnava tilaka on his forehead glowed with a light of its own. The crown that he wore of burnished gold shone dully, plunging his eyes in relative darkness. Only the pupils shone through, betraying intelligent eyes which saw beyond the here and now.

After a moment's pause, the daitya king stirred, his locks of grey hair moving as he shifted his position in the dark, the light now illuminating his face.

---

[190]*Adhish* means master. Here it can mean captain or leader of people.

'There is no dishonour in a challenge. No rules will be broken and daitya honour will be restored. Manobhuva Indra can agree to our terms and accept daitya overlordship to keep the peace. He will continue to rule over the heavens. Or he can take up our challenge and fight an honourable battle to decide who is more powerful. The only condition is that all the daityas MUST remember their pledge and not do anything dishonourable or I will dissociate from this venture midway,' the daitya king pronounced his verdict.

Bana and his friends smiled and heaved a sigh of relief. Victory was in sight now.

'Jayam,' Bana said.

'Jayam,' the other daityas repeated.

'Jayam,' Bali intoned.

Later, following Bali's instructions, a swift messenger was dispatched to Amravati carrying a message to Manobhuva Indra, the ruler of the heavens.

The message was short, just two words, '*Yuddham dehi.*'[191]

2

The war council sat in the royal assembly of Bali's palace discussing strategies. There were several generals, some prominent warlords and some leaders of independent daitya states. All of them sat around a huge rectangular

---

[191] '*Yuddham dehi*' literally translates to 'give me war'. It was an old code for challenging a rival for a duel, or a war, to prove the superiority of one over the other. The person who was being challenged could either accept defeat or accept the challenge and fight the challenger. It was a time-honoured tradition, and could not be ignored without ignominy, not even by the devas.

table with Bali's throne positioned at one end and Bana's seat on his right. Bali had handed charge of the war preparation to Bana and he sat listening carefully to strategies and preparations, sometimes clarifying a point, sometimes clearing a doubt. He rarely interfered with the discussions unless it was necessary and he thought the council was losing its way. Otherwise, he let the discussion progress under Bana's leadership. This would be a good learning experience for him and would prepare the daitya people for his future leadership.

Bana was standing now, addressing all the generals and warlords.

'Please make sure to deposit all your weapons in the royal armoury and collect new ones. Keep an inventory of all your weapons, large and small, and all metallic implements used for warfare like the axle of your chariots, the hooks used for hauling weight and even the instruments used for repairing and sharpening weapons. Deposit them all and collect new ones, checking each against your inventory. There is no use for the old weapons now. We are giving away the new ones to all the daityas for free.'

There were murmurs in the assembly.

'What is this new metal that we hear about, prince Bana?' someone asked.

'It is not a 'new' metal. The devas have used it for ages and this is the reason for their military superiority over us. I cannot divulge any further details regarding this for your own benefit. The metal is forged in our foundries and the weapons made in our workshops. You only need to collect them,' Bana responded.

His answer seemed to satisfy everyone and so the

discussion turned to other things.

'But the devas are immortal now after consuming the amrit. How can we defeat them?' another voice said.

'Immortal is a strong word,' Bana said, looking at Bali as if to ask if he would like to speak.

Bali nodded and Bana sat down motioning towards the daitya king.

'Yes, immortal is a strong word. There is no such thing as immortal, not even for the devas,' Bali said and a huge furore erupted in the house. The daityas were all suddenly talking to each other. No immortality? Then why the amrit? Were they taken for a ride? Did the devas do the manthan without a cause? What does the amrit do then?

Bali raised his hand, silencing the unruly crowd.

'Listen,' he said. 'Listen well.'

'Immortality is an illusion. Everyone has a lifetime, even the grandfather Brahma. Only Narayana and Shiva from what I hear from Bana, are beyond life and death.'

'Then what is the amrit?' someone shouted.

'Listen, don't interrupt,' Bali growled and everyone quietened down.

'The amrit is a medicine, an elixir. It confers a healthy and long life, long enough to last throughout the manvantar, so that the present Indra can complete his term. It delays aging and death but cannot prevent it altogether. It also has several healing properties. The devas who consume amrit heal from their wounds quickly, almost magically, within a nimesha. Even apparently fatal injuries can heal quickly, rendering the devas almost immortal. Almost!'

'But it is no magic, it is just advanced medicine of a kind we have never seen.'

The hall was as silent as the lull before a storm.

'The amrit is made for a very specific purpose—to prolong the life of the reigning Indra and the principal devas. But it is not for all the devas. So the deva army is not invincible as you fear. Only their leaders are now stronger, faster, healthier and heal faster. They will be difficult to kill,' Bali continued.

He paused, letting his words sink in.

'However, one need not kill the principal devas, the adityas, to win the war,' Bali smiled, his eyes twinkling, and nodded at Bana.

'We do not plan on killing the adityas,' Bana said. Again, a murmur went up in the hall, forcing him to raise his hand for silence.

'We only have to capture the adityas, and their army having been rendered leaderless, will be routed.'

Silence. And then a murmur of approval. The daityas were nodding, talking amongst themselves, letting the simple logic of Bana's plan sink in. As this met with greater and greater approval, the sound in the hall rose again and soon the daityas were beaming and shouting with happiness.

Bali smiled at Bana. This is how he liked the daityas, loud, boisterous, confident, war-like. Bali got up to leave the assembly and the hall fell silent once more.

'I will leave the details to Bana and my capable generals,' Bali said. 'I will go and finish my *sandhya vandan* (evening prayers). Bana can fill me in later.'

Bali then left the assembly and the daityas rose from their seats to bid him goodbye. Bana was officially in charge now.

The deva and the asura armies met again in the valley that lay between the two northern mountain ranges, east of the land of the seven rivers. It was a battle of honour, for redemption, for establishing supremacy, for declaring to the world that the daitya kingdom had come of age.

Over time the daitya army had improved in their battle etiquette, their formations, their battle gear and their mannerisms. They looked as resplendent as the deva army. Gone were the days of Hiranyakashyap when the daityas looked like the infernal kalakeyas, wild, untamed, uncivilized. The sobering and civilizing influence of Prahlad and Bali were clearly visible. The daityas were a standard army like any other, a force to reckon with, their chaturanga forces arrayed in standard formations or vyuha.

The colours of the deva army were red and silver; those of the daityas black and gold. The deva army stood in *makara vyuha,* the crocodile formation,[192] and the daitya army had chosen the *garuda vyuha* or eagle formation. Thus the red-white makara faced the black-gold garuda.

In the deva army, Indra stood near the head of the makara, resplendent on his Airavata, the milk-white elephant with ten tusks that was obtained during the

---

[192]The *makara,* commonly understood to be a crocodile, is the source for the Hindi word for crocodile, *magar.* The makara, however, is not a crocodile, and is a mythical half mammal-half amphibious creature depicted at several places in the Vedic iconography. Most commonly the makara is shown as having the head of an elephant and the tail of a fish or a crocodile. The makara is the mount of the Vedic god Varun, the master of the seas and a storehouse of all divine weapons, and also serves as a mount of the deified river Ganga. The makara also appears on the flag of Kamadeva, the god of love, who is therefore called Makaradhwaj.

Saagara Manthan. Flanking him, near the eyes and the jaws of the makara, stood the principal devas, the adityas. The snout was formed of soldiers with huge shields and long spears. The body of the makara was similarly made of soldiers with heavily armoured shields and thick, movable armour on wheels made up of wood and metal. The elephants and the cavalry were evenly interspersed from the snout to the tail of the makara. Small, agile attack units on horses, carrying light weapons, were present near the feet of the makara, crouched near the belly. Inside the belly of the makara were the catapults and the shataghnis, the machines which could kill one hundred enemies at one time. Indra, confident of his army's martial prowess and of the immortality offered by the amrit to his chief devas, looked around the vyuha with satisfaction. His elephants, his mobile armour, the long shields, the cavalry, the swordsmen—everything was ready. It was difficult, he thought, for the daityas to pierce his armour with their primitive weapons. They would tire themselves out trying and he would wear them out using his shataghnis from inside the belly of the makara. Then when they were weakened, he would let loose his cavalry with their light longswords, their fine armour and their swift steeds. The daityas would be cut to pieces before they knew what hit them. Going over his preparedness and his plan of action mentally, Indra smiled to himself and raised his sword hand as a signal for his forces to be ready to attack.

The daitya forces on the other hand were in the garuda formation with Bali riding his Ucchaishrava horse, the celestial, winged equine, right near the beak. He wanted to be seen from afar and wanted the message to be loud and clear that he would not hide behind his soldiers. He would go in with the first wave and meet the enemy headlong. Flanking him, forming the elliptical head of the eagle, stood his main generals on their respective horses leading their men. This time the daityas were using regular war animals like horses and a few elephants, not wild animals like the last time. Each adhish or warlord was given charge of a small portion of the eagle. The wings of the eagle spread out far and wide and in a gentle curve ended in the tail which was commanded by Bana, giving him a complete view of the battlefield. Adjacent to him was his signal man, carrying an assortment of flags to relay Bana's orders to the rest of the army. Inside both the wings of the eagle were a few elephants, a couple of catapults and lots of horses with armoured plates on their foreheads and torsos. The catapults, instead of carrying boulders, had been refitted to throw large arrows the size of trees and now stood loaded. The elephants stood in pairs, loosely tied to each other by a system of chains and carrying a huge log of wood like a battering ram between them. The horsemen inside the wings of the garuda travelled light. They had light armour and used either the longsword or the long spear. Bana's army was lightweight, meant for swift movements, while Indra's army was heavily fortified to stand assault but could not move very swiftly.

Indra could see Bali riding out in front of his army, talking to the soldiers; not the generals but the ordinary soldiers, getting them ready for the imminent assault. It was a standard procedure with Bali, talking to his brother soldiers who stood beside him! He would ask after them, encourage them, tell them that he had their back and that he would die before he would let any harm come to any of them, that he would look after their families should they fall!

This feeling was reciprocated by all the soldiers with great enthusiasm and thus they formed a sort of suicide squad surrounding their king, which would fight to death before any harm befell him. This battle strategy always worked and Bali had inspired generations of soldiers with his pep talk before the war.

Indra also noticed the unusual absence of heavy war machinery and elephants in the daityas army and was suspicious. But they were committed now, he himself had already given the sign and could not reconsider his strategy. Something was amiss, he thought. He quickly re-strategized.

'Varun,' Indra shouted. 'The daitya army is designed for quick movements. It will try to assault us from different angles. We must ensure good fortifications and disperse them early with our catapults. Aim for the junction of the body of the bird with the wings. Once the junction is broken, the army will disperse.'

'Ho!' Varun, the sea god, harrumphed in reply and got busy in relaying the instructions to the deva army.

Suddenly and instinctively, both armies went completely silent, sensing the moment to be at hand. Still. Waiting. Indra and Bali, looking at each other from a distance, raised their arms and brought them down simultaneously, giving the order to charge. After the pause, the collective war cry from both sides was deafening. The armies moves forward, keeping their formations and with the clanging of weapons and shouting of men and beasts alike, clashed in the middle of the field. Sparks flew as white met black and red met gold. As the colours mixed, new colours erupted from the field; the dark dust, copper blood and crimson sludge where the two of them mixed. Horses neighed, elephants trumpeted and men shouted and screamed and howled in pain. Deadly weapons flew around killing and maiming every living thing in their path.

'Aim the catapults at the junction,' Indra shouted over the din to Varun.

'Fire,' Varun, the man-at-arms of the devas, shouted. The shataghnis were fired with a great swooshing noise, aimed at the junction, ready to dismember the bird.

As hundreds of arrows rose into the sky, blotting out the sun for an instant, the bird came apart by itself, as if anticipating its dismemberment. The wings separated from the torso, leaving a wide-open space where the missiles thudded harmlessly into the ground, making the earth tremble. Indra and the devas watched in amazement as the wings of the eagle continued to separate, to move, to fly apart, while at the same time moving a little forward thus flanking the makara. In a matter of minutes, the wings dispersed and reassembled in a circular formation, the chakra vyuha. The body of the bird had reassembled and stood in the *suchi vyuha* or the needle formation. At the tail end of the needle, Bana could be seen giving instructions furiously, his flags rising, changing and waving at an alarming speed.

The deva army was flanked now by the two chakras and in front of the makara stood the needle.

'Charge,' Bali said and the realigned daitya army charged into the head of the makara with renewed vigour, their long spears pointed forwards.

While Indra's attention was diverted by Bali's headlong charge, the two chakras near the flanks of the makara rotated on their axis and opened up to reveal several pairs of elephants tied together with a contraption made of chains and carrying a large log with a pointed tip between them. Very soon, as the deva army watched, the elephants had battered a hole in the flank of the makara and the daitya cavalry came pouring in, slashing and cutting the deva soldiers as they went, surprised that the deva soldiers were not immortal. Along with the cavalry charge from both sides, the daitya catapults were also pulled inside the belly of the makara.

The hind parts of the makara had started to disintegrate by the time the daitya cavalry opened a space inside the belly and positioned the catapults facing forwards from inside the belly. Now the deva army was under assault from inside its own formation. Indra and the other adityas at the head of the makara were perplexed. On one hand their army which formed the tail of the makara was being routed and battered, and on the other hand they were being pincer attacked from the front as well as from inside the belly of the makara.

The adityas fought valiantly, knowing that they had taken the amrit and could not be killed easily. But the daitya army was whittling away the foot soldiers of the deva army. Soon the daitya legions had full control of the belly and they had positioned their catapults, waiting for Bana's orders.

As soon as they saw the red flag waving, the daityas released the long missiles loaded on the catapults, carrying an enormous net made of metallic ropes hitched on to the tail of the arrows. As the long arrows rose into the sky, the metallic net rose with it, swishing and cutting through the air, screeching as it rushed forward. The arrows thudded into the ground in front of the deva army, sinking deep into the ground through force and their sheer weight, splaying the metallic net over the head of the remaining makara, trapping Indra and the other adityas under it. The other devas fled after seeing the plight of their leaders and the daitya soldiers quickly hammered the remaining net into the ground, firmly and completely imprisoning the deva leaders. They were trapped!

The adityas struggled to free themselves to no avail. They saw their army being chased away and the daitya legions consolidateing their position around the mass of deva soldiers trapped under the gigantic metallic net along with their Indra. Soon the field was overrun by daitya forces and the last remaining deva had been chased away; those that remained were under the net. Bana walked up to the net, eyeing the mass of trapped, struggling men, assessing them as a sense of satisfaction filled his eyes. He looked at Indra, still seated on his Airavata but pinned down by the net squirming, and laughed. Bana's laughter echoed across the plains like a thunderclap, booming, silencing the chatter of lesser mortals and shaming the devas.

Bana stood quietly in front of Indra, looking at him as if he was a war trophy and waited.

'What is he waiting for?' Indra thought. He did not have to wait long for his answer.

Bali rode in from behind Bana, looking majestic on his Uchhaishrava, the magical horse obtained from the great churning of the ocean. As his horse trotted close to where the devas struggled under the weight of the massive net of metal, the daitya soldiers gave way and stood some distance away, their heads bowed respectfully. Bana looked at his father and nodded, a gesture returned by Bali. A few paces behind Bali were Ugra, Vikaraal and Durmukha, the daitya commanders who had along with Bana requested Bali to lead them in this expedition. They had also stopped at a respectable distance and now looked on curiously as did hundreds of other daityas who had formed a huge circle around the net. Indra struggled, his face red with anger and shame. He had been made a spectacle by Bali. His friends, the adityas, were trapped with him too.

'This cannot be good,' thought Indra. 'Why is Bali doing this? He, of all people, understands the delicate balance, the order of things and the daityas' unsuitability to govern and rule the kingdom of the gods. Then why has he attacked us? He cannot expect the daityas to rule over Amravati, this will be disastrous. The cosmic order will crash. The daityas are undisciplined and cannot handle responsibility. Why is he helping them do something which he himself knows is not right?'

Indra's mental torment must have showed on his face for soon enough Bali addressed him.

'Don't worry, Indra,' Bali said. 'We do not plan to ransack or to rule Amravati.'

Indra was surprised. This seemed even more useless. Why risk a war if they did not plan on ruling over the defeated? Indra sensed that Bali must have had his own reasons to support the daityas' cause. He waited patiently for Bali to explain, all the while writhing inside the net.

Bali noticed his discomfiture and ordered his soldiers

to release the king of the devas immediately.

'Release Indra, accord him all the respect due to him and escort him for parley to my camp. The other devas can go back to Amravati,' Bali ordered the daityas.

A murmur of disapproval went up from the daitya soldiers. They were unhappy. Bali looked at Bana and then at Ugra, Durmukha and Vikaraal, his eyes admonishing them. Bana raised an arm and the murmur immediately died down. The importance of this was not lost on Indra. He could sense a divided house when he saw one. Obviously, Bali and the other daityas were not on the same page here.

'That explains some things,' Indra thought.

Still staring at Bana, Bali turned his horse and trotted away, motioning to his son to release the other devas and send Indra to his camp.

Bali sat in his tent with Indra seated comfortably and respectfully in front of him. Both had had time for their personal ablutions and having rested and refreshed themselves with fruits and drinks were now ready to discuss difficult political matters. The other adityas had been released and had gone back to Amravati reluctantly, leaving Indra as a 'guest' with Bali. The daitya soldiers were happy at having defeated the deva army convincingly and at having captured the adityas like a hunter catches game but resented letting them all go after having caught them alive. Even in their celebrations, an undercurrent of discontent simmered. For now Bali was blissfully unaware of this as he sat down for parley with his deva counterpart in his regal tent. The cacophony of daitya soldiers celebrating, Bana's voice the loudest of them all, served as the background music to their discussions.

'The purpose of the war, Indra, was not to snatch Amravati from you. You can have your kingdom and rule it but you have to accept the fact that the daitya army has defeated you and your people in battle and thus we are your superiors,' Bali said. 'This will be enough to please the daityas and they will leave you and your kingdom unmolested. They have fought this war only to redeem their honour which they thought they had lost when you routed them ignominiously after the manthan. They have fought with honour and have not so far crossed boundaries of civility or breached the codes of war. They have adhered to all the principles of honourable combat and will continue to behave honourably if you concede defeat publicly.'

'This is a little difficult to believe, Bali,' Indra said. 'You know it. Going by the history of the daitya people, we know that they have never behaved responsibly, and far less honourably especially when in power. Why should they be any different now?' Indra chose his next words carefully, scrutinizing Bali's face to understand what was going on inside that brilliant mind.

'Bali, you of all people should know that the daityas have always been unreliable, unpredictable and prone to violence but if you say that they will mend their ways, I will believe it, upon your honour, for I trust you. I am ready to risk my ignominy and a potential threat to the sacred order, the ritam, which I am bound to uphold, if you say so, for you are an honourable man. Between the two of us, Bali, I am ready to make peace on your terms if you guarantee the daityas will keep the peace. However, if they don't, the next time I will be better prepared. The cosmic balance has a tendency of correcting itself. If I am unable to protect it as a guardian, it will protect itself. The balance of *karma* and *phala* is divine and will be maintained at all costs.'[193]

'Accepted,' Bali said. 'You accept daitya overlordship and the daityas will keep their end of the bargain. All the generals, warlords and adhishas of the daitya people have promised me, upon their honour, that this will be a turning point in daitya history, that they will forthwith work to develop a civilized and cultured state. I have decided to trust them and you should trust me. Between us, we can discuss any misgivings at any point of time, should they arise in the future. But you must relinquish your overlordship of the ritam. Only when you abdicate will the daityas be peaceful. You can continue to rule Amravati but the matters of the rest of the world need not concern you. The daityas will look after the law and order of the world. I will see to it that the ritam is maintained. I do understand the importance of the order as well as you do and will do my utmost to uphold it.'

Indra nodded, knowing there was no other way out. He had to relinquish power to Bali and see what happened, although this was something not ordained by the powers that be and would have consequences.

The two men rose and embraced and a peace was thus brokered. Indra accepted defeat publicly, suffering the humiliation and relinquished his hold over the order of things. The devas would no longer enforce order in the universe and the daityas would ensure peace and

---

[193]*Karma* refers to actions, and *phala* refers to results or consequences

prosperity in all the realms as the guardians of the ritam. Bali publicly promised that the daityas would mend their ways, follow the eternal rules of the ritam, enforce peace, eschew violence and uphold dharma in all the realms. Thus, peace was brought to the world once more. But how long would it last? For peace, like war, like all things worldly, is ephemeral, that is what the Vedas have told us.

3

The daityas were soon drunk on power. They had defeated the devas! There was no one to challenge their power, and their supremacy in the world. They were the guardians of the cosmic balance. Invincibility and absolute power are great responsibilities and, like Indra said, the daityas were not ready, for it was ill-gotten power. Unknown to Bali, the terms of the treaty were broken almost as soon as they were agreed upon. The daitya legions went back to their kingdoms singing with joy, indulging in useless and indiscriminate molestation of innocent people. They looted towns and villages, killed anyone who resisted and plundered merchants and farmers alike—everything that they had promised not to do. The devas could not do anything because they had publicly been declared underlings and had been stripped of their role as peacekeepers. They had no power over the situation since Indra had relinquished his duties as the keeper of the ritam. The cosmic balance, delicate as it is always, had been disturbed. There would be consequences!

Bana learned of what was happening and and tried to control it but only half-heartedly. He knew the daityas were a violent people and there was a limit to which they could be tamed or controlled. Strain the leash too tightly and it might break! He decided to let them enjoy their newfound power and glory a little. Maybe they would get used to it, get tired and settle down. Maybe the people of the different realms would adapt to the ways of their new masters. Time is a great healer; it can work miracles. There is a limit to which mortals can force things to happen, sometimes it is just wiser to wait for the right time, Bana thought.

The adityas also learned of the situation and went to Indra to seek advice but even he was helpless. Short of declaring an all-out war again there was not much to be done, and a war so soon after the mauling they had received would be disastrous. The daityas were riding high on confidence and the morale of the deva forces was low. A war cannot be fought with demoralized soldiers. They needed another way out. It was true that daitya supremacy had plunged the world into chaos and this had been brought about with the consent of Bali and Indra. The situation could not be helped, not by the devas at least. They decided to seek the help of the only person in the world who had always helped them when they had fallen into bad times, when they were too weak to uphold the order, to sustain the ritam. He was the one who had incarnated as the boar, as the man-lion, as the kurma and as Mohini. Only he could help them now, only he could restore balance and return them to their status as the upholders of the dharma, the ritam.

'It is the power, the piety of Bali that sustains them, O Hari!' Indra pleaded.

'He does not know whom he supports. We cannot win over the daityas, cannot beat them back, till Bali is with them. The daityas are violating the time-honoured code, the ritam, as they always have. They are the guardians, yet they are the ones who violate it. We are powerless to fight them as our forces are demoralized, beaten and broken. Bali supports the daityas and sustains them. He has appointed them as guardians, O Narayana. Bali wants to be Indra, O Sridhar, but his generals and his soldiers do not honour the ritam. Till Bali stands with the daityas we cannot defeat them. He needs to go,' the devas pleaded.

'No! Bali is my devotee. He is flawless. No one can harm him. I will see to it that no harm comes to him. But the order, the ritam, must be restored. You will have your chance to enforce the right order, Indra. For this manvantar you are the Indra, Manobhuva, and you shall continue to be Indra. Bali will be the next Indra but for that he has to wait till the end of the manvantar. I shall convince him; I will give him a new realm to rule. The daityas do not deserve his leadership. Go and wait for my sign,' said Madhav, the slayer of Madhu-Kaitabh, smiling, for he knew what the devas did not. Only he could know what was in store for Bali.

Bali was performing the *rajasuya yagya.*[194] He had finally

[194] *Rajasuya yagya* and *ashwamedha yagya* were ceremonies performed by kings or emperors who want to declare their suzerainty, their overlordship over the other contemporary kings. In the rajasuya this was done by inviting all the reigning monarchs, who offer homage and tribute to the one performing the rajasuya, thus symbolically accepting his superiority. In the ashwamedha, a horse with royal emblems and accompanied by the army, is let loose through the country and wherever he goes, that land comes under the lordship of the king performing the ashwamedha. These yagyas were thus a means of forming a loose confederation of states within the nominal rule of one emperor.

defeated the devas and had arbitered a treaty with them wherein Indra had stepped down from his position as the upholder of the ritam in all the realms. He had also defeated the danavas, the nagas, the yakshas and the gandharvas. All of them had bowed down before his power. Thus the rajasuya ceremony was an open declaration of his overlordship and a formal announcement that he was now the ruler of the earth and the heavens. All the kings would be invited to pay tribute to him and accept him as their emperor publicly. He had also invited Indra. When and if Indra came and accepted Bali's superiority publicly by paying him tribute, the ritam would effectively be reversed. and Bali would be Indra and Manobhuva Indra would just be a king ruling in Amravati in his stead. This would be the most revolutionary thing to have ever happened since the creation of the world!

A huge *mandapam* had been constructed with a large *vedi* for the yagya, the fire worship.[195] The mandapam was in the shape of a large rectangle with the sides sheltered by a temporary structure made of bamboo and cloth, and the middle area containing the vedi was open to the sky. The royal enclosure was on one side of the rectangle and had several seats to accommodate royal guests and dignitaries. On the other three sides of the rectangle were more frugal seats for the priests, sages, brahmanas and lay visitors, each with their own

[195] *Mandapam* is a temporary structure used for ceremonial purposes. The *vedi* is the fire altar and is made according to extensive geometrical instructions given in the Shatpath Brahmana and in the Shulbha Sutras. The Shulbha Sutras are addendums to Vedas and the source of all Vedic mathematics, including geometry, ratio-proportion, algebra and trigonometry.

enclosures. In the middle of the mandapam, in the area open to the sky, a huge fire altar in the shape of a falcon had been constructed. Around the vedi sat four types of priests with Shukracharya, the guru of the daityas, playing the lead role.[196] Among the priests, at one end of the vedi facing guru Shukracharya, sat the great asura emperor, Mahabali.

He was taller than those around him even sitting, with fair skin like burnished gold. He had a broad forehead, wide chest, arms like the trunk of an elephant and long greying hair falling over his shoulders. His ageing face, wrinkled with time, was handsome and well-proportioned. His torso was marked with the scars of the several battles he had fought and won. He had marked his forehead with a long Vaishnava tilaka, the mark of Vishnu, made of sandalwood paste and vermilion. His torso was bare, covered with just the angavastram, a piece of cloth thrown over one shoulder. He wore the sacred thread which was looped across his chest obliquely and lay on his left shoulder. Bali sat with his priests, participating in the yagya while the visitors, guests, royal family, courtiers, generals and lay soldiers looked on. Most of the guests he had invited had come and paid him the due homage. Only Indra, the ruler of Amravati, the king of the devas, was conspicuous by his absence. Bali had noted this lapse but had stayed quiet

---

[196]The four types of priests at a fire ceremony or *agnihotra,* are the *hotr,* the *adhvaryu,* the *udgatr* and the *brahman.* The hotr is the chief priest and recites hymns from the Rig Veda. The rest are assistant priests. The adhvaryu is the one who helps with altar construction and recites hymns from the Yajur Veda. The udgatr chants hymns from the Sama Veda and the brahman from the Atharva Veda.

since the ceremony needed to be completed first.

On one side of the mandapam was a crowd of commoners, mendicants and brahmanas who had come to seek alms. The king, as per tradition, would give away considerable wealth today after the ceremonies and he would refuse none! The word had spread and thus a huge crowd had assembled in the field where the mandapam had been constructed, waiting patiently for their king to distribute alms.

One session of the yagya having been completed, the king got up and folded his hands in respect to the priests who were helping him conduct the ceremony. They responded likewise, paying their respects to their benefactor. Shurkracharya rose with Bali, he had to oversee the alms distribution that the king had scheduled.

There was a commotion as the king walked towards the open area where the crowd waited, a posse of soldiers maintaining order. A few royal stewards hurried with carts full of clothes, money, food, fruits and other articles which would be distributed among the poor and the needy. When Bali reached the area designated for the daanam ceremony, the distribution of alms, he motioned to the palace staff to quickly help him speedily distribute the clothes and the money. The king stood to one side and the guards brought people to him one by one to receive the gifts. After several hours of distribution, the crowds were finally finished, as was the material to be distributed.

At the very end of the line, a lone brahmana had stood patiently throughout the day, a dwarf wearing only a loincloth and carrying a small bamboo umbrella in his left hand. In his other hand he carried a *kamandalu* and a yoga danda.[197] His sacred thread was slung over his left shoulder and his body bore all the auspicious marks. His dark skin was marked with sandalwood paste on the forehead, the ears, the neck and the upper arms. His head was shaved except for a shikha, a tuft of hair at the very top which he had braided and stringed with rudraksha beads. He was barefoot and even though he stood erect, he barely reached a few feet in height. However, his face radiated with piety and inner peace. He smiled lightly when his eyes met Bali's and the daitya king felt his tiredness drain away. He was suddenly happy; he did not know why! The sight of this *vamana*, this dwarf brahmana, made him immeasurably happy. He saw the glow which emanated from this young ascetic and wondered if the others could see it too. His whole body was radiant! From the top of his head, right down to the nails of his small, dark feet, the dwarf was glowing! Bali wondered if the others really couldn't smell the fragrance of sandal and vaijyanti flowers spreading through the mandapam even though he could not see them anywhere.[198]

The vamana was looking directly at the daitya king, smiling. His eyes looked into Bali's tired soul, talking, communicating and soothing him. Bali felt happy and weak looking at this dwarf brahmana. He could not take his eyes off him; such was the hold that the vamana

---

[197]A *kamandalu* is a water carrier made by hollowing out the gourd fruit. The yoga danda is a stick used by ascetics to rest their hand on while praying with the string of beads.

[198]Vaijyanti flowers are the favourite flowers of Vishnu and Krishna, and both are portrayed as wearing a garland of vaijyanti flowers, called the vaijyanti mala, or the garland of victory. The vaijyanti flower has not been identified but is supposed to have been some form of non-wilting lotus.

had over him. As the vamana, supplicant to Bali's court, walked up to him, the king felt himself kneel and bow to the dwarf. The assembly watched in shocked silence as the daitya king bent down and touched the vamana's feet with his forehead. Mahabali had never experienced such peace and tranquillity, such an invigorating feeling; it flooded over him now, in cold waves. He was born again, his sins erased, his past rectified, his future secured in the feet of Sri Hari.

Bali raised his head and looked directly at the vamana, still kneeling in front of him, the assembly still deathly quiet.

'What can I do for you, O Brahmana? Command me, for I am your servant. I shall give what you ask of me.' Bali said.

'You are generous, O King,' the vamana smiled. 'My needs, however, are few. I only need three paces of land to sustain my family, to restore order among my *kutumb*.'[199]

'Three paces of earth?' Bali repeated, as if in a trance.

'Yes, Mahabali, just three small steps of land,' the vamana said.

Shukracharya stirred and said to Bali, 'This must be a trick, O King. This is one of the devas come to cheat us. Or maybe he is Vishnu come to take back from you what you valiantly won from Indra. Beware, sir!'

'I have promised to give away anything anyone asks of me today, guruji. Even if it is the devas, I will give them what they ask if they have come to my court as a mendicant. But I know this is is not the devas. If it is indeed Narayana who has come to ask something from

---

[199]Family

me, I will be the luckiest person in this whole world. I will consider my life well-spent if it is indeed Mukunda asking alms from me. Look how this vamana glows, how his fragrance of the vaijyanti flowers fills the air. This is no ordinary brahmana. And he will not go back empty-handed, not from Bali's home,' Bali said.

'You will have three paces of land, O Vamana. Measure them!' Bali said, with his right arm raised.

The vamana smiled at the generosity of his devotee, at his devotion, and then he started to grow in size. In front of the whole assembly, in front of the daitya king who had granted him the three paces of land, and in front of the daitya priest Shukracharya who had warned his king against it, the vamana grew. He grew taller than Bali, taller than the elephants that stood guard at the gates, taller than the gates themselves, taller even than the royal palace. Then he continued growing, taller and taller, till he was no longer visible. The assembly watched wonderstruck and Bali watched in pious wonder as the vamana grew taller than the skies, taller than the sun and the moon, taller than the galaxies that dot the sky. He seemed to engulf all of creation within him, the stars were his crown, the earth was his pedestal. And then he started to measure!

With one stride he had measured the heavens, striding across the Milky Way, striding across the unknown galaxies that lie in the cosmic void, striding across the great, black emptiness the sages call the Shesha, the cosmic serpent. He strode across the universe, across the Hiranyagarbha, the nucleus, the nidus of creation, the ball of fire which began it all. He measured it all in one pace.

Then he took his second pace and measured the earth

and all that is encompassed within it, its mountains, rivers, oceans, deserts, its ponds and lakes, forests, kingdoms, men and women, beasts and birds and fishes—all were his in the second pace. After he had measured the earth and the heaven in his two paces, he paused. His booming voice filled the sky, coming from the stars, even like the pranav, the aum, the sound of the universe turning in its orbit, the cosmic sound, the sound that was there before anyone else, the sound that is God!

The vamana's voice addressed Bali, testing him, reprimanding, challenging.

'Where is the third pace, O Generous King?' the vamana said and laughed. His laughter shook the stars, the earth trembled under his weight, the mountains were crushed and released their ores.

'You promised me three paces, Mahabali. Where is my third pace?' the vamana was insistent.

Mahabali thought for a moment, then stood up, folded his hands, bowed his head, and said, 'O Narayana. Place your foot on my head. I am your third pace. I offer you my head and with it my soul.'

Tears streamed down the cheeks of the great king Mahabali at this experience, at this encounter with the creator of the universe, the progenitor of the gods, the one who created the cosmic order, the one who balances the ritam. With great humility, devotion and piety, the great asura king, the generous Mahabali, offered his head to Sri Hari, the god of gods. The vamana laughed, decreased in size and put his foot on the head of Mahabali, blessing him with immortality, with everlasting life, with undying devotion and a place in Vaikuntha, Sri Hari's abode, inaccessible even to the gods, when he should finish his work on the earth. Mahabali was appointed the ruler of the *patala*, the nether regions, and Vishnu promised to be his *dwarapala*, his guard and his doorman, guarding the entrance to the nether regions. He forbade Bali to come up to the earth except once a year and told him to wait for the next manvantar to be named the Indra.

Bali accepted the command of his deity, his Vishnu, his Trivikram[200] with humility and great happiness. At the end of the manvantar, when the time of Manobhuva ended, Mahabali was appointed the Indra of the heavens and he was charged with maintaining the cosmic order, the ritam. Mahabali is still remembered today by pious Hindus as one of the greatest devotees of Vishnu who rose to great heights through his valour and piety.

Author's Note

The great Vishnu devotee Bali is revered by several pious Hindus across India. His ascension to the earth once in a year is celebrated all over the country at different times of the year in different communities. In the south, chiefly Kerala, he is remembered during Onam, a harvest festival. In other states, especially Karnataka, he is remembered as Bali Indra during the Bali Pratipada, the first day of the bright fortnight following the festival of lights, Deepawali.

---

[200]Trivikram is one of Vishnu's names since he measured the world in three strides. Literally translated the word means 'victory in three (paces)'.

Epilogue

After investing more than twenty-five years in the service of mankind through the practice of medicine, I have just begun my journey of discovering the wealth that lies within the Vedic texts as well as the beauty that lies within the Itihasas, the Puranas, the Samhitas, the Vedantas and the Vedangas. I hope others start on this journey sooner and this book is an attempt to help them do that. In this age of 'mythological fiction', it is easy to lose sight of the treasure trove, the Amrit Kalash that lies within our reach, full of the nectar of science, philosophy, metaphysics, mathematics, art, poetry, literature and all the beautiful things that thousands of years of human civilization have to offer.

It will be my constant effort to fathom this ocean, borrow from this pot of nectar, and bring to my readers the pearls that ancient Indian wisdom has to offer. I hope HIS hands and HIS spirit continues to guide my buddhi and my medha so I can measure up to this tall order.

Till the next book—Hari Har!

—Divya Narain Upadhyaya